HYDE'S ABSOLUTION

NINA LEVINE

Editing by Becky Johnson, Hot Tree Editing

Cover Design ©2017 by Romantic Book Affair Designs

Cover photography Wander Aguiar

Cover model Nick Bennett

To My Mother

You taught me that there can be beauty in pain.

I love you xx

PROLOGUE

Hyde
Twenty Years Old

Do babies ever stop crying? That was the only thought running through my head while I watched my wife struggle with our one-and-a-half-week-old daughter three days after we brought her home. Charlotte hadn't stopped crying in those three days, and I was certain Tenille was about to have a mental breakdown. I'd watched her steadily withdraw since giving birth, and between the never-ending crying and the fussy feeding, the vacant look I dreaded seeing in Tenille's eyes had returned. The look that she'd had back in school when we'd first started dating. *The look I'd worked hard to erase.*

Reaching for Charlotte, I said, "Here, let me take her. You go lie down."

She stared at me for a long moment before doing as I said. "I'll just have an hour or so."

I shook my head while ignoring the cries coming from my child. "You need longer. You're fucking exhausted."

The frown that crossed her face highlighted that exhaustion. "She needs to be fed soon, Aiden."

Fucking breastfeeding. It was the thing coming between us more than Tenille's tiredness. Charlotte didn't want a bar of it, but after a nurse had lectured Tenille at two fucking a.m. one morning in the hospital about the importance of breast milk, my wife had been adamant that our child would be breastfed.

I took a deep breath to calm myself. We'd had a few arguments over this, and I didn't want another one. I just wanted Tenille to get some sleep. "There's enough milk in the fridge for one feed. I can give that to her, so all you need to focus on is lying your ass down on that bed, closing your eyes, and not waking up for hours."

Charlotte stopped crying at the same time that Tenille's eyes widened. "I haven't heard that bossy tone from you in a few weeks," she said quietly, a slow smile touching her lips. Dropping her gaze to the baby, she murmured, "I think Charlie likes it, too."

I held Charlotte close to my chest with one arm and wrapped my spare one around Tenille's waist, settling my hand on her ass. "Charlie, huh?"

Her smile grew, and my dick twitched. Nearly four weeks of not being inside her was far too fucking long. "Yeah, Charlie. It was on your list of possible boy names. I think it makes a great nickname for her."

Glancing down at my daughter, I took in the way her eyes fluttered closed as her chest rose and fell before she finally drifted off to sleep. Looking back up at Tenille, I said, "It seems she likes that, too."

Tenille shook her head. "No, I think what she really likes

is being in her daddy's arms, which I totally get. It's the best place in the world to be."

"Jesus, woman, you need sleep, and here you are turning me on so fucking much that I want to keep you awake all night."

"Uh-uh, no sex for six weeks. Doctor's orders."

I raised my brows. "You think I give a fuck what the doctor says? And besides, I don't need my dick inside you to keep you awake all night."

She was silent for a few moments, just watching me intently before cradling Charlotte's head and bending to place a kiss on her forehead. "Are you sure you'll be okay with her while I sleep?" The smile on her face and in her eyes disappeared.

I frowned. One minute we were in the moment together, the next she'd fucking exited without stopping to take a breath. I moved my hand to her waist and pulled her closer to me. "What the fuck just happened there?"

Blinking, she shifted her gaze to the floor. "Nothing. I'm just really tired and want to go to bed, but I want to make sure you—"

"No," I cut her off, "something happened in your head, Tenille, and I want to know what it was."

She kept her eyes down for far too long before meeting mine again. "Can we please just leave it for now?" Her question came out more like a plea.

"No. Tell me." If there was one thing I'd learnt in the four years we'd been together, it was that when she retreated like that, it was always something that needed to be talked about. Tenille was the queen of avoidance. Her shitty family had taught her that. But it did her no favours.

"God, you're a pushy bastard sometimes," she muttered as she attempted to move out of my embrace.

I tightened my hold on her. "Yeah, welcome to the rest of your life, but you already knew that about me."

"Fine," she started before snapping her mouth shut as if she had changed her mind. But she knew from experience that there was no way I was dropping this, so she finally blurted out, "Sex with me isn't going to be the same. I just need you to know that."

I frowned again. "How do you figure that?"

She stared at me as if I was the crazy one. "How do you figure it *won't* be? I mean, I birthed an eight-pound baby out of my vagina, and my stomach is stretched and flabby. And I was already overweight. And on top of that, I don't even feel like having sex or sucking your dick or doing any of the shit you like to do. Everything has changed!" Tears trickled from her eyes, and a moment later, they fell in gushing streams.

"Fuck, baby, that's a lot of shit to be carrying around in your head and keeping to yourself. You need to be talking to me about this stuff."

She madly wiped her tears away, not having much success because as soon as she wiped them, more fell. "This isn't stuff I want to discuss with anyone, let alone with you."

Always my strong girl, trying to deal with everything on her own. "Okay, so let's go through it all, starting with your pussy. I don't care if it's pushed ten babies out, there will never be a day I won't want my dick inside of it. As for your curves, I fucking live for them. I wake up thinking about them, and I count down the hours during the day until I can get my hands all over them at night. If you ever try to starve yourself to get rid of them, you're going to have a huge fucking fight on your hands with me." I let go of her so I could place my hand on her cheek. Stroking her jaw with my thumb, I added, "If you never want to suck my dick again, I'll deal with it. I won't love it, but I love you, so I'll fucking deal. But I read some of the shit your doctor gave you to read, and it's normal for you to not want sex straight away, so I'm fairly fucking sure that the time is going to come soon where you won't be able to keep yourself off my dick."

"You read that stuff?" She forced her words out between sobs, and it fucking killed me that she was so upset over this. She was supposed to be on a high after having Charlotte, and yet the last week had been nothing but tears and anxiety.

"Of course I read that stuff. I'm your partner in all this, Tenille. You've done the physical stuff. Let me help you with everything else."

Something I said clicked with her, and she sagged against me, her arms tight around my body. The three of us stood together for a long time while she cried and allowed me to comfort her. We'd been together for a while, but I knew she'd always held a piece of herself back. It was in the way she refused to cry in front of me, and the way she clammed up when we talked about certain topics, and the way she was guarded about her dreams for the future. I'd always vowed to break those walls down; I'd just never known how to do it. Maybe this would be the beginning of those walls shattering.

After I'd settled her in our bed and Charlotte in her cot, I headed into the kitchen to find something to cook for dinner. My mother's voice drifted from the lounge room. "You're just like your daddy. Smooth with your words. I hope you don't turn out like him when it comes to sticking around long term."

I stilled in the hallway, her words cutting through me like sharp blades. Turning, I entered the lounge room and found her sitting in the corner, taking a swig from her bottle of scotch, watching me through eyes that betrayed so many toxic emotions. My mother and I had always had a hard relationship, but the birth of my child had stirred some nasty shit in her, and I'd dealt with nine months of this bullshit.

"How long will you be staying with us this time?" I asked, choosing to ignore what she'd said.

"What? You don't want your mother staying with you?"

Not particularly. "Answer my question."

She narrowed her eyes at me as she stood and walked my way. "That right there, that's your father coming out in you. Refusing to answer my question, but demanding I answer yours."

My patience frayed at the edges, and I couldn't hold my asshole side back. She'd turned up on our doorstep three days ago, and if her history was anything to go by, she'd still be with us in three weeks. Tenille didn't need her around, and I sure as fuck didn't need to listen to shit about my father for another minute. "I never knew my father, so I wouldn't know if I was like him or not."

She stiffened. She hated being reminded of the fact the only man she'd ever loved had walked out on her when their child was seven months old. The sting I'd intended hit its mark. Pushing her shoulders back, she said, "Take my word for it, you have plenty of your father in you. I've never felt as abandoned as I did when I was quitting the coke. The way you chose Shane Gibson over me hurt in a way I'll never forget. And that was true McVeigh style."

Fuck. She liked to throw out the shit about "McVeigh style" as often as she could. It was the surname I shared with my father—the one he never gave her but that she made sure to give me in her desperate effort to keep him. "What the fuck are you going on about? I was there for you when you quit the drugs." Hell, I was seventeen at the time and knew more about surviving in this shitty world than most adults. I'd made sure my mother made it through the detox, and I kept our home running while finishing my last year of high school and holding down a fucking job.

"Shane Gibson offered you a job and you jumped at it.

You did everything to help that man, and I was the one who suffered. You might have been around a few hours a day, but I needed you more than that. It was the only time I ever really needed you, and you let me down." She paused for a beat. "I hope your wife and child never know the coldness of your back to them or the despair of you deserting them."

Before I had a chance to reply, she exited the room, leaving me alone with my thoughts. I had no desire to go after her. This was the way our interactions tended to go. She unleashed her mean streak on me when she'd been drinking, only to take it all back the next day. It was our vicious cycle.

But her words clung, and I spent far too long thinking back over that time in our lives when she'd finally kicked her drug addiction. It hadn't been her first attempt, and perhaps there was something to what she'd said. I hadn't had faith in her. Not after all the other times she'd half-heartedly tried. And I'd been tired of dealing with her crap. So when Gibson offered me that job, I'd taken it and given him 200 percent. I'd wanted to escape the hell of my life. So I had to admit to myself that there was some truth in my mother's words. But the shit she'd said about me abandoning my wife and child? That would never happen. Tenille and Charlotte were everything to me. There was no way I'd ever turn my back on the two people I loved more than life itself. I was not that kind of man. I was not my father.

CHAPTER 1

Hyde
Current Day – Sixteen Years Later

Removing my sunglasses, I met Sully's gaze. "So you're telling me that her bank account is down fifty grand, and you can't track where it went?"

He nodded. "Yes. The cash was withdrawn a week ago, and they've made no significant purchases that I can see. I've been tailing all three of them and nothing seems out of the ordinary in their behaviour. Tenille and Craig go to work the same as usual, Charlotte goes to school, mostly, and the way they spend their free time hasn't changed. Like I mentioned on the phone, though, Charlotte has started smoking, cutting class, and fighting with her mother a lot more. And Tenille and Craig have had a few fights in public that bordered on violent. She appears to be drinking heavily. The bank statements verify that, as does her public behaviour."

I glanced around the pub as I sifted through his information. Two in the afternoon was a time you saw the dedicated drinkers, and there were a few there that afternoon. I recognised them just as easily as they recognised me. But none of us acknowledged the other.

Turning back to Sully, I said, "Something's not right with the family."

"Agreed. You want me to do some more digging?"

I drained the glass of whisky in front of me. "No, I'm going to pay them a visit and find out for myself what's going on."

"You think that's a good idea, son?"

I wasn't his son, but he was the closest thing I had to a father. Sully had been working for me, reporting back on my wife and daughter, for fourteen years. He knew my history, and over time, we'd developed the kind of friendship that resulted in the occasional meal together. Outside of Storm, Sully was the only person who showed any interest or care in my life. That interest wasn't requested, but I'd grown to tolerate it.

"No, it's a really bad fucking idea, Sully, but I don't see that I have any other choice. I walked away from my family once. I won't do it again. Not when they need me."

"And Gibson?"

I clenched my jaw. "Fuck him. He wants to come at me? Let him fucking come."

"You'll take some club members with you for backup?"

I shook my head. "No. I'm doing this on my own."

His forehead creased. "Now *that's* a really bad fucking idea, Aiden."

I pushed my chair back and stood, my tolerance for his interest having met its limits. "We're done here. I'll call you if I need any further information."

As I watched him leave, a voice filtered through my thoughts. "You want another drink?"

I turned to find Jilly, the waitress, waiting for my answer. Her eyes ran over my body in the same way they always did. I ignored the heat in those eyes. "Yeah, another whisky."

She finally met my gaze. "I finish up in an hour. You wanna come back to my place? We could have some fun like we used to."

My irritation flared. I'd made it clear to her on numerous occasions that I wasn't interested in more time between her legs. "No, just the whisky."

She opened her mouth to speak, but King cut her off when he joined me. "I'll have a whisky, too." His eyes met hers. "And some privacy."

After she threw a pout my way, she left us alone, and I directed my attention to King. "I thought we were meeting later at your place."

"Something's come up that I need to take care of, and I figured I'd find you here."

"Everything okay?"

"Yeah, just some family bullshit." He settled into the seat across from me and crossed his arms over his chest. "You leaving tonight?"

I nodded. "I want to get there early tomorrow morning."

King remained silent for a few moments. "I don't fucking get why you never told me about your family, brother. Not after the shit we went through together years ago."

I hadn't told anyone about my family, but I'd come close more than once with King. Staring at him, I thought back to the night he saved my ass the first time. "Do you remember how fucked up I was the night you saved my life?"

Jilly placed our drinks on the table, and King reached for his. After drinking some, he said, "The night you decided you could take five assholes on and win? I'd seen you at that pub a few times, always jacked up on something, and I remember thinking you were one crazy motherfucker. The way I recall it, though, is that you didn't really need me to help you that night. I was just looking for a fight, and yours seemed like a good one to get in on. I didn't save your life, that's for fucking sure. You were capable of doing that yourself."

"No, I wasn't. And you know that. Saving my life had nothing to do with that fight." I knocked back some whisky, savouring the burn as it slid down my throat. "If I'd never met you that night, I'd have been dead within weeks. I wanted to fucking die back then."

"I know. But no one wants to die in a filthy back alley with a needle stuck in his fucking arm or beaten to death by a bunch of assholes he doesn't even know."

"I did. I didn't want to deal with life. And I sure as hell didn't want to talk about it or my family. Not to you. Not to anyone." I threw back some more whisky. "Fuck, King... you're always saving the fucking strays. What the hell possessed you to save me from myself?"

He didn't have to think about his answer. "I knew you'd make a fucking good VP."

I stared at him, processing that. King had been twenty-three at the time, seven years off becoming president. I was twenty-two and a man with no future. King had helped me win that fight, and then he'd given me a reason to live. He'd also spent months making sure I kicked my drug habit. "How the fuck did you figure that?"

He held my gaze, his eyes hard. "You were almost as crazy as me, but every now and then you hesitated and thought shit through. And you never failed to tell me when you thought I was wrong. I knew I'd need someone like that." He glanced around the pub for a moment before looking back at me. "Turns out I was right to fight for you. Some of the shit you've done for me...."

I shrugged. "It's what we do."

He lifted his drink to his mouth. "You gonna tell me why your wife thinks you're dead?"

I ran my finger around the rim of the glass in front of me. "There was a fire, and our home burnt to the ground. My remains were supposedly found in it."

King didn't blink, didn't show any reaction at all. He simply said, "Why?"

I emptied my glass and signalled to Jilly to bring us another. Getting into this with King wasn't something I had the patience for without more alcohol. "Let's just say I was young and made a fatal error about where to put my loyalties. The guy I worked for, Gibson, was being investigated for all sorts of shit, but mostly they were desperate to pin two murders on him. I was the guy he called on to handle any problems in the business, so the cops hauled me in for questioning. After I was released, Gibson gave me an ultimatum —fake my death and walk away or he'd get rid of me his way. Part of the choice involved Tenille and Charlotte's safety. If I didn't choose to walk away, he'd kill us all."

King frowned. "Walking away doesn't sound like your style, Hyde."

The guilt I'd carried with me for fourteen years roared to life, squeezing the fucking air out of my lungs and coming dangerously close to flipping the switch that sent me from controlled to crazed in under a second. "Jesus, King, I was a fucking twenty-two-year-old with no family and no fucking resources. They caged me in and threatened me, beating the shit out of me and almost killing me in the process. It wasn't like I had much fucking choice. And back then, I wasn't the man I am today, that's for fucking sure."

"Why didn't you use Storm's resources once you had access to them? I would have helped you get your family back."

I scrubbed my hand over my face while my gut churned

with regret. "I was damned if I did and damned if I didn't. In the end, though, I didn't want to put Tenille through that. She remarried within a year and was happy. I've kept an eye on them, and the guy seems to have done right by Charlotte. Me going back would only have stirred shit up for them."

"So now you're ready to deal with this Gibson asshole?"

"No, now I'm simply heading to Melbourne to find out what shit my family is in and help get them out of it. Then I'm back here."

King stared at me like I had two fucking heads. After drinking more of his whisky, he said, "Who the fuck are you today? Because you aren't the Hyde I fucking know."

I scowled at him. "You know much about Gibson Transport, King?"

His movements slowed as understanding dawned on him. Whistling low, he said, "Fuck me. Shane fucking Gibson is the asshole you used to work for?"

"Yeah."

The hard determination King was well known for returned to his eyes. "Storm is behind you, brother. Whatever you need, you have."

Fuck. No. Not what I was looking for. "It's not as clear cut as you think. I need to think about how anything I do could affect Tenille and Charlotte." *And how it will affect Storm.* No fucking way was I involving King or any of the club in this shit.

King was smart, but he always proved you didn't know the half of it. Leaning forward, he said, "I don't give a fuck who he is or who he's connected to. And I sure as hell don't give a fuck that you're trying to protect the club. Storm doesn't let a brother handle shit on their own, especially not when the stench of that shit comes from the places I suspect it comes from. You go see what your family is dealing with. I'll give you enough time to do that, and then I want you checking in with me so we can figure out how to take this motherfucker down."

I pushed out a harsh breath. "Fuck, King, this isn't something Storm needs at the moment. Not with all the heat we're under. That *you're* under."

His chair scraped against the floor as he abruptly stood. "I won't leave you out in the fucking cold on your own, Hyde. That's not how I operate. And if it brings me more heat, so fucking be it." He threw some money down on the table before stalking out of the pub.

Fuck.

Fuck.

Shane Gibson was not a man that Storm wanted to cross. Any power that King had, Gibson had it ten-fucking-fold. I threw back the rest of my whisky as I resolved to make it my mission to find a way to keep King out of this shit.

CHAPTER 2

Hyde

My wife was a beautiful woman. Even half drunk, stumbling across her front lawn screaming at her husband, she was stunningly beautiful. Fourteen years after I'd last laid eyes on her, she still took my breath away.

Tenille had made some changes, though. The long black hair I'd loved had been replaced with a shorter cut that hit her shoulders. Still looked good, but not my preference. And the curves I'd loved on her had been ditched. Her body was stick-thin instead, and that was a fucking shame as far as I was concerned.

I stood in the shadows of her neighbour's house watching her argue with her husband, Craig. It was just after nine at night, and he'd come home late. She'd started in on him immediately, until they'd brought the fight outside. He'd exited their home first, and she'd chased after him. Her drunken state didn't help her. She'd almost tripped in her haste to catch him before he got in his car. He'd caught her before she fell, but had pushed her away while they continued arguing about her drinking and the money missing from their bank account.

I'd arrived in Melbourne late that afternoon and had intended to get eyes on Tenille's place, suss out the area and then crash at my motel before going back to see her in the morning. I didn't want our first conversation after fourteen years to be late at night when everyone was tired. However, my plans changed when their fight became physical. No fucking way would I stand by and watch a woman get hurt. Especially not my wife.

I covered the distance between the three of us fast but not fast enough to stop his palm from connecting with her cheek. Everything that happened in the few moments after was a blur. Between them yelling at each other, Tenille trying to hit him back, me trying to intercept, and Tenille's shock when she realised who I was, I wasn't sure how it all went down. But I would never forget the look on her face as recognition set in.

"Aiden?" My name fell from her lips on a strangled cry. I felt every ounce of her pain and confusion in that cry. And the knowledge that I'd caused her any kind of agony cut deeper than it had in the past fourteen years.

"What the fuck?" Craig's confusion mirrored Tenille's. We'd never met, so he had no way of knowing me, but he knew my name.

"No... it can't be. You're dead," Tenille said as she lurched my way, bewilderment splashed across her face.

"Tenille," I started, but stopped when she gasped.

"Oh my God!" She stood in front of me, eyes wide, and placed her hand against my cheek. "You look different, but I would know that voice anywhere," she said as she brought her other hand to my face also.

I did look different. I'd packed on a fuckload of muscle, inked half of my skin and grown a beard. I sure as hell wasn't the scrawny kid she'd married.

She madly moved her hands over my face, as if she was trying to feel for something she recognised. I gave her a few moments and then reached for one of her hands to stop her. "It's me."

Her breathing slowed at the same time her hands did. Her body stilled also. And then she slapped me, right about the same time her eyes flashed with anger. "You fucking bastard! Where the fuck have you been?"

I deserved that slap, so I took it. But when she started in on me by punching my chest, I shut that shit down fast. Grabbing both her hands, I pulled them away from my body. "I see some things haven't changed," I muttered. Tenille had often used physical violence in an attempt to get her point across.

"Yeah, well when I discover my husband didn't really die, but rather just left me without another word, you can bet your fucking ass I'm going to react this way."

Craig took that moment to step in. Finally. If I were him, I would have involved myself from the beginning. "You've got a fucking nerve showing up like this. I dragged Tenille from the shit you left her in. If you think I'm about to let you back into her life, to screw her over again, you're seriously mistaken, asshole."

I'd held my temper in check because I owed Tenille the space to be angry and hurt. But I didn't fucking owe this asshole a thing. My shoulder's tensed as I met his gaze. "I don't want a fucking thing. But let's get something straight here, Craig. You didn't drag Tenille from any-fucking-thing. I made sure she was set up financially before I left. I made sure she had everything she needed. By the time you came on the scene, she wasn't in any shit. But you've sure as fuck put here there now, haven't you, motherfucker?"

"Fuck you!" he spat as he threw a punch at me.

I'd seen that coming and blocked it by grabbing hold of his arm and shoving him with enough force to knock him flat on his ass. Ignoring Tenille's shocked gasp, I stepped over his body and pushed him so he was on his back. Pinning his hands to the ground, I said, "A lot of shit has gone down in this family, and I'm here to sort it out for you. I may have walked away from Tenille and Charlotte once, but I'll be fucked if I'll stand back and watch them suffer again. I suggest you get on board with that or else you and I are gonna have trouble. And trouble with me is the last fucking thing you want." Men like Craig—small men who paraded as big fucking men—were best dealt with fast. He needed to know where we both stood. And although he was married to Tenille, that meant very little to me. As far as I was concerned, it was my job to make sure she was okay.

"Mum, what's going on?"

The air in my lungs disappeared at the sound of my daughter's voice. It felt like a hammer had hit my chest, causing my heart to beat in erratic, painful throbs that roared in my ears and screamed through my body.

I stood hunched over Craig, frozen to the spot, unable to look up. Fourteen fucking years without that voice in my life, without *her* in my life, had caused me more torment than anything else had ever come close to causing me.

I desperately wanted to look at her, but my greatest fear stood between us, almost suffocating the life out of me. I hadn't expected that, and it threw me. I didn't fucking acknowledge fear in my life, but this one had haunted me for so long that it had rooted itself deep inside.

What if Charlotte refused to accept me?

Fuck.

"Go back inside, Charlotte," Tenille urged.

"Not until you tell me who that is and why he's threatening Dad."

Dad.

That word slashed right through me as the world began to spin. Jesus, I was losing my shit. And still struggling for fucking air.

It was Craig who snapped me out of it when he pushed me away and yelled, "Charlie, for fuck's sake, go back inside! This has nothing to do with you."

Charlie.

She was *my* fucking Charlie, not his.

My head snapped up, and I finally caught a glimpse of the child I'd missed every single day since I'd left. If I thought I'd been frozen a moment ago, I was completely and utterly rooted to the spot now. Every inch of my skin shivered with a sensation I hadn't felt in sixteen years. It was as if I was seeing her for the very first time again. This was the same feeling I'd felt when I'd laid eyes on her at birth.

Wonder.

Awe.

Disbelief.

Love.

As I stood staring at her long dark curls that were an exact replica of my mother's, and lips that were the same as Tenille's, she placed her hands on her hips and snapped, "God, you can be such an asshole!" With a huff, she spun and stomped back into the house.

I tracked her movements until I couldn't see her anymore. Craig took the opportunity to attack while my attention was elsewhere.

His fist smashed into my face hard, leaving the kind of

pain that usually sent me into a rage. This time, however, I locked that shit down tight. The last thing I wanted to chance was Charlotte seeing that from inside the house. Instead, my hard glare met his as I moved directly in front of him. "The only thing holding me back from knocking you the fuck out is my daughter. You do that—"

"She's not your daughter, asshole. You gave up that right the minute you left town and never looked back."

I took a deep breath as I clenched my fists by my side. "She *is* my daughter. Yeah, I left town, but I never stopped watching over her. You think you and Tenille have been getting by on your own all these years? Think back to the time you lost your job because you smashed your boss's face in at the pub that Friday night. You ever wonder how you had a job offer on the Monday morning? And the time you blew through five grand at the casino? You never stopped to ask how that money magically appeared back in your account the next day?" At the shock lining his face, I nodded. "Yeah, you get the idea. We won't rehash every single time you fucked up and I fixed it before Tenille ever had to know."

Craig didn't have a comeback, but Tenille delivered one that did the work of a thousand armies deployed to destroy. "A man who isn't there to kiss their child's fears away, and bandage their wounds, and help with homework, and tuck them in at night while telling them monsters don't exist, and teach them that they are enough is *not* a father, Aiden. He's simply the guy that donated some fucking sperm. Don't get the two mixed up." I met her hard gaze right before she added, "Helping me and Craig get by certainly doesn't make you a father. Whatever help you think we need right now, we don't, so just go back to wherever you came from and leave us alone."

I watched in silence as she stalked back inside, her earlier drunken wobble almost gone completely. The sound of the door slamming closed behind her filled the night air with a reminder that I was going to have to work hard to gain her trust back. I had expected that, but reality was always a harsh bitch compared to expectations.

CHAPTER 3

Hyde

Tenille and I met when we were sixteen. She was the chick who stood up for the underdog whenever given a chance, and I fell for that trait long before I fell for her beauty. I loved her fire and the fierce way she lived her life—always giving anyone who criticised her the middle finger.

She was fiery back then, and stubborn as hell. Convincing her to marry me at nineteen took over a year to do. She held strong views on marriage after watching her father control her mother. Tenille wanted to stay single; she didn't see the need to declare our relationship with a piece of paper. What she didn't count on was my determination to make her mine. I'd been fucking relieved, though, that talking her into having a baby was a lot easier. I'd always wanted lots of kids, and it turned out Tenille was down with that. Both of us came from shitty families; replacing them with our own was a dream we'd shared.

As I sat on my bike in the undercover car park of the shopping centre where she worked, the day after she slapped me and told me I was merely a sperm donor, I realised she hadn't changed much. She exited the shopping centre after work, at the time Sully informed me she would, and began the short trek to her car. Right before she arrived at her old beat-up Corolla, a guy had almost reversed into her. An honest mistake because the 4WD next to his car would have blocked his vision. Still as fiery as ever though, Tenille let loose on him, giving him a piece of her mind.

I left my bike and approached them as the guy lost his cool.

He ripped his sunglasses off, demanding, "Fuck, are you this bitchy to everyone you meet or just us unlucky bastards?"

She placed her hand on her hip and raised her brows at him. "Just the assholes who don't watch where they're driving."

His glare deepened. "Yeah well, lady, I told you I couldn't see shit because of that 4WD in the way, so back the fuck off, okay."

I moved next to Tenille. "This is done," I directed at him before turning to her. Wrapping my hand around her forearm, I said, in a tone that asked for no arguments, "Let's go."

The guy nodded his agreement and turned to leave. Tenille, on the other hand, didn't take heed of my tone. Her wild eyes met mine as she pulled her arm from my grip. "What the fuck, Aiden? What are you doing here? And since when do you get to tell me what to do?"

"Just helping you make a better decision, Tee."

"I don't need your help. I could have done with it fourteen years ago, but not now. And don't call me that. You don't get to call me that anymore," she snapped.

Her anger was justified. I'd give her that. But letting her

make the mistake of riling this guy up any further wasn't something I was about to do. Hooking my arm around her waist, I lifted her and walked both of us away from him before she could continue her tirade. She fought me all the way, legs kicking and arms swinging, but I managed to keep hold of her until he was settled back in his car.

When I finally let her go, she straightened her clothes and shot me a filthy look. "Is that how you get women to do what you want these days? Just manhandle them however you please?" Her voice wobbled on the last few words she spat my way, letting me know a softening was coming.

I remembered clear as day how Tenille's bursts of anger went. First, the passionate outburst that she didn't put much thought into; then a moment of confusion when her brain kicked into gear; and then the softening as she came around and realised there might be more to the argument than she first saw.

Pushing a flyaway strand of hair out of her eyes, I said, "I don't get women to do what I want these days, Tee."

She stilled and her breathing slowed. Understanding dawned on her face, and her mouth fell open. Lastly, a frown wrinkled her forehead. "You're not with anyone?"

I shook my head. "No."

Confusion riddled her face. "But you have been, right? Like, I can't imagine you not being with a woman since you left me."

I scrubbed my hand over my face. This was not what I came here to discuss. "Out of everything we could be talking about right now, you want to discuss my sex life?"

The confusion on her face gave way to the shitty look she'd given me earlier. And the hand that landed on her hip told me I'd said the wrong fucking thing. Story of my life with Tenille. She blew hot and cold as easily as she breathed. "Do you know how it makes me feel knowing that you walked away from me and faked your own fucking death? Besides being upset and angry that you could do that to your wife and your child, it makes me, as a woman, feel like shit. Like I wasn't good enough for you. So yeah, I want to discuss your sex life, because I'm kind of wondering whether you found better out there. Whether you found what you were looking for." She worked herself up into such a state that her breaths came out unevenly as she tried to swallow her hurt. There was no hiding it, though—I'd wounded her horribly.

I stared at her, my mind splintering with a hundred different thoughts as I took in everything she said. It had never occurred to me that she would assume I left because she wasn't good enough. That I was looking for some tits and ass somewhere else.

Fuck.

Reaching for her, I said, "Tee, me leaving had nothing to do with not being happy with you or looking to get laid elsewhere."

She shrugged away from me. Wrapping her arms around her body, she said, "Why else would you leave? It doesn't make any sense."

I'd known this question would need to be answered when I decided to come back, but I still wasn't sure how much information to share with her. The need to make her understand clashed with my commitment to keeping her and Charlie safe, leaving me with a tough decision. On top of that, I'd sheltered Tenille from the harsh truth of working for Shane Gibson all those years ago. As far as she knew, he was simply the father of our old schoolmate, and a nice guy who cared enough to give me a job when I'd needed one. He was also the man who looked out for her when her husband died and gave her second husband a job when he needed one. She didn't know that he'd happily put a bullet in a man as naturally as he'd hold a newborn baby.

"I got tied up in some bad stuff at work. The cops started investigating, and Shane told me to get out of town to save us all going down. He was the one who organised the fire at our house—"

"Bullshit." She cut me off. "Shane would never do that." The fierce way she defended him was like a knife twisting in my chest. The motherfucker had clearly won her over while helping her pick up the pieces of her life.

"It's not bullshit. You don't know half the truth about Shane."

"I know more than you think I do, Aiden. Remember, it's been a long time since you left. A lot has happened in that time, and Shane has been a good friend to me."

I narrowed my eyes at her. Something she said, or the way she said it, triggered a warning deep in my gut. "What did he tell you after I left?" I kept a firm grip on my temper while waiting for her answer, but I was dangerously close to losing it. Not at her, but at the situation that Gibson had put me in.

"About what?"

My shoulders tensed as I took a long, calming breath. It didn't do much good, though. "About me, Tee. What the fuck did he tell you about me?"

She blinked a couple of times at my raised voice. "Don't yell at me!" At my silence that smacked of anything but pleased, she added, "Nothing. He didn't tell me anything about you. All I know is that he misses you. Still to this day, he goes on benders when he thinks about you and Brad too much."

Stunned, I tried to process that. Brad was Shane's son and had been my best mate in high school. He'd died in a freak accident just before Charlotte was born. I could believe that Gibson still mourned his son's death, but what I could never believe was that he still cared for me. Not after what he'd done to me all those years ago.

"So you're close to Gibson?" Sully's information over the years painted a picture of Gibson helping her out, but I wasn't sure just how close he'd become to my family. It wouldn't have surprised me if he'd stayed near to keep an eye out for my return.

She didn't answer me straight away, just kept her eyes firmly on mine while she stayed silent. Finally, she blinked and glanced at her feet briefly before looking back up at me and nodding. "Yeah, kind of."

Something felt off here. I couldn't put my finger on it, but Tenille seemed to be acting strangely. She was hiding something from me. I guessed, though, that she had no reason to trust me these days. I'd have to rebuild that. However, in the meantime, I needed answers, and I also needed to make sure she understood a few things about the situation we were in.

"I'm telling you the truth, Tee, but I get it if you can't trust me on that for now. All I ask is that you don't tell Shane I'm back."

"Stop calling me that!" She rummaged in her bag for a moment, pulled her keys out, and added, "I'm going home now. To my *husband*. I don't want to see you again, and as far as keeping secrets from Shane Gibson, I'm not sure that's even possible. He's the kind of man who seems to know everything that's going on."

The displeasure written all over her face, coupled with the wariness flashing in her eyes and the bite in her words, hurt more than I ever thought it would. Where was the girl I'd loved more than anyone before or after her? I'd at least assumed she'd still be in there somewhere, giving me a sliver of an opportunity to show her the truth of the situation.

I reached for her, curling my hand tightly around her forearm. As our skin connected, a spark blazed through me, jolting long-forgotten memories to the surface. Or maybe they were buried in an effort to move on. Her eyes sliced to mine. I ignored the warning in them, in much the same way I'd done many times during our relationship. It was what Tenille and I were good at—ignoring signals and pushing our way in or out of situations. It didn't always work in our favour, but that never stopped me from trying.

"Do you remember the day we were married? I promised you forever that day, and you cried as you promised me the same. It was the first time I ever saw you cry, and it made me understand how deep you were in with me, because getting you to that point had taken me some hard fucking work, and I hadn't always been sure you really wanted to marry me." I paused for a moment, searching her face to make sure she was still with me. She was. In fact, she held her breath while she took in everything I said. "I fucked up our forever, Tenille. I'm sorry for that. But I'll be damned if I'll sit back and watch any more of your life get screwed over. When I tell you that Gibson isn't who he shows to the world, I need you to remember the trust you used to have in me and trust what I'm saying now, too. I need you to know that even though you and I don't have a forever anymore, I never stopped loving you. And anything I'm trying to do now to help you is because of that. Dig deep, Tee, and think back to who I used to be before I left. For you, I'm still that person."

I laid myself out in a way I hadn't had to in over a decade, hoping like hell that she'd respond and give me an inch.

But she didn't.

Reefing her arm out of my hold, she shook her head like a mad woman. "You took all my trust, Aiden, and threw it in my face. And it makes me question everything about you and who you were before you walked away. You knew everything about me and all the shit I'd been through, so I feel like if you really loved me like you say you did, you would never have left me alone to raise Charlotte and deal with shit on my own." She drew a long breath as her fight faded. Staring at me with eyes that revealed her turmoil, she added, "Just leave again. We don't need you here."

No fucking way was I backing down. She'd just have to find a way to deal with me being around.

"No, you do need me here, Tenille. I've had a guy keeping an eye on you and Charlie since I left—"

She frowned as her fight flared up again. "What the fuck? Like a stalker watching over us?"

I kept my own fight in check. I'd forgotten just how argumentative my wife could be. Sometimes, it had been like going to war every day with her irrational thoughts and emotions that she flung at me. "No, like a private investigator who made sure you guys were okay. He checked in with me regularly, letting me know how you both were."

"Jesus, Aiden, that's a little extreme, don't you think?"

"Clearly not, if the shit you and Craig are in at the moment is anything to go by."

She straightened, pushing her shoulders back. I remembered this move—it was what she did when she tried to appear confident. What it told me, though, was that whatever came out of her mouth next would be a lie. "If you're talking about the fights we've been having, they're nothing. We love each other and are working things out."

I narrowed my eyes at her. "I'm talking about that, along with your drinking, Charlie's school grades going down, and the money missing from your bank account. Are you working all that out, too?" My last words came out a little too harshly, but fuck, this wasn't shit to be avoided.

She stilled. "Your PI is a nosy bastard. None of those things are your business."

"I would argue with that. They are all my business because you and Charlie are my business, and I plan to get to the bottom of every single one of them. With or without your help."

Silence for a beat. And then—"You know what would have been nice? If you'd been this intent on getting to the bottom of shit fourteen years ago when you and I were having problems. When you tell me to think back to who you were then, and to know you're that same man for me now, it doesn't mean much, because back then all you focused on was working. You were hardly home, and when you were, you and I spent most of that time arguing." She jabbed a finger against my chest. "So don't come back here now and tell me you know all about my marriage to Craig and the shit my family is in, and that you're going to fix it, when you couldn't even fix your own shit years ago." She turned to get in her car, leaving me staring after her with no comeback.

She was right. I hadn't been there for her when she'd needed me. I'd been so fucking focused on providing for our family that I'd ended up neglecting them. And as the weeks and months passed, and the small wounds between us had turned to gaping ones that I didn't even know how to begin to fix, it just became easier to fight with her or to retreat completely. At the end, we'd both been like casualties of war who stared at each other through vacant eyes, hurling words intended to hurt the other because that felt like the only way to allow the pain out.

The guilt I carried over that and over leaving them never eased up. It was like a hammer chipping away at me all the fucking time. I was certain that the only way I'd ever get rid of it was to make things right with Tenille again. We couldn't go back, but we could sure as fuck go forward. But only if I could convince her to let me in.

CHAPTER 4

Hyde

Four hours after seeing Tenille in the car park outside her work, I made my way up the path towards the front door of her house. This wasn't the home we'd lived in. I hadn't seen the inside of it yet, but if the outside was anything to go by, this house was much nicer than the one we'd rented. The well-maintained garden with colour everywhere was only the first clue. The recently painted wood was another. On top of that, the neighbourhood was respectable. I'd been relieved when Sully had told me Tenille had chosen to raise our daughter here. I may not have been around to help her do that, but at least the money I'd left her ensured she could afford to give Charlie a good start in life.

As my boot landed on Tenille's front porch, I slowed and took a moment to get my head together. Not something I was used to doing. My usual method for getting what I wanted was to charge in and do whatever it took, regardless of the consequences, because they meant very little to me. But in this situation, the consequences were everything. They would never be anything less than that when they involved my daughter.

Taking a deep breath, I knocked on the door and waited. Raised voices coming from inside told me that Tenille and Craig were most likely arguing again. The way Craig ripped open the front door a couple of minutes later, confirmed that.

He scowled as our eyes met. "What the fuck are you doing back here? I thought we made it clear last night that you aren't welcome."

Not waiting for an invitation, I forced my way into their home. "I obviously didn't make it clear enough that I don't give a fuck."

I didn't wait for his reply. Instead, I walked the length of the hallway until I found Tenille in their kitchen. The smell of roast filled my nostrils in much the same way the homely feel of their house filled every cold part of me. Family photos, plants, warm light, books, the television running in the background, a cat that rubbed up against my legs, and Tenille chopping potatoes in the kitchen—it was all there.

She'd done it.

Tenille had created the family we always wanted.

I'd always known it, but now I fucking *felt* it.

The ache in my chest came out of nowhere as I watched her. Really, it was so much more than an ache, but that was all I would acknowledge it as. I'd spent years figuring out ways to avoid this kind of pain; I wasn't going to let it in now. I just needed to get through this conversation and then I'd drown that fucking pain at the nearest pub.

Tenille stopped chopping and placed her knife down. "You just don't give up, do you?"

Before I could answer, Craig stormed into the kitchen. He'd been yelling at me as I walked down the hall, but I'd shut him out. "Motherfucker! You can't fucking come into our house and—"

"Craig," Tenille hissed. "Charlotte can hear everything you're saying."

I faced him, doing my best to ignore the way my chest tightened knowing that my daughter was so close. I hadn't been sure if she'd be home. Figured she might have been out with friends or at the ice skating rink where I knew she spent a lot of time.

Fury riddled his body, and I wondered how close he was to punching me again. "You need to get used to the idea that I'm back in Tenille's life now. And Charlie's."

His nostrils flared. "Tenille told me you cornered her after work today. And that you want to play Good fucking Samaritan and fix our problems. We don't need you, Aiden. We're already working on our own shit."

"I'm here for a lot fucking more than that."

Tenille's sharp intake of breath filled the room. "I knew it. You want Charlie."

Fear laced her words, and that fear sliced into my heart. I never wanted her to fear me. Fuck, me being back was supposed to do the opposite.

My gaze found hers. "I'm not here to take Charlie, Tee. But she is mine, and I would like to get to know her."

She paled. "Do you realise the impact that might have on her, Aiden? She thinks you're dead. All these years, you've let her think that. And now you want to come back, when she's sixteen and already going through so much shit in her life with school and friends. She doesn't need you to add to the stress she's already under." Her voice trembled as her anxiety increased.

I moved closer to her, surprised that Craig hadn't. His wife was visibly upset, but he made no move to console her. "We can go slowly. I don't expect to just come back and to suddenly be deep in your lives. She and I can find our way to each other over time."

Her eyes narrowed at me. "Have you had anything to do with teenage girls in the last fourteen years?"

I frowned, not understanding where she was going with this. "No."

Shaking her head, she muttered, "Fuck, I didn't think so. Let me tell you, sixteen-year-old girls are a handful. And while they slap on a mask for the world, underneath that bullshit they're vulnerable and sensitive. This kind of news will confuse the hell out of Charlie, and I don't want to put her through that at the moment."

"So when do you propose, Tee?" My question was genuine, but I couldn't hide my impatience.

"Never!"

Craig finally manned up and stepped around me to pull Tenille into his arms. In a hushed voice, he said, "Can we at least agree to make a time to meet to discuss this? I don't want Charlie to come out and meet you without us preparing her first."

His use of *Charlie* grated again, but I bit my tongue in order to keep the peace. "Agreed."

Craig and I may have come to an agreement, however forced, but Tenille didn't appear to want any part of it. "I'll meet you to discuss this, but I'm not promising anything will happen soon. I want to make sure Charlie is more settled at school before we do this. She's been having problems so far this year."

Charlie had just started her second last year of high school. It was an important year, so it concerned me to hear she was experiencing difficulties. "Okay, we'll meet tomorrow and talk more about this. The last thing I want is to cause more issues. You'll guide me on this."

Her eyes widened at my acceptance of what she said.

When they softened a little, I knew I'd made the right step. "Thank you."

I held her gaze for a moment as I gave her a nod, before looking at Craig again. "I also want to discuss the money that's missing from your bank account."

"Jesus, you're a fucking asshole, aren't you? I'm beginning to wonder what Tenille ever saw in you. For the fucking record, that money is sorted, and I'm not fucking discussing it with you."

His voice grew louder as he spoke, and Tenille placed her palm against his chest as she said, "He's right, Aiden. The money is back in our account and all sorted out, so you don't need to worry about that anymore."

I lifted a brow as I glanced between the two of them. "You miraculously found fifty grand?"

Craig stiffened as he continued to glare at me. "Because I know you're not gonna fucking let this go, I'm doing some extra work for Gibson. He's paid me in advance."

I whistled low as I crossed my arms over my chest and planted my feet wide. "Must be some hard-core work, Craig. Tell me, what kind of work does Gibson ask for these days to pay someone that amount of money?" I knew from Sully that Gibson had hired Craig about a year ago to drive trucks for him after Craig lost his job. Driving trucks, however, didn't earn you fifty grand fast.

Tenille slid out of her husband's embrace. "Don't be a prick, Aiden."

I probably was being a prick, but I gave no shits. I'd watched Craig gamble away their cash for years. I refused to watch any longer. And Tenille needed to see Gibson for the person he truly was. If she thought he'd advance Craig that kind of money out of the goodness of his fucking heart, she lived in fantasyland. And I fucking needed her to understand that fairy tales didn't exist when Gibson was involved. Maybe then she'd realise the truth of why I left her all those years ago.

I jerked my chin at Craig. "I know what kind of work you used to have to do for Gibson to earn good money. I'm wondering if it's the same these days."

Craig swallowed hard, and I knew I was right. Gibson had him getting his hands really fucking filthy for that cash.

"Mum, is dinner nearly ready? I've got a stack of homework to do tonight, and I want to get started."

I spun around to find my daughter watching me warily. The sounds of Tenille and Craig cursing behind me faded away until all that surrounded me and Charlie was silence while we took each other in.

I committed her face to memory—every perfect curve of it —while I tried to ignore the fear rushing at me. *Fuck.* I needed to get this shit under control. Fast.

Her forehead wrinkled slightly. "You're the guy from last night. On the front lawn."

I nodded, unable to form an answer. I wanted to wrap her in my arms and take the fourteen years of hugs I'd missed out on in one go. Wanted to take her pinky in mine like I did when she was a baby. Hell, I wanted to tell her exactly who I was, but I reined in my own desires and upheld my end of the bargain I'd just made. Finally, I managed to grind out, "Yeah."

Tenille pushed past me and took hold of Charlotte, guiding her out of the kitchen as she murmured something I couldn't make out.

As I stood staring after them, Craig said, "You need to go now. Come back tomorrow morning at nine, and we'll talk more." He shoved my back as he added, "And if you ever fucking say a word to Tenille about the work I do for Gibson, I'll make sure you never have anything to do with Charlie."

Every ounce of control I'd worked hard to maintain while

in his presence snapped. I turned to him, curled my hand around his neck and rammed him against the pantry door. A storm raged in me as I squeezed his neck. This man had everything that should have been mine. It wasn't his fault, though, and I needed to remember that. It was *my* fucking fault. But it didn't give him the right to threaten me. No one fucking threatened me and got away with it. The only reason he was still standing was because my daughter was somewhere in this house.

"Don't ever threaten me again," I snarled. "I'm playing this the way Tenille wants to. For now. But don't fucking mistake my acceptance for weakness. I am not a weak fucking man, Craig, and I won't hesitate to show you exactly who I am if I need to. As for Gibson, we both know the level of shit you're in with him. I just hope you have a fucking clue how to get yourself out of it, because trust me when I tell you, he is not a man to stay involved with." I knew I'd hit my mark by the way his face whitened and his breathing slowed.

As I exited their home, I wondered just how deep Craig was in with Gibson. From the information Sully had given me over the years, I hadn't thought they were close. I guessed, though, that a year working for him had drawn Craig closer. And that was how Shane Gibson got blood out of a stone. He sucked you in and gave you everything until the day he started slowly demanding some of it back. He moved with stealth, so that you didn't even realise what he was doing until it was too late and you were handing your life over to him.

CHAPTER 5

Hyde

Motherfucker.

I blinked my eyes a few times in an effort to open them, while at the same time reaching for my phone. As the sunlight blinded me, I muttered, "Fuck."

What fucking time was it anyway? Whoever was calling had better have a good fucking reason for waking me up.

Swiping my phone off the bedside table, I barked, "What?" and immediately regretted it when the headache I'd woken up with intensified

"Late night, brother?" King's voice boomed through the phone. Fuck, could he talk any fucking louder?

"What time is it?"

"Time to get the fuck up."

I slowly swung my legs over the side of the bed and sat on the edge. Cracking one eye open, I took note of the time blaring from the clock in the motel room. Almost seven.

I scrubbed my face. "Why are you calling me so fucking early?"

"We've got a situation here. Might need you to come home sooner than planned, so I wanted to see where you were at with everything down there."

"Just getting started. What's going on with the club?"

"Marx is fucking with us. He just drowned Sydney in cheap drugs. I need to find him fast before he kills our business, but the fucking feds are making that a little hard."

Figuring out who was backing Marx was Storm's top priority, but after we'd taken down the entire Sydney chapter of the Silver Hell MC, Detective Ryland had upped his surveillance of our club. In particular, he had eyes on King every minute of the day and also kept a close watch on Nitro, Devil, and me. Kick had managed to slip through his net somehow.

"I lost my tail on the way down here. They still all over you?"

"Can't shake the fuckers. How long do you think you're gonna need with your family?"

For the first time since I'd joined the club, I felt conflicted. My loyalties were divided. Letting King down was the last thing I wanted to do, but the unwavering certainty I'd felt for over a decade that I would never do that wasn't there anymore. Truth be told, I'd been fighting this for around six months. The pull to my family had grown stronger, until I couldn't ignore it any longer. Fucking shit up with the club like I'd been doing seemed to be my way of not facing it. At least that was Sully's take on this shit. He'd wasted a lot of fucking breath on telling me to get my head out of my ass.

"Hyde," King snapped when I didn't answer him. "How long?"

"I don't know. When you get to the point that you really need me, let me know. I'll be there."

"Yeah." He paused for a beat. "How's your kid?" The demanding tone he'd been using disappeared with his last question. This didn't happen often, but I knew from experience that kids were a trigger for him. They brought out a side to him we hardly ever witnessed. I had to wonder whether having a kid of his own one day would soften him at all. I'd lay bets that it wouldn't, but there were moments where I caught a glimpse of him that made me question that.

"Not sure yet. My wife's playing hardball."

"She won't let you see your daughter?"

"Not yet, but she will. I'll make sure of it."

"I have no doubt, Jekyll."

"Fuck you, brother," I muttered. He liked to call me that when referencing my moods. He'd given me the name Hyde for the same reason, but his use of Jekyll as an alternative stemmed from an argument we'd had way back when. He'd been right during that argument, but I'd refused to budge. Every now and then he threw this name at me to remind me of what an asshole I was.

He chuckled. "You reckon she remembers what a prick you can be?"

I reached for the painkillers I'd dropped beside the bed the night before. "I was a different man back then."

"So she has no idea what's coming for her?"

My headache increased its efforts to destroy me, and my chest tightened as I listened to him. This conversation irritated me.

As I shook two pills out of the bottle, I snapped, "I've got shit to do, King. Are we done here?"

His easy mood disappeared as fast as it came. "Yeah."

I exhaled my relief when the line went dead. I hadn't told anyone about Tenille for a good fucking reason. Talking about her and Charlie stirred feelings I didn't want to have to deal with.

I dropped my phone on the bed and grabbed the bottle of whisky that sat next to the bottle of painkillers. A moment later, I washed the two pills down. Before I screwed the cap back on the bottle, I guzzled enough whisky to get me through the morning. Fuck knew I was gonna need it.

***

"Where's Craig?"

Tenille finished stirring the coffees she'd made us, threw the dirty spoon in the sink and slid my mug across the kitchen counter to me. Lifting her mug, she wrapped both hands around it and drank some while looking at me over the rim. As she placed the drink back down, she said, "He got called into work last minute. He's on his way to Perth now."

This news was the best thing I'd heard in a couple of days. Now she and I could start working through some shit. "Good."

She eyed me silently for a few moments, and I wondered what thoughts ran through her mind. Tenille had never been an easy woman to read, but I'd usually managed to have some clue as to what she'd come out with next. Flying blind with her put me at a disadvantage. One I'd rather not have.

"Why did you leave, Aiden? And what's the real reason you're back?" All the fight she'd had the day before was gone. In its place, was a simple plea, and it seemed to me that she'd finally come to the place in our journey where she was ready to listen.

I moved my hand to hers and held it. Surprisingly, she let me. Trying to figure out where to start to answer her question took me a minute. I had to get this right if I had any hope of convincing her to give me what I wanted. I wasn't opposed to being more forceful if I had to, but things would be a lot easier if she came around willingly.

"Do you remember the times I came home from work with blood on my shirt? You used to ask me why, and I used to—"

"You used to avoid my questions and try to distract me with sex. Yeah, I remember."

"Did you ever wonder what the hell I was keeping from you?"

I expected her to throw something snarky back at me, but she didn't. Instead, she pulled her hand from mine and said, "At first, yes, but by then we weren't in a good place. We were both keeping so much from each other and just trying to get through the day. I did anything to avoid an argument with you, including turning a blind eye to whatever you were getting up to outside of work."

"The blood on my clothes was from work, Tee."

She blinked a couple of times, but other than that, she gave no other reaction that what I'd said shocked her. Tenille had seen a lot in her life as a teen, so I knew not much surprised her, but I'd expected more than what she was giving me. Hell, some nights after work, I'd come home almost soaked in blood.

When she didn't say anything, I demanded, "Did you hear what I said?" No way was she not going to take this in. By the time I was finished, she would have some idea of what Shane Gibson was capable of.

"Yes, but I'm not sure where you're going with this. I asked you two questions, and this doesn't seem to have anything to do with those."

"This has every-fucking-thing to do with those questions." It suddenly felt like we were back where we were fourteen years ago. Snapping and snarling at each other, and not getting anywhere. "Look, I didn't come back here to argue with you—"

She cut me off, her eyes flashing with that wild anger I knew all too well. "I don't know what you expected then, Aiden. You don't get to walk out on your family and come back years later to smiles and fucking gratitude."

Fuck it. I'd been trying to ease her into it, but I could see that wasn't going to work. She appeared closed off to any talk of what Gibson had me doing. Maybe shocking her would be the only way. "Gibson made threats against our family to get me to leave." She blanched at that, but didn't say anything, so I kept going. "He demanded I fake my death and leave town. The fire was his idea, not mine. Fuck, none of it was my idea or what I wanted. I tried to find another way, but there wasn't anything else he would agree to."

"Why would he ask you to do something like that? It doesn't make any sense to me."

"The Gibson you know is not the one I knew. He didn't build his business by smart decisions alone; he used ruthless tactics, and he wasn't afraid to get his hands dirty to make money. I was the person he called on to help him do that."

She swallowed hard a couple of times. "What kind of threats did he make against us?"

"The cops obviously had something on me about what I'd done for him, and he knew it. He threatened to hurt you and Charlotte if I didn't leave and also if I ever came back. That's why I've stayed away. But I never stopped caring about you and Charlie. And like I told you yesterday, I always made sure you were both okay."

She sat back in her chair and ran her fingers through her hair the way she used to when she was nervous. "Jesus, Aiden. I don't know…. This doesn't even sound like something Gibson would do."

"Does it sound like something *I* would have done?"

"No."

"Well there's your answer. I *did* do it, and only because he taught me to."

She frowned. "What do you mean he taught you to?"

"I'm fairly sure that he always intended for me to do his dirty work. He took Brad and me out shooting from about the age of fifteen, and he also made sure we knew how to fight. At the time, I thought he was the kind of dad I would have loved to have, but now I see that he wanted us familiar with guns and able to handle ourselves. He encouraged the darker side of me, Tee."

"So, what, you just happily did all this stuff for him?"

I kept my irritation in check and reminded myself that she had every right to ask these questions. "What I'm trying to say is that I did shit for Gibson that led to him forcing me out of town. And yes, I'm not a good man, Tee. I'm not the man you thought I was, but neither is he. *That's* what I need you to understand here."

She moved off the stool she sat on and commenced pacing her small kitchen. I didn't speak again because I wanted to give her the space to process this new information. Even when the silence became deafening, I kept my mouth shut.

Finally, she met my gaze again. "I'm finding it hard to believe all this, but I can't think that you'd make something up like this just so I'd believe you didn't want to leave me."

I heard the confusion in her voice and knew I'd succeeded in helping move her closer to the truth. She wasn't quite there yet, though, so I needed to do a little more work.

"Do you remember your twenty-third birthday?"

Her eyes narrowed as she thought back to that day. Nodding slowly, she said, "Yeah, kind of. Why?"

"You worked that day, and while you were at work, flowers were delivered. The note said—"

Her memory kicked in and surprise flickered across her

face. "Holy fuck, I didn't even put it together. They were from you."

Moving to where she stood, I ran my finger lightly down her cheek as I nodded. "Yeah, they were from me."

The card had read *Happy birthday. It's time to move on and live again. If you fall, I'll be there.* It referenced a sappy quote that I'd found about six months after we started dating. She'd been going through some shit with her family, and I'd told her if she fell, I'd be there for her. She'd made fun of me for it because she hadn't thought a dickhead like me would say something like that. She was right; they weren't words I would have ever said, but I'd been young, dumb, and in love, so I'd gone out of my way to impress her. It'd worked. After she'd made fun, she'd fallen harder for me and gave up her virginity about a month later.

She stared up at me, seemingly lost in her memories. A moment later, a tear slid down her cheek. Only one, but I'd never known Tenille to be a crier, so this was significant. "It took me so long to get over you. Even after I married Craig, I still wasn't over you," she whispered, her voice full of raw emotion. "I loved you so damn much, but we were in such a bad place, and I hadn't said all the things I wanted to say to you. I hated that the most. I really fucking hated that the last time I saw you, I yelled at you for being a fucking asshole to me, because even though that was true, I still loved you, and I'd wished that the last thing you ever heard me say was *I love you.*"

I nodded, not taking my eyes off hers for even a second. "I knew you loved me. I never cared when you called me an asshole, because at least you were still communicating with me. There were months after Charlie was born that I doubted we'd ever make it out of that black hole. I'll never forget that first huge fight we had when you started to find yourself

46

again. It was one of the best fucking days of my life, because I knew I was getting you back."

Her breaths came faster. "I'm sorry that I fucked it all up back then."

I gripped her cheek and shook my head. "No, you have nothing to apologise for, Tee. You had no control over that depression, and when you worked out what it was, you did everything in your power to fight it. So don't you ever fucking apologise for it again."

She placed her hand on mine as another tear fell. "Where have you been living all this time? What have you been doing?"

My chest squeezed with regret and hatred towards Gibson. He'd taken this woman from me. And everything we might have been able to build together. I fought the urge to kiss her. It wasn't that I was still in love with her—I'd had to find a way to move past that over the years—but the familiarity I felt pulled me towards wanting a taste of her again. I knew she felt it too by the way she was looking at me. Maybe we never got over our first love, regardless of what we went through with them.

I let my hand fall away from her and took a step back. While I would always think of her as my wife, she wasn't mine anymore, and I needed to remember that. I wouldn't drag her through any further heartache with me. "I moved to Sydney."

We sat talking for close to two hours. I filled her in on what I'd been doing with my life since she'd last seen me. Not that there was much to tell, because mostly I'd been taking care of club shit and doing anything to avoid thinking about the way my life had turned out. Those things involved drinking and sex—two things I was sure Tenille wouldn't want to hear about, so I did my best to steer the conversation away from me, to her and Charlie.

Our conversation would have lasted longer, but I received a call from King. Excusing myself, I went outside to take the call. I knew instantly that something was up. King's hard tone gave that away. "Hyde, need you back here now. Sorry, brother. Got a situation that calls for you."

"What?"

"Jacko was killed last night. And when I say killed, I mean fucking executed. I need you to help me figure out who it was because Kick's dealing with baby stuff, and Nitro and Devil are busy with other shit. And at this point, you're the only other person I trust for this job."

"Fuck," I muttered. Not because this would drag me away from Charlie and Tenille, but because it was just one thing after another with the club. And, fuck… Jacko. We hadn't been close, but I'd always liked him. "Give me an hour to leave. I'll tie up some shit here first." That'd put me back in Sydney by ten tonight, maybe earlier depending on traffic.

"Call me when you get back." With that, he ended the call.

"Everything okay?"

I turned to find Tenille watching me hesitantly. Her new acceptance of me seemed a little shaky. I'd need to get back to Melbourne soon so I could strengthen that.

"No, some club business has come up. I need to go home and sort it out."

She wrapped her arms around herself, and I sensed her retreat. "Okay."

"I'll be back as soon as it's dealt with. I want time with Charlie. I figure me going home will give you a chance to talk with her and help prepare her for seeing me."

Taking a deep breath, she nodded. "Yeah, I guess."

I stepped closer to her. "You're not going to change your mind on this, are you?" Not that I would let her, but I wanted her to be comfortable with it.

She shook her head. "No. But it's complicated, you know? I've gotta get Craig on board with it, too. And God knows how Charlie will take the news. I'm just worried, is all."

I stopped myself from telling her that if Craig had a problem with it, I'd settle that fast. Taking shit slowly wasn't how I usually ran my life, but on this occasion it was called for. "I'll give you my number. Keep me updated."

We exchanged numbers and I gave her my address before leaving her to head back to the motel so I could grab my gear and make the trip home. Disappointment that I hadn't had any time with Charlie sat heavy in my gut, but it was a feeling I was old friends with, so I simply carried it with me like I always did.

CHAPTER 6

Monroe

"Did you end up getting any last night?" Savannah asked me as she handed the bowl of potato salad over. It was our weekly dinner at our parents' house, and we were all in attendance—my sister, Savannah, my brother, David, his wife, Nikita, and me. I'd also dragged Tatum along because Nitro was busy with work.

"No." She was talking about the guy I'd met at the club where we'd danced all night. "Which was a crying shame because he had it all going on. I bet he was even pierced under all those clothes."

"You mean you didn't check?" Mum asked.

I turned to my mother who had cocked her head to the side while she waited impatiently for my answer to her question. Laughing, I said, "No, Mum, I don't go around randomly checking men's cocks for jewellery."

"You may as well with the addiction you have," my brother muttered from across the table.

I drank some of my wine and caught David's eye. "It's a good addiction. Better than drugs, don't you think?" David was the prude in our family. Hell, even my parents talked openly about sex with us, but David always found the sex talk a little too much. I liked to mess with him as often as I could.

He shook his head at me in mock exasperation. "It's not the kind of addiction I would choose."

I rolled my eyes. My brother was the complete opposite of me. Where I was impulsive, he had everything in his life planned down to the finest detail. Where I was what you could call a little dramatic, he was calm. And while I was the dreamer in the family, he was the sensible one.

"You'd prefer to be addicted to checking the stock market, right?"

A smile touched his face, but only fleetingly, because God forbid he express his emotions for longer than necessary. "I'd prefer to have no addictions, Roe."

I returned his smile. I did love him, even though he wore me out sometimes with his dry personality. David was the kind of man you wanted in your corner when the shit hit the fan in your life. He'd never failed to come through for me when I needed him. He was solid and always did right by those he loved. Truth be told, I wanted to find a man like him. I just wanted said man to live on the wild side a little and know how to have fun. A little spontaneity never killed anyone.

I raised my wine glass. "I would give up all my addictions to food and clothes and make-up and shoes and bags if I could just have a pierced cock in my life regularly."

My father laughed from the other end of the table. Raising his glass, he said, "Cheers to happiness, baby."

I flashed him a huge smile. My dad was my biggest champion. "Cheers, Dad."

David groaned as he leant back in his seat. "Jesus, don't encourage her."

Dad looked around the table with a smile. "I encourage all my girls."

"Yeah, and look at what you've created," David said. "Three women who walk all over you and spend all your money."

My mother waved her hand dismissively at him. "Pooh to you, too. So we like to live a little. Your father understands the needs of a woman." She threw a wink at Nikita as she tacked on, "And it seems you've followed in his footsteps. Nikita is a woman after my own heart."

David took after Dad in a lot of ways. Both men were quite serious and anal in the way they ran their lives, but Dad had wisdom when it came to women that my brother at thirty-two was yet to learn. David's analysis of my father allowing the women in his life to walk all over him was off base. It probably seemed that way to most, but Dad had learnt how to handle his wife and his daughters. He knew when to push and when to ease off in a way that still got him everything he wanted in life.

Nikita sent Mum a smile. I loved the relationship they'd nurtured since David started dating her four years ago. They were close in a way a lot of women in their positions weren't. "I think Colin could teach his son a few things."

David muttered something under his breath, but at the same time, he looked at his wife with eyes that told everyone how much he loved her. Sliding his arm around her shoulders, he pulled her close and kissed her. They shared the kind of intimate moment that caused my heart to constrict with jealousy. I wanted that kind of connection with a man. I was a thirty-one-year-old single woman with no men in my life that I would even consider sleeping with, let alone dating.

Tatum leant close. "What are you thinking, Roe? I saw the way you just sighed."

My cousin knew me so well. "Why is it so hard to find a man? I feel like it shouldn't be this hard."

"Maybe it's time to take a break. You've been going at it pretty hard for a long time."

She was right—I had dedicated years to my search. And when I did something, I did it well. I left no stone unturned. But besides a two-year relationship that ended badly a few years ago, I hadn't found a man who held my attention for longer than five months.

"I'm not ready to give up yet."

"I'm not talking about giving up. I'm suggesting you ease up, because I think you're getting a little disheartened with it all, and I don't want that for you."

"Tatum's right," Mum said, listening in on our conversation. "Finding a man has become your sole focus lately, and to be quite frank, I'm missing my Monroe time. We haven't been to the spa in months. And do you remember the last time we went shopping together? I don't."

"Right," Savannah said, joining in. "We're hitting the spa this Saturday. All of us. No excuses."

"I'm in," Tatum said as she drank some of her wine. Her eyes sparkled with fun, which was odd for her, but then again, dating Nitro had changed her. She was all about the fun these days.

"Me too," Nikita agreed, smacking David as he muttered something under his breath again.

Mum's face lit up with happiness. She eyed Dad. "Looks like you've got some peace and quiet on the agenda for this weekend, Col. I'll pick up a roast tomorrow. You can cook it while we're all at the spa on Saturday. Family dinner twice in one week is exactly what Monroe needs."

"And some shoe shopping on Sunday," I said. "That's the other thing I need."

Dad chuckled. "Of course it is. I've heard shoes fix everything."

They didn't fix everything, but I didn't tell him that. I didn't want my family to know just how disappointed I was becoming over being single. I wasn't the kind of person to get down, but lately I'd felt every bit of being single, and it sucked.

"Nitro's been really busy with the club lately. Is everything okay?" I asked Tatum a few hours later at the pub after dinner.

Shaking her head, she said, "No, they've got a lot of problems at the moment. I'm hoping they can figure them all out soon, because he's so tense and hardly ever at home."

"How's the wedding preparations going?"

"Don't ask. We've got less than two months to finalise it all, and I feel like I'm drowning in plans."

"That's because your man was so bloody adamant that he wanted that ring on your finger fast. Maybe you should tell him you're pushing the date out."

She lifted a brow. "You think Nitro is going to go for that? I'd have more luck telling him I was knocking our house down and pitching a tent for us to live in."

I smiled. "I love the way he's changed you."

"He's changed me in so many ways. Which one are you referring to?"

"All of it. If there was ever meant to be a couple, it was you two. And I actually don't know if you have changed each other or if you've just changed yourselves so you can love each other and yourselves better."

She finished her glass of wine. "You're just a big old romantic, Roe. I don't know anyone else who loves love like you do. You're going to find your man one day, and he's going to love you so hard."

"Yes, and until then, I'm going to buy shoes and hit day spas with my mum." *God help me.*

Tatum laughed. "I do love your mother, but there is no way I'll ever allow you to spend all your weekends with her."

"Thank fuck. I was beginning to think I'd turn into a crazy old cat lady living on my own."

She grinned. "With all your shoes. Don't forget them."

"Fuck. I need another drink. And then maybe I'll just take a quick peek around the club and see if there are any men I wanna talk to." At the shake of her head, I added, "Just a really quick peek. Like, five minutes max."

"Five minutes!" She tapped her imaginary watch. "I'm counting those minutes."

I left her and headed towards the bar, checking the pub out for men as I walked. It was Wednesday, not a busy night, so I lucked out on finding anyone that matched my list of requirements.

As I handed Tatum her drink a few moments later, she said, "That was quick. Let me guess, none of the guys in here were a fit."

I ignored her sarcasm. She made fun of my list, but I held fast to it. And the longer it took me to find *the one*, the more items were added to it. "I don't think there are any men in here taller than me, Tatum. That's an automatic strike."

"Yeah, I don't blame you. I couldn't imagine being with a man shorter than me." She placed her drink down on the table. "Okay, enough talk about men. Tell me how the gym's going."

I pulled a face. "How the fuck do you think the gym is going? You know of my hate affair with the fucking gym." I'd joined for the fifth time in my life two days ago in my latest attempt at shifting some weight. And it was still the home of horror as far as I was concerned.

"What are you doing there?"

"They've written me up a weights programme and recommended some classes, including a pilates one that I'm dreading. It starts next Tuesday, so I have almost a week to psych myself up for that one."

"I was surprised when you said you were going back to the gym. I thought you were done with that place."

"Yeah, I was. But I got caught at the shopping centre the other day at one of those bloody stands where they talk you into all kinds of shit. I signed up for three months. I was proud of myself for resisting the guy's charms when he tried to convince me that I was made for a year's membership. I mean, do I fucking look like I'm made for twelve months of horror?"

"You know those agreements have a cooling off period? You can get out of it if you want."

"Yeah, I know." I fell silent for a moment before admitting the truth to her. It was a truth I struggled with, because honestly, I would have preferred to be completely confident in my body, but I wasn't. "I think I actually want to do this, though. I act like I don't care about my curves, and mostly I do love them, but there's this tiny part of me that secretly wants to know what it's like to be your shape. I want to know how it feels to be able to walk into any clothes shop and choose a sexy dress knowing it will definitely fit me. And then to wear that dress out and receive the kind of attention you do when you enter a room."

Her face softened. "Oh, babe, you do realise that you

attract a lot of attention, right? And when I say a lot, I mean a fuckload. I see guys ogling you from miles away."

A wolf whistle and then a lot of cheering from a group of guys cut through the noise of the pub, breaking up our conversation. Turning, I saw a guy down on one knee making what looked like a marriage proposal to his girlfriend. When they quietened down, Tatum said, "Okay, I don't have to work tomorrow, so I'm gonna have a few drinks. You in?"

"Fuck yes!" I pulled out my phone. "I'll text Fox. He can open up at work for me tomorrow so I can go in late."

"Perfect."

It was just what we needed. Between our hectic schedules lately, we hadn't managed Friday drinks together in weeks. And I needed my drinks with Tatum to keep my sanity. Well, the drinks were optional, but she was the keeper of my sanity. I wasn't sure what I would do without her in my life.

CHAPTER 7

Hyde

I watched from where my bike was parked on the other side of the street as the redhead stumbled down the path to her front door. She was clearly drunk, which meant she was of no use to me tonight.

I'd arrived back in Sydney an hour earlier, and King had given me instructions to come here and get as much information out of her as possible about the guy she worked with and who he bought his drugs from. She'd just arrived home in a cab, thank fuck. I'd started to think she was out for the entire night. King was on the warpath trying to figure out who was behind Jacko's death, and for some reason, he thought she would have information that'd help us.

Monroe—the redhead—tripped just as she almost made it to her front door. It wasn't a surprise. The heels she wore were so fucking high I wasn't sure how she even managed to stand in them, let alone walk in them.

"Fuck," I muttered when she landed on her ass. Moving off my bike, I crossed the street and jogged to where she sat.

"Why the fuck do women insist on wearing heels like that?"

Her back was to me when I asked my question. She swiftly turned her upper body to look at me. "Jesus, do you always sneak up on women near midnight?" I didn't miss the panic in her eyes before she realised it was me. Couldn't blame her—it was fucking late. I'd tried to talk King into putting this visit off until the morning, but he'd been forceful in his desire to see it done tonight. I guessed the fact she'd met me once helped ease some of her concern.

"Can't say it's on my regular list of jobs, no." I watched as her eyes traced every inch of my body. Monroe appeared to be a woman who wasn't afraid to show her healthy appreciation for men. I crouched next to her. "See anything you like?"

My question didn't even come close to interrupting her appraisal. She continued to silently check me out before slowly bringing her eyes back up to meet mine. A smile danced across her lips. "How tall are you?"

My lips twitched with amusement. She was fucking drunk. And that was the strangest fucking question I'd ever been asked by a woman. "Six foot five."

The lazy smile on her face grew into the kind of smile that could knock a man on his ass. "Well look at that," she murmured, making absolutely no sense to me.

"Look at what?"

"A man who is taller than me. I vaguely remember that about you, but I wasn't sure if my memory was right."

She moved in an effort to stand, but her drunken state didn't allow that to go too smoothly. She'd almost made it off her knees when she started to go down again. I reached for her and helped her up. By the time we were both standing, my hands were firmly around her waist and her tits were pressed up against my chest.

Her face lit up and she hit me with that dazzling smile again. "I'd say it's a good thing you dropped by unannounced so late. Otherwise I would have probably had to sleep out here tonight."

I jerked my chin at the door. "How about you unlock that door so I can get you inside before you pass out."

"Oh good lord, not only are you tall, but you're helpful, too. It's not often a girl can tick two items off her list in such a short space of time."

I let her go so she could turn and take the last few steps to the door, but made sure to keep my hands close in case she fell again. "What list are we ticking items off?" I'd expected to cop an earful for waking her when I arrived at her place, not this.

She stopped abruptly and turned back to face me. I hadn't been expecting that, so I collided with her. She wobbled on unsteady legs, but my arms were around her in an instant, holding her up.

"What list do you think?"

"I've no fucking clue. That's why I asked."

Her hands landed on my chest and she pressed herself closer against me.

Fuck.

This was getting dangerous. *Monroe was dangerous.* Those curves called to me. Fuck, everything about this woman called to me. I remembered the first time I'd laid eyes on her. She'd been in her kitchen rambling on about broken doors and religious shit or something. I'd copped one look at those curves and I'd been fucking lost for words for a minute. It wasn't just her body that did it for me; it was everything about her. From that red hair, to her voice, to the way she'd handled herself when Devil and I had come over—she had something I couldn't put my finger on or describe. But whatever it was, I wanted a taste.

"You had much experience with women, tiger?"

Tiger?

Fuck, though, I'd answer to that.

"Depends on your definition of much."

"Mmm, I'm betting that by your definition, you probably have. I can't imagine a man like you not getting your fill. But I'm asking about your experience with dating and relationships, not purely sex."

"A man like me?"

"Yeah, tall, hot with muscles for miles, and a voice that makes me wanna beg you to take my vibrator away and replace it with your cock."

I raised a brow. "Is this the alcohol talking or do you talk to all men this way?"

She ignored that question. "So, do you have much experience?"

I gripped her waist and moved her away from me. "Can't say I do."

"I figured. It's a damn shame you're not into dating. But I'm taking a break anyway, apparently. If you listen to my mother and Tatum. They think shoes can make up for cock. Pfft. That's what women with cock in their life say. Us singles girls would give up shoes in a heartbeat."

I stared at her, no clue what she was going on about. But then, that seemed to be how most of this conversation was going down. "Okay, let's get you inside."

She placed a hand on her hip. "You trying to tell me to stop talking?"

I chuckled. "I doubt any man could tell you that and get away with it."

My answer seemed to work for her. She finally turned, unlocked the door and entered her house. I followed close behind, steadying her when she stumbled. We walked the short distance to her kitchen where she threw her bag on the counter, kicked off her shoes, and poured herself a drink of water.

Eyeing me, she said, "What are you doing here? We never did cover that."

It had surprised me that she'd allowed me into her home so easily, but I figured her drunken state had a lot to do with that decision.

"King sent me to ask you about the guy you work with and who he gets his drugs from."

"You think I know that kind of information? I don't do drugs, so I'm not up on who the drug dealers are in this town."

It was what I'd suspected and had said as much to King. "Yeah, I figured. I'll need to talk with your guy tomorrow. You know where I'll be able to find him?"

"He's working." She reached for one of the pens she had stashed in a mug on the counter, and a piece of paper. Scribbling an address down, she said, "He'll be here from about nine until three."

I took the paper when she offered it to me. "You good from here?"

She smiled and cocked her head. "You offering to help me some more?"

I was far from a fucking saint, but taking advantage of drunk women wasn't something I did. Even when that was *all* I wanted to do. "I think it'd be best if I didn't help you too much tonight."

She continued to watch me with appreciation. "You sure do know how to make a woman feel good. I'll let you off the hook since you appear hell-bent on not touching me. But let the record show that I may not let you walk away a second time if, say, you were to show up here again."

Jesus, it had been a long fucking time since I'd wanted to flirt with a woman rather than simply fucking her. I pushed off from the counter I was leaning against. "Is that an invitation?"

She shrugged drunkenly. Her body moved with an easy and natural sexiness that sucked me right in. Even when she was intoxicated and not trying to be sexy, she fucking was. "I'll leave that up to you."

Not a smart move. If shit were up to me, I'd be back to fuck her tomorrow. But with all her talk of dating, I figured Monroe was probably looking for a relationship rather than what I had to offer. And again, for the first time in a long time, I wasn't sure I wanted to chance disappointing a woman.

CHAPTER 8

Monroe

"You wishing you hadn't had all those drinks last night yet?" Fox asked me as I dropped my head into my hands and groaned for about the hundredth time. Well a hundred was an exaggeration, but not by much.

I cracked an eye open to look at him but didn't lift my head. It hurt too much to move, so I restricted that to only when it was absolutely necessary. "You think if I promised God I'd clean up my act, he'd wipe this headache?"

"You don't believe in God."

"Just because I don't go to church, doesn't mean I don't believe."

He glanced towards the front door of the shop as a guy entered. "You reckon you've got it in you to clean up your act, Roe? Like, I don't see that happening at all."

He was right. I didn't. But a girl could pretend.

I straightened because we had a customer. Thank God for

Fox—he'd opened up this morning and had taken care of almost all the customers so that I could rest and feel sorry for myself over how damn hung-over and sick I was.

"You okay on your own for a bit while I do this tat?" Fox asked after chatting with the guy about what he wanted.

"Yeah." I didn't even have it in me to talk much. Everything I did or said exacerbated the headache.

He narrowed his eyes at me. "You sure? It looks like you're getting worse rather than better."

I waved him away. "It's a slow day. I'll be fine."

With some hesitation, he left me, and I sighed with relief as I settled into the chair we had at the front counter and rested my head again. The day had been a waste. I'd achieved none of my goals, but at that point, I didn't have it in me to care.

Fifteen minutes later, my headache eased a little thanks to the silence. I was beginning to drift off to sleep when a deep voice rumbled, "How's that head, sugar?"

I'd know that voice anywhere. It was the voice of sin and sex. Well, at least, that was what it made me want to do. However, it was also the voice of danger, and it set alarm bells ringing all over the place. Hyde was a biker and best to avoid when it came to sex.

Without lifting my head, I mumbled, "How do you think?"

His chuckle filled the room, and I cursed him silently for being so damn sexy. "Gotta say, I'm surprised to see you here. Figured you'd stay home and sleep it off."

I was beginning to wish I had, too, as my memory reminded me of what I'd said to him last night. Not to mention the fact I'd fallen on my ass and stumbled all over the place. Sure, I was a woman who liked to flirt with men, but I usually refrained from doing that with men who could bring trouble into my life. It was okay to have Storm around in the form of Nitro, but I didn't want to invite one of them into my life on a regular basis. And yet, I'd pretty much invited him to pop on by for a quickie when he was next in the neighbourhood.

Reluctantly, I met his gaze. The heat I found there caused my legs to squeeze together. *Shit.* "Look, about last night, I was so drunk I hardly remember any of it, but I do remember you helping me into my house. Thank you for that." I prayed hard that he'd let me off the hook and not bring up anything I'd said to him.

His eyes firmly held mine, but his face gave nothing away. I couldn't tell what he was thinking. Finally, though, he nodded. "No worries." Then, glancing around the shop, he said, "Is your workmate in?"

I could have kissed him for not pushing the point. But, kissing him was off the table. *Must remember that.* "Yeah, but he's with a customer. He'll be a while. I could get him to call you when he's finished."

Those dark eyes of his found mine again. With a shake of his head, he said, "No, I need to speak to him now."

I lifted a brow. God these bikers could be pushy. Nitro sure as hell was, and it seemed Hyde had the same bossy streak. "So when I said he's busy, I meant he can't speak with you now."

"I won't be long." With that, he walked away from the counter and towards where Fox was working.

Oh no he didn't.

"Hey, this is *my* business, dude. And when I say that one of my staff members is busy working and can't see you, I mean it. So back the fuck up and turn your ass around." My headache returned full force, which only made me crankier. I wasn't sure exactly what caused me to snap at him, but it was probably the fact I felt so ill combined with the fact that it annoyed me when men didn't listen to me.

He came to an abrupt halt and turned to face me. The heat in his gaze had disappeared completely. In its place was a dark expression that, along with the hard set of his shoulders, told me I'd pissed him off. Well, fuck him. He was the one in the wrong here. Not me.

Taking a step towards me, he said in a low voice, "You care to repeat that?"

I crossed my arms in front of me. "No, not really. I'm fairly certain you heard what I said."

"I heard it, but I didn't fucking like it."

"Do I look like I care whether you liked it?" This conversation was going downhill at a rapid rate of knots.

"You should care."

"Yeah, so I've heard. But I've had a long day and am in too much pain to even think about caring. All that matters to me at this point is that my guy finishes the tattoo he's working on and that my customer is happy with the work. I've got bills coming out of my ass, so I kinda need the cash from that job so I can pay them. You barging in there demanding Fox's time could piss my customer off, which may mean I can't pay my bills. You see where I'm coming from?"

He watched me in silence for a few moments. I couldn't tell if he was calming down or getting more worked up. He still looked angry, but his body language told another story.

Just when I was beginning to settle in to go another round with him, he said, "I'll leave my number. Get him to call me."

"God, could you be any more bossy?" I muttered before stalking back to the front counter. Locating a pen and paper, I shoved them at him when he joined me there, and said, "And just so we're clear on something, that invitation to come back to my place for sex no longer stands."

I couldn't be sure, but I would have sworn he almost

smiled. He jotted down his number as he said, "I see you remember something from last night."

I snatched the paper from him when he was done. "It just came back to me, so I wanted you to know I'm actually not interested. It was all that damn alcohol I drank that made me say shit I didn't mean."

Resting his hands on the counter, he leant over it so our faces were close. "Just so *you* know, that vibrator of yours has got nothing on my cock." He tapped the piece of paper with his number on it. "You change your mind, you use that."

Without another word, he exited my shop, and I stared after him, unable to process the thoughts rushing through my mind. He had me so worked up and so damn confused. On the one hand, I never wanted to see him again. The absolute nerve of him to come to my business and try to tell me how things were going to go down. But on the other hand, the man was hot as hell, and I was more attracted to him than any man I'd met in a long time.

I looked up at the roof, towards the heavens.

Why God?

Why is the only man I want to sleep with a moody asshole?

CHAPTER 9

Hyde

Women.

Fuck.

Dealing with them was fast becoming the norm in my life. And after all these years of *not* having to deal with them, it was doing my fucking head in.

For what felt like the fiftieth fucking time that day, I checked my phone for a text from Tenille. It had been over twenty-four hours since I'd left Melbourne, and I was yet to hear from her. My natural instinct was to call and demand to know what was happening with Charlie, but the rational side of me won out, so I shoved my phone back into my pocket and blew out a long, frustrated breath.

"Fucking women," I muttered under my breath. I was sitting at the bar in the clubhouse waiting for King. Being mid-afternoon Thursday, it wasn't busy, but the few guys there were fucking noisy. I turned to face them and called out, "Can you assholes keep the fucking noise down?"

They scowled at me. I wasn't anyone's favourite person, but at least when I wanted something it was usually given. As they quietened, I turned back to my drink and took a swig, my eyes meeting Kree's.

"Rough day?"

I didn't like many people. Not easily, anyway. But Kree was someone I did like. Probably because she knew when to involve herself in something and when to back off. She was smart as hell, too, a trait I valued in a person.

I drained my glass, the second whisky I'd had that afternoon after returning from Monroe's shop. "Tell me something, Kree. You've got kids, right?"

She stopped what she was doing and put down the glasses she was clearing away. Kree had this way of giving her full attention when she had a conversation. You knew she was fully in it, and that was another thing I liked about her. "Yes."

"If you had a teen daughter who hadn't seen her father since she was a toddler, how do you think she'd take the news that he was back?"

"My daughter is only young, so I have no experience with teens yet, but I can tell you how I reacted when my dad came back into my life when I was fifteen. I desperately wanted him around, but he'd walked out on us when I was five, so I was angry with him. Ten years without him built enough anger to cause some explosive fights. And fifteen was an age where I liked to express my anger a lot. So I took it out on him." She rested her elbows on the bar and leant closer to me. "I'll tell you this, though—if he'd been man enough to stick that anger out, I would have forgiven him and accepted him. But he didn't. We haven't seen each other since."

"And your mum? How did she deal with all that?"

She straightened. "She hated him more than I did, so it wasn't pretty. Maybe if she hadn't shared that anger with me, it might have been different with my dad. I may not have been so mad at him. But at the end of the day, my father was a weak man. A child—especially a teen—needs strength from their parents." She paused for a beat before adding, "I presume we're talking about your daughter here. You show her even a fraction of the grit I've seen in you, and you'll get through to her. But you may need to curb that temper of yours. Teens don't respond well to your kind of impatience and moods."

I gripped the empty glass in front of me and then slid it towards her. A headache screamed at me, and I did my best to ignore it. Depending on what King had on my agenda for the rest of the day, whisky would do the trick.

Kree took the glass. "The same?"

I nodded, and she left me to my thoughts. It was only a few moments, though, before I was interrupted.

"You get anything out of Monroe?"

I glanced up to find King taking a seat next to me. He jerked his chin at Kree, indicating he wanted a drink, and then looked back at me.

Did I get anything out of Monroe? The answer to that was nothing but hell, and a hard-on that she'd never wrap her lips around. She'd fired up at me fast earlier and given me a tongue-lashing that had tripped my own temper. The surprise in it all, though, was that she'd managed to ease my mood swing almost as fast. That wasn't something that happened often, if ever.

I'd had a foul temper for as long as I could remember. Apparently it ran in my family. Over the years, I'd just accepted it, but it had dragged me into some shitty situations. Tenille and I had spent half our marriage fighting over shit because of our temper clashes, and I often found myself in fights I usually refused to back down from with my brothers. Backing down wasn't in my personality, so it had surprised me when I did so with Monroe.

"She's a fucking handful, King, but yeah, her guy called me this afternoon and gave me some info. Not sure that it's useful, though. Turns out the kid he buys the drugs from has a dad who forces him to sell them. I've got his address, but he's out of town for a few days. Fox thinks he'll be back either Saturday or Sunday."

"Get one of the prospects to watch the address and let us know when he returns. I talked with Max James and Calvin Ryan today. Neither seems to know anything about Jacko's murder. I would have thought if anyone would know something, it'd be one of them. Whoever is behind this, is keeping a low fucking profile." Max and Calvin had their fingers in a lot of pies. It surprised me, too, that they didn't know anything.

King's phone rang, and he was silent for a few moments while he listened to what was being said. His face morphed into a scowl before he said, "Let him in. I'll deal with him." After he had shoved his phone back in his pocket, he said, "Ryland's here. Wants a chat."

"Has Bronze heard any more about the investigation?" The last I knew, he was having trouble digging up any info for us as to what Ryland had on the club. Unusual for Bronze, which made me think the feds were working hard to keep shit under wraps.

King shook his head. "Haven't heard from him for days. I'll call him after I hear what Ryland has to say."

The detective entered the bar, drawing our attention to him. King's body tensed as he watched Ryland walk towards us. With everything going on in the club and with Jen, he was wound tighter than I'd ever seen him.

"Ryland," King greeted him, "What the fuck do you want

now? I'd have thought keeping your eyes on me twenty-four-fucking-seven would be enough for you."

Ryland was good at his job. I'd give him that. His face remained blank, not registering any reaction to what King said. "I thought we had a deal, King."

"I don't make deals with cops."

"Yeah well, you did with this one." He waited for King to reply, but when King simply stared at him in silence, he added, "I want your guys off Gambarro."

King crossed his arms. "No."

Ryland's carefully controlled composure finally cracked a little. "No? You do realise what will happen to you if you don't comply, right?"

King's jaw clenched. "How about you waste your breath and tell me again."

Ryland stepped closer to King in what appeared to be an effort to intimidate him. He shouldn't have bothered; nothing intimidated King. It would only piss him off more than he already was. "You're playing with fire here, King. You remove the men you've got watching Gambarro, otherwise I'll be stepping up my investigation of your club. And I think we both know how that will end up. I'll also find a way to take over the investigation of Jacko's murder, which will only increase my surveillance of your members."

King's nostrils flared as he looked at Ryland with every ounce of contempt he felt towards the man. I didn't know what had happened to King when he was younger, but I would have put money on him having an altercation with the cops, because I didn't know anyone to hate them as much as he did. "You do whatever the fuck you have to, Ryland, and leave me to do whatever the fuck *I* need to. Investigate the shit out of Storm. You won't find anything that others haven't been able to find over the years. But let me be crystal fucking clear—*you're* the one playing with fire here, not me.

73

And when that fire gets hotter than you ever realised it could, you'll be wishing you never knew me or threatened me."

Neither moved for a good few moments, each staring the other one down. Ryland was the first to move, taking a step back. "I've warned you. Let the chips fall where they may." He stalked out of the clubhouse after that, leaving King to track his movements with disgust as he left.

"You think he's got much on us?" I asked.

"He's got something. But whether or not he can back it with evidence is another story. I'm not fucking removing our eyes off Gambarro, though, so Bronze better come through with something soon."

We were dangerously close to the kind of shit we'd managed to avoid for a long time. Bronze had kept us off the cop radar most of the time, and whenever we'd hit it, he'd dragged us off it fast. But this time felt different; this time I was actually concerned about where it would all end up. Where *we'd* end up.

CHAPTER 10

Monroe

"So, do we think this is going to become a thing?" Tatum asked as she stirred our Milos and passed me mine.

"God, I hope not. Milo Fridays suck. But I can't handle another night of too much alcohol this week. I'm barely recovering from Wednesday night."

"How sick were you yesterday?"

I groaned as I sat on the stool at her kitchen counter. I loved being in her house. Since she'd moved in with Nitro, Tatum had decorated and made it a beautiful home for them. One of the things she'd scattered throughout was plants. The kitchen alone had three in it. Every time I visited, I thought about how much I would love some plants in my home, but I was certain they wouldn't survive. I had a tendency to kill them.

"I felt ill all day and most of the night. I'm beginning to think I'm getting too old for hangovers."

"Jesus, Roe, you're only thirty-one. That's not old."

My phone rang, drawing my attention away from how old I really did feel. "Hey, Robyn, what's up, girl?" It was one of my oldest friends.

"I'm calling to beg you for a favour next week, but I totally understand if you can't do it, okay?"

I'd do pretty much anything for Robyn if I could swing it. She was the kind of friend every girl should have—loyal, kind and giving—and she'd never once let me down when I needed her. "Sure, what is it?"

"Bree has ice skating on Tuesday night, but I also have to go to John's parent-teacher interview. And Matty isn't home until Wednesday. Are you able to take Bree to ice skating?"

Her hubby worked away from home, and she often struggled with being able to do it all on her own. But she wasn't the kind of woman to ask for help very often, so when she did, I knew she was desperate. And I loved Bree, her fifteen-year-old, so of course I would do this for her. "Just let me know the time, and I'm there."

The relief was clear in her voice. "Thank you so much, Roe. I owe you huge."

"You don't owe me a thing, girlfriend."

After I ended the call, Tatum asked, "Is she okay?"

I drank some of my Milo and nodded. "Yeah. Matty's away, so she needs some help juggling the kids. I'm taking Bree ice-skating on Tuesday night. You wanna come?"

"I can't. Nitro and I are going to check out cakes for the wedding."

I almost spat out the Milo I'd just drunk. "*Nitro's* checking out cakes? How the hell did you convince him to do that?"

She shrugged. "Sex. And well, the man loves cake, and I told him he'd get to sample lots of it."

"That man loves *you*. I'd say that has a lot more to do with it than cake."

She smiled. "And sex. Let's not forget that."

She was right. Nitro couldn't keep his hands off Tatum. "Yeah, but he can get that from you whenever he wants."

Her smile dimmed. "We've been a bit hit and miss lately. He's been so busy with club stuff, and on edge, too. He comes home tense as hell and exhausted after the long days he's putting in, and pretty much just falls into bed. I told him enough was enough and that he had to finish work early on Tuesday night to come to this with me."

"He didn't argue?"

"Well, that's where the sex came in. I told him I'd make it worth his while and may have mentioned something about installing a mirror on the roof above our bed. He likes to fuck me in front of the mirror, so I figured we needed one in the bedroom. It arrives on Monday."

I raised my mug. "Nice work, sister."

She clinked mugs with me. "I thought so." After she drank some Milo, she said, "How's Bree these days?"

Bree had been a handful for the past three years, but was beginning to mature into the kind of daughter any mother would want. "Let's just say that I think they've turned a corner with her. Robyn's not reporting half as many arguments as she used to."

"So you and Bree are still getting on okay?"

My face spread out into a smile. Bree was like the daughter I'd never had. I loved Robyn's son, too, but I'd always wanted a little girl, so I felt a special bond with Bree. "We have our moments, but I never let her walk away angry with me. I always make sure we resolve any issues before they can become a problem."

"You'll make a good mum one day, Roe." Tatum wasn't really a kid person, but she always supported my dream of having a large family.

"That's if I ever manage to have one before my eggs shrivel up."

"Oh God, sometimes you are overly dramatic. You've still got years to go before that's a concern."

I lifted my brows. "You saw what happened to my friend, Davinda. That shit could happen to me, too."

Tatum waved her hand in the air dismissively. "That's not going to happen to you. Davinda will grow old alone because she was too much of a bitch to hold her marriage together. And then when it fell apart, she was too much of a bitch to find another man who would put up with her shit. She's childless because of her personality. You don't have that problem. Men fall over themselves to be with you. You're just too damn fussy."

"I'm not fussy. I just have extremely high standards."

It was Tatum's turn to raise her brows. "Look, I'm all for high standards, but yours are out of this world. I mean, what woman ditches a man because she discovers he doesn't eat meat?"

"You know why I did that. I'm not going to spend the rest of my life arguing with my husband over what we eat. I like my meat, and I refuse to give it up."

"Did he ask you to give it up?"

I put my hand on my hip. "No, but he would have."

She shook her head in frustration. "You don't know that, Roe. But that's the thing you always do—you assume to know what will happen down the track and you make rash decisions based on those assumptions. I'm beginning to think you sabotage your relationships before they can even get started."

"I do not. I—"

I was cut off by Nitro's booming voice from the front door. "Vegas, you got a minute?"

She moved off her stool, a look of confusion on her face. I

78

was confused also. He'd told her he wouldn't be home for hours. Leaving me, she headed towards the front of the house.

I listened as he said something to her and then the door closed, leaving the house in silence. Guessing they'd gone outside together, I decided to fill in the time waiting for her by making us some tea. I was rummaging through Tatum's teas when the front door opened and boots thudded down the hallway towards the kitchen.

Turning when they stopped, I expected to find Nitro, but instead found Hyde standing in the kitchen doorway.

Good God, the man was impressively built. So much so, that I found it hard to keep my eyes on his face. All I wanted to do was let them drop so I could take a good long look at his body. But I managed to stay strong and hold his gaze.

He had the darkest eyes. They matched everything else about him—his dark hair that hung in tangled waves around his face, his dark beard, and his tanned skin. And not to forget, his dark moods. I'd only seen one of them, but I got the distinct impression they made up his personality. He seemed to be an intense man, that was for sure.

"I need your car keys," he said after a few moments of silence.

I frowned. "Why?"

"So I can move your car."

"You don't think I could do that myself?" My tone got a little snarky even though I tried to keep it in check. I was acting weirdly, which annoyed even me, so who knew how he would take it. There was just something about this man—something that drew me to him when all I wanted to do was run the other way. Snapping at him would hopefully keep him at arm's length.

His jaw clenched and he took a minute. Finally, he nodded

and said, "I do. Could you move it so I can pull Nitro's ute out of the garage?"

Well shit. I had to give him points for not losing his cool. Grabbing my keys, I made my way out to the driveway. As I brushed past him, I did my best to ignore his masculine scent and the hard muscles I grazed. The muscles that practically pleaded with me to reach out and touch them.

Stay strong, Monroe. You do not need a biker in your life. Not even for sex.

I reversed my car out onto the footpath and then joined Nitro and Tatum in the front yard. They were deep in conversation but glanced at me as I made my way to them.

Nitro raked his fingers through his hair as he lifted his chin at me. "Thanks."

I took a good look at him. Tatum wasn't kidding when she said he was exhausted. It was written all over him. "You doing okay, Nitro?"

Hyde interrupted us with an impatient look. "King just texted. He wants us back at the clubhouse."

Nitro nodded and dropped a quick kiss on Tatum's lips. "Don't wait up, I'll be late."

She reached for him as he stepped away from her. "Be safe." She spoke softly, but I heard the concern in her tone. Something was off here because it was unlike Tatum to speak like that to Nitro. She knew he was capable of looking out for himself, and while she always worried, she never felt the need to voice it to him.

He stopped and turned back to her. Taking her face in both his hands, he said, "I'll call you as soon as I can after this is done." For a man who wasn't tender, Nitro had a way with Tatum that was as close to tender as I was sure he'd ever get. It seemed to do the trick. She nodded and motioned for him to go.

A few moments later, Hyde took off in Nitro's ute while Nitro's bike roared down the street.

Looking at Tatum, I said, "What's going on? I've not seen you this worried before."

She took a deep breath, straightening her body and pushing her shoulders back. Anyone would have thought she was the one going into battle. Some days, I figured she probably felt like it. "One of their guys was murdered. They're looking for payback, and I know it's not going to be pretty."

"Shit." No wonder she was concerned. I wasn't sure how she managed to cope with this type of stuff. If the man I was dating went to work with the threat of murder over his head, it would be enough to make me spend my days worrying.

She nodded. "Yeah, that's one way to put it. This isn't going to end well for someone. I just hope that someone isn't going to be Storm."

CHAPTER 11

Hyde

Someone was banging on my front door. Loudly and fucking insistently.

"Jesus," I muttered to myself as I left my bed, pulled my jeans on and stalked down the hallway towards the door.

What fucking time was it anyway? It couldn't be later than eight. After only getting to bed at about three this morning, the last thing I wanted to be dealing with was some asshole wanting shit from me.

The bashing on the door quietened before a female voice called out, "Aiden, are you home?"

I slowed.

My heart rate kicked up a notch.

Charlie.

What the fuck was she doing here?

She commenced bashing on the door again. "Fuck, Aiden, open the door."

I yanked the door open and stared at my daughter. On one hand, I wanted to welcome her with open arms. On the other, the father in me kicked in and I knew I had two things to do here—pull her up on her attitude and call her mother to make sure she knew where her daughter was.

Our eyes met. Hers swirled with emotions I wasn't sure I was ready for. I'd imagined this moment thousands of times over the years, but I hadn't nailed it in my mind. Not if the way my daughter glared at me was anything to go by. I'd expected anger, but not this attitude rolling off her.

Crossing my arms, I said, "Does your mother allow you to swear in her house?"

My question caused her to hesitate, but only for a moment. "No, but this isn't her house, is it?"

"I don't appreciate it in mine either."

Her brows lifted before she casually ran her gaze over me, zeroing in on the ink covering my chest and arms. "You look like the kind of man who couldn't give a shit about swearing."

"I'm the kind of man who gives a shit about how his daughter grows up, and growing up with a foul mouth isn't how I imagined that to go. When you're in my house, you don't swear."

She blinked. This time I managed to cause her a few more moments of hesitation. And then she simply shrugged and said, "Fine." With that, she pushed her way past me and entered my home without another word. I stood in silence and watched with a full chest as the child I loved more than anyone in this world finally merged her world with mine.

Nope, I definitely hadn't nailed this moment in my imagination. I hadn't realised the depth of emotion I'd feel. My chest filled to overflowing, and feelings I wasn't sure I'd ever experienced roared through me.

She's here.

Charlie's home.

With me.

I closed the front door and followed her into the kitchen where she dumped her backpack on the counter before opening the fridge.

"You got any juice in here?"

I pushed against the refrigerator door and closed it. "No. And how about we start again? Does your mother know you're here?"

"No. And she doesn't need to know."

I reached for my phone. "Yeah, she does."

When I started hitting numbers on my phone to dial Tenille, she blurted, "We had a huge fight. I just need somewhere to crash for a bit, okay?"

I stopped what I was doing and stared at her. "You plan on staying with me?"

"You're my father, right?"

Fuck, I was so out of my depth here. I knew how to deal with assholes and motherfuckers, but a teenager? No fucking clue. I placed my phone back down on the kitchen counter. "Yes, I'm your father."

"Good. So I'm staying."

"How did you get here if your mother didn't bring you?" I hoped like fuck she didn't say she hitchhiked.

"By bus."

It was clear she didn't want to discuss that, so I let it go for now. "What did your mother tell you about me?"

"Everything." She didn't volunteer any further information until she grew tired of waiting for me to speak again, which I didn't do because I figured whoever spoke first lost in this situation. And I needed to get the upper hand here if I was going to have any hope of controlling this. "Fine, she told me you didn't really die in that fire, that you faked your death and left town because of shit that was going down at your work."

Her tone was indifferent, like she was detached from the whole thing. I wasn't a man too interested in feelings, but I had to know how she felt about this. "Does that piss you off?" Fuck, this was the strangest fucking conversation. Asking my daughter if me faking my death and walking away from her pissed her off. Based on the way my father abandoning me as a child made me feel, I could only assume Charlie was angry and hurt.

Her shoulders lifted in a shrug. "Yeah, but I don't blame you for wanting to get away from Gibson. He's an asshole."

That threw me. After Tenille had defended him, I hadn't expected Charlie to dislike him. But that wasn't what I needed to focus on. For now, I needed to work on my relationship with my daughter. "Did she tell you anything else?"

She blew out a long breath, looking more pissed off about this conversation than any emotion I detected in her voice. "Look, I'm not into discussing how I feel, okay? It's not what I do. I just want somewhere to crash until I get over this shit with Mum. You think we could do that?"

I recalled something Tenille had said about teenage girls slapping on a mask to hide their vulnerabilities, so I decided to let both this conversation and her attitude go for the moment. It was going to take us some time to work our way towards each other, and in the meantime, I was just going to have to ease into my role as her father. Unfortunately, patience wasn't my strong suit, so fuck knew how this would go.

I picked up her bag. "Follow me." I led her to one of the spare bedrooms. "You can stay here as long as you want, but I'm calling your mother now to let her know where you are."

"She's not going to come get me if that's what you're

hoping for. All she cares about at the moment is getting drunk and avoiding her problems."

I knew she was close to the mark with the getting drunk bit, but she was way off base if she thought Tenille didn't care about her. In the small amount of time I'd spent with Tenille, the love she had for Charlie had been evident. However, I figured that getting into a discussion about that now wouldn't get me anywhere.

I lifted my chin at her. "You want some breakfast?"

She stared at me like I had two heads. As if having breakfast with me was the last thing on her agenda. Moving to the bed, she sat on it and pulled her bag into her lap. "No, thanks."

"I'll be in the kitchen if you change your mind."

I didn't wait for her answer. She'd made it clear she wanted to be by herself. Forcing her to do anything with me would probably just push her away, and that was the last thing I wanted. It had been too fucking long since I'd had my child close; I wouldn't screw this up.

I headed into the kitchen to make a coffee and call Tenille.

She answered the call straight away "Aiden, I can't talk for long. I need to keep the phone free in case Charlie calls. She took off yesterday and I have no idea where she is." The panic and worry in her voice bled through the phone.

"Tee, she's here."

Silence.

And then a sob broke from her. "Oh, God. Thank God." She exhaled her relief, and I imagined her doubling over as she heard this news, in the same way she had years ago whenever she was relieved about something. Not that I knew if she did that anymore, but my memories were clear as day where Tee was concerned, and they flashed through my mind whenever we spoke or when I caught a glimpse of her. I wondered how our relationship would pan out now and whether she'd allow me close enough to learn who she had become. It wasn't my intent to force that, but I would welcome it.

"She showed up just now. Said something about a fight you'd had and that she needed a place to stay while she calmed down."

"Yeah, we had a fight about you. She said she didn't want anything to do with you, and I told her she should give you a chance and get to know you before making that decision. And now look where she is. I'll come get her." Tenille sounded drained, exhausted. She probably was. Between a husband with a gambling addiction, thousands of dollars disappearing from her bank account, a husband she thought dead turning back up, and a daughter going missing, I guessed she was running on emotional fumes right about now.

Opening the cupboard above where I stood, I grabbed the bottle of whisky from it and splashed some into my coffee. Fuck knew I was gonna need it today. As I stored it back in the cupboard, I said, "How about she stays here for a couple of days while she blows off steam, and then you come and get her?"

Silence again. And then—"I'm not sure about that, Aiden. She doesn't know you. And you have no experience dealing with teens. I should probably just come today and take her home. By the time I get there, she'll have calmed down enough to talk to me."

"Tee, stay put. I've dealt with worse than teens in my life. I can handle Charlie. You need a break."

She barked out a laugh. "And what do you propose I do with myself while taking a break?"

I frowned as I downed some coffee and waited for the whisky to hit my bloodstream. "I don't know. Whatever the fuck mothers do when they get some alone time."

"You really do have a lot to learn about parenting," she muttered. "Fine, I'll call Charlie and tell her I'll be there in a few days. She's all yours. Don't kill each other, okay?"

Jesus, how fucking bad was this going to be? "I'll keep you updated."

We ended the call, and I reached for the bottle of whisky again. Filling my cup, I took a long gulp, closing my eyes briefly as the alcohol began to take the edge off.

How hard could this be? I could put up with a bit of teenage attitude for a few days. Anything to keep Charlie with me.

Three hours passed without a word from Charlie. Not a sound. Nothing. Those three hours felt like three fucking days to me. I fought an inner battle between leaving her alone and going in there to make her come out and spend time with me. In the end, I left her alone and went outside to the gym I'd built in my garage.

I'd just finished with the weights when she wandered into the garage. Wiping the sweat from my face, I watched her silently, waiting for her to speak.

Her gaze travelled around the gym before coming back to me. "You've got a good setup here. Would you mind if I did a workout later?"

"You box?"

"Yeah."

"How about you do that workout now?"

Her eyes widened a fraction. "With you?"

I nodded.

She hesitated for a moment before shaking her head. "Nah, I prefer to work out on my own."

"Fair enough. I'll be finished in about half an hour. The gym's all yours then."

"Thanks." With that, she turned and left.

As I watched her go, I wondered if she'd inherited my preference to be alone most of the time. She certainly seemed to have inherited my desire to avoid needless conversation. And I wasn't sure yet, but perhaps my moodiness as well.

My phone rang, and I quickly swiped it off the bench. I'd been expecting a call from King all morning. Nitro and I had paid some visits around town last night looking for anyone who knew anything about Jacko's murder. Sydney wasn't talking, though, and we'd almost called it a night when we finally found someone who knew something. He'd given us a guy's name, said the guy could probably help us. King had been adamant he wanted to be present if we found someone who might squeal, so we'd called it in to him and he'd told me to be ready today to drag information out of the asshole. I was more than fucking ready to do that.

King wasted no time on small talk. "I'm gonna text you an address. Meet me there in half an hour." And then he was gone. A moment later, an address came through, and I headed inside to get dressed.

"Charlie," I called out as I walked the length of the hallway. When she didn't answer me, I knocked on her closed bedroom door. "I've gotta go out for a while. You okay here on your own?" I figured she would be. I just wasn't sure *I* would be. My protective instincts were kicking into high gear, and leaving her was the last thing I wanted to do.

She still didn't answer me, so I knocked loudly a few more times, and when no answer came still, I opened the door without waiting any longer.

I found her lying on her bed, earphones in, eyes closed. Fuck, this was frustrating. She couldn't fucking hear me and still had no clue I was in the room.

Pulling one of her earphones out, I said, "These things are a pain in my ass. I've been calling out to you, trying to get your attention."

She scrambled into a sitting position as she shot me a filthy look. "I could have been naked! You can't just barge into my bedroom."

I ignored the way she referred to this room as her bedroom, and how much I liked that, to instead address what she'd said. "I can barge in if I've been trying to get your attention for a while with no response. You stop with the earphones and I'll stop with the barging in."

"No one listens to music without earphones. That's a dumb idea."

"Suit yourself, but expect me to enter your room if I need you and you don't hear me."

Scowling, she muttered, "Screw you."

I raised a brow. "You care to alter that?"

Eyes steady on mine, she refused to budge. "No."

She was my daughter all right. The way she held her ground and refused to back down was exactly how I would have handled this situation. But that didn't mean I would encourage it.

"Charlie, we need to get something straight here. I want you to stay with me, and I want to get to know you and have a relationship with you, but no way am I putting up with you disrespecting me. You wanna tell me to go screw myself, you do that when I can't hear you."

Her turn to lift a brow. "Oh, so now you wanna get to know me? *Now* you wanna be my father?" She moved off the bed and stepped close to me. Her shoulders tensed as she spat out, "You talk about me disrespecting you. Well, how about we talk about the way you disrespected me for the last fourteen years by ignoring me? That kinda felt like a big screw you from you to me."

And there was the anger I'd been waiting for. It hit me like a tidal wave, causing my chest to constrict with all the guilt I'd been trying to shove away for years, and then some. I deserved everything she said.

"Yeah, I guess it did. The only excuse I have is that I was trying to keep you safe." Fuck, I wasn't prepared for this. I should have been. I'd had fourteen fucking years to prepare for it, and yet there I fucking was fumbling for words that would never ease her hurt or adequately tell her how sorry I was.

Her eyes searched mine furiously, looking for what, I wasn't sure. Short, harsh breaths pumped from her as she worked herself up with more anger. "That's all you have to say? *Really?*" She shook her head at me, but she had the kind of look on her face that told me she wasn't hearing anything she hadn't expected. "Fuck, I've got a father anyway. I didn't need you."

With that, she spun on her heel and stalked out of the bedroom while I stared after her processing what she'd said about not needing me.

Who would have thought a child could inflict so much hurt with four words? The pain was instant and deep as fuck. And unlike any pain I'd ever experienced in my life. But I didn't have time to feel it; I had to go after her and attempt to fix the mess I was making.

"Charlie!" I called out as I followed her out of the house. "I fucked that up. Let me try again."

She didn't stop, though. Instead, she picked up the pace and jogged away from the house. I followed suit and eventually caught up to her four houses down the street.

Grabbing her arm, I stopped her and turned her to face me. Almost breathless, she stared at me through tears that streamed down her face. No words came, though. The only thing that sat between us was heartache and misery. We were both hurting, and I had to begin repairing the damage I'd done all those years ago.

Wiping away her tears, I said, "I'm sorry, baby. There's nothing I can say or do that will make up for all the years I wasn't there. At the time, I did what I thought was right for everyone. I was young and had no resources to do anything else. But I fucked up. I see that now. I should have tried harder to fix the situation without doing what I did."

When she didn't argue with me or attempt to walk away again, I moved closer. I wanted to take her into my arms and wrap her up in them, but it was too soon for that. Even though she lived and breathed in my soul, I wasn't in hers. She didn't know me, and she had no reason to trust me. So I gave her the only thing I could. The only thing I thought she might respond to. "I know you have no reason to believe anything I say, but I'm gonna say it anyway. There hasn't been a day gone by that I haven't thought of you. The day you were born was the happiest day of my life. I've missed seeing you grow up, but I've been watching you and keeping track of everything you've done. Don't think that I didn't care, because I do. And I'm going to be there for you now, however you need me to be."

I'd hoped my words would help stop her tears, but they seemed to have the opposite effect. She madly wiped them from her cheeks. "You think that an apology and a promise to do better will magically fix everything, Aiden? You have no fucking idea. Even though I had a dad growing up, I always wondered what it would have been like having my *real* dad there. I wondered if *you'd* been there, would we have been like those fathers and daughters who did everything together. Would you have taken me fishing or camping or taught me stuff about cars or shit like that? Dad never really did that stuff with me, and while I'm not sure I would have wanted to do any of it, maybe if you'd been around, you would have taken me." She paused for a beat before her face twisted and more tears fell. "Just because you say you want to be there for me, doesn't mean you will be." Her voice cracked as she uttered those last few words, slicing more guilt through me. Fuck, I'd screwed every-fucking-thing up.

"Give me a chance, Charlie. That's all I'm asking. I don't expect you to suddenly trust me or believe in what I say, but let's take it a day at a time and see where we end up. I'm not fucking around here. I want you in my life more than I've wanted anything." My voice turned gruff and I almost held my breath waiting for her reply. She was everything to me, but I had no idea how to make her understand that.

Her tears slowed as she quietly watched me. Weighing up which way to choose. Something I'd said must have reached her because she finally said, "A day at a time. And I'm not making any promises to you."

I exhaled and nodded. "Fair enough."

Another silent few moments passed between us as we settled into this new phase of our relationship. I wasn't sure where to go with it next. I felt like a fucking parenting manual would be good right about now. In the end, she broke the silence. "You're gonna have to get used to me wearing earphones, though. When you want me and I can't hear you, just message me."

Fuck. This was a whole new world to me. "I've got a lot to learn, haven't I?"

She raised her brows and nodded. "Yeah, and one other thing? Don't call me baby. I'm not your baby anymore, Aiden."

She'd always be my baby. One day she'd grasp that. I'd make fucking sure of it.

CHAPTER 12

Hyde

"You're late," King said when I showed up ten minutes late at the address he'd sent me.

"Had some kid trouble, brother."

His forehead wrinkled in a frown. "What happened?"

"My kid showed up on my doorstep this morning. She wants to stay with me for a few days or so after having a fight with her mother, which is good, but we got into it just before I was about to leave."

"You got it sorted?"

I blew out a breath. "Fuck knows. I'm drowning here, man. Got no fucking clue what I'm doing, but I managed to calm her down enough to know she'd be at my place when I get home later. Now I've just gotta figure out how to get through to her that I want to be in her life."

"Talk to her mother and find out what shit she likes to do

and then spend time doing that with her. It'll be a start. Time's what you've gotta give."

King never failed to surprise me with the shit he knew. He'd never had kids, but he'd spent a lot of time around them, so I figured he was probably onto something here.

Changing the subject, I said, "How'd you evade the feds?"

"Devil and Nitro caused a scene outside the clubhouse. Distracted Ryland enough for me to leave." He nodded before casting his gaze towards a house down the street. Jerking his chin at it, he said, "That's Dean's house." The asshole we'd been told could help us find Jacko's murder. "I did some digging on him and he deals in stolen cars. Recently took up a heavy coke addiction and gets it from Marx. We're not leaving here today until we get something out of him."

"Agreed."

We made the short walk to the house, and King took the front while I took the back. The place looked abandoned and filthy. The person who lived there didn't appear to care about their surroundings. Overgrown grass and weeds filled the yard, peeling paint and dirt made up the outside of the house, and the backyard was a mess of old tyres and rusted car parts.

Finding a back door open, I easily entered the house and headed towards the bedroom where I could hear someone talking. Dean was on his phone. As I came into view, his eyes widened and he muttered, "Fuck, I gotta go, babe," before dropping the phone and demanding, "What the fuck?" Yanking his gun out, he pointed it at me and pulled the trigger.

I ducked and narrowly avoided getting a fucking bullet in my chest. King was right behind me. Without hesitation, he entered the bedroom, taking purposeful strides towards the asshole. Dean shifted the aim of his gun and shot at King who took a bullet in his arm. That didn't slow him down, though.

He grunted through the pain and bellowed, "Welcome to your worst fucking nightmare, Dean," right before he punched him so hard in the face that it almost knocked him out.

By the time I joined them, King had the guy down, flat out on his back. He'd straddled him and pinned his hands to the floor above his head. No amount of fighting King helped the asshole; he was stuck beneath him, caged in by King's legs that refused to budge. King had strength and grit that not many men I knew possessed. When he set his mind to something, nothing stood in his way.

"You good?" I asked King as I took a look at his arm where the bullet hit.

"Yeah, it just grazed me. Nothing I haven't dealt with before."

I bent to get a better look at Dean. Eyes full of hatred stared up at me, and I wondered how long and what efforts we'd have to go to in order to change that hatred to fear. And whether we'd have to introduce some horror to make that happen. After being shot at, I was itching for some of that, and I figured King would be too.

"Next time you wanna shoot a man, make sure you know who the fuck you're shooting first," I barked. "King here doesn't appreciate bullets in his body."

Dean spat up at King. "Go fuck yourself."

His spit landed on King's face, and I felt the energy change in the room as King reared backwards, a look of absolute rage settling over his face. After he had wiped the spit away, he spoke, his tone low and murderous. "You'll regret that."

Without pause, he swiftly stood, bringing Dean up with him. Grabbing him by the shirt, he pulled him out of the room, down the hallway and into the small, dirty kitchen. Yanking out a chair at the kitchen table, he shoved him down onto it. He then took both of Dean's hands and bound them together tightly with a large tea towel he found next to the kitchen sink.

Gripping Dean's hair, he wrenched Dean's head back and demanded, "Tell us everything you know about Marx and the drugs he's dealing. And once you've done that, tell me who killed one of my men this week."

Sweat beaded on Dean's forehead as his eyes met King's, but he refused to give up what he knew. "Like I said before, motherfucker, go fuck yourself. You're getting nothing out of me today."

"We'll fucking see about that." King slammed his face into the table and then jerked it right back up again.

Blood streamed from Dean's nose, and I figured King had broken it with the force he'd used. Dean glared up at King as he kicked and thrashed his legs in an attempt to move off the chair. I reached down to grab his legs to prevent him from breaking free.

"I've got all fucking day, asshole," King said. "Longer if needed. And I'm in the kind of mood to inflict some pain, so I suggest you stop fighting us and start fucking talking or this isn't gonna go well for you."

Dean didn't reply. He simply sat there staring at King defiantly. I knew then that my itch for violence was about to get scratched. King did, too. His eyes met mine and he nodded at the knife block sitting on the kitchen counter. "Time for some Jekyll time."

"You read my mind, brother."

I selected a knife from the block and stood in front of Dean after King swung the chair around to face me. I undid the binding holding his wrists together and splayed his hands out on the table, holding them down in place with my free hand. I then dug the tip of the knife into the back of one of his hands. "You want that through your hand, Dean?"

When he didn't answer, I sliced into his hand. Not too deep, but enough to give him a reason to start talking.

"Fuck!" His body jerked and he tried to pull his hand away, but I pressed my hand down on his harder keeping them there.

"I can go deeper if you want."

His eyes met mine, and I saw some of the fear I was aiming for. "You're fucking crazy! I don't know anything that you want to know."

I bent and pushed my face close to his. "Your reaction to us showing up here tells me otherwise." To give him more incentive to start talking, I ran the blade of the knife along his throat, making sure to draw some blood there too.

His hostility intensified at that, and instead of volunteering information, he spat at me like he'd spat at King. "Fuck. You."

Anger rolled through me, and the fine line I walked between surviving in this world with a touch of rage and sliding over the edge into full-blown madness was crossed. Slamming the knife down, I grabbed his shirt with both hands and lifted him out of the chair. The adrenaline coursing through me gave me the kind of strength that took over and achieved my goal. Barrelling him into the wall, I shoved him with enough force that he dented it. Not giving him a second to catch up with what was going on, I smashed my fist into his face. Again. And again. Over and over, until his face was a bloody, unrecognisable mess.

My mind ceased to process my actions. Instead, my rage controlled me.

I wanted to inflict as much pain as I could.

Misery and blood fuelled me.

To cause it and to see it.

I wanted to inhale his pain.

I wanted to draw it in to my soul and breathe through it.

All I lived for right then was his torment. It would match my own raging storm of pain. Being in the moment with him —*with his agony*—would ease mine for a brief time. I would be able to forget it. His suffering would wipe mine, even for just a moment.

"Hyde. Enough." King stepped in and dragged me off Dean.

I blinked a few times as my surroundings came back into focus. I'd beaten Dean so badly that he'd slumped to the ground, covered in blood, half unconscious.

After he had pushed me out of the way, King crouched down and slapped Dean's face a few times. "You still with us, asshole? Ready to talk? Or do I need to finish what Hyde started?"

Dean coughed a couple of times and attempted to sit up straight, but he cried out in pain and swore as he failed. After spitting some blood out onto the ground, he managed to get out, "I've never met Marx, but I'm pretty sure he's tied to that murder. I overheard my dealer talking about it yesterday. That's all I fucking know."

King shook his head as he took hold of Dean's throat. "No, you know something else. Keep fucking talking."

Barely able to talk thanks to the unyielding grip King had on his throat, Dean choked out, "Whoever organised the murder is Italian."

King grunted and let Dean go, shoving him hard as he did so. Standing, he looked at me and said, "Well that narrows it down."

By my count, there were six major Italian players in Sydney. "Shouldn't take us too long to go through them all."

King pulled his phone out. "I've got something I've gotta do for the next couple of hours and then I want you, me,

Nitro and Devil on this. I want to find that motherfucker and end this shit now."

An hour later, I entered my house after leaving King and grabbing some food on the way home. I hadn't restocked after being away in Melbourne, and I figured Charlie would be hungry.

The house I'd left a couple of hours earlier and the house I walked into were like two completely different places. I stood in silence at the living room entry when I found Charlie in there. I was silent, the room was not. She had rap music blaring from the speakers and was sitting on the floor in the middle of the room smoking and drinking what I was pretty fucking sure was whisky from my cupboard.

"What the fuck?" I barked loud enough that she heard me over the music. Any attempt at keeping my outrage in check would have been futile so I skipped that. The sight of my sixteen-year-old daughter smoking and drinking slapped me in the face with a level of shock I found confusing. I didn't give a shit if people did those things—teens even—but not *my* fucking kid.

Her head whipped around so she faced me. After she had taken a swig of her drink, she said, "What?"

I stalked into the room and turned the music down. "You don't smoke or drink. Not in this house. Not fucking ever."

Her brows lifted and it appeared she was settling in for a fight by the way her shoulders squared and her back straightened. "Yeah, I do."

Shaking my head, I snapped, "No, you don't." I motioned for the glass. "Give me that."

She held her drink close. "No. And you can't tell me what to do."

"Oh yes I can. This is my house and you are my kid. I make the rules here. Not you."

Pushing up and onto her feet, she threw back, "If this is how it's gonna be around here, I'm out. I can get this at home from Mum. I don't need it from you too."

I reached for her arm as she turned to exit the room, halting her. "You're fucking sixteen, Charlie. Don't fuck your life up this early by drinking and smoking. I can promise you that's the last thing you'll be happy about when you look back on your life as you get older."

"So that's why you've got a kitchen full of booze then? You are so full of shit."

"No, I'm full of honesty. I want so much better for you than I have in life. I don't want you to make the same mistakes I did."

She rolled her eyes as she shrugged out of my grip. "You and Mum must have taken parenting lessons from the same manual. That's exactly what she says."

I raked my fingers through my hair. I wasn't sure if I was fucking shit up here or not, but no way would I stand back and watch her do what she was doing. "Do you know why we both say the same shit? Because we both came from families who didn't give a fuck about us. They let us do whatever the hell we wanted and couldn't care less what the consequences were for us. My mother was a drug addict from the age of fifteen and she died from a drug overdose when she was thirty-eight. She was a selfish woman whose only desire in life was to make herself feel good. Taking time for me wasn't in those plans. And she sure as shit never worried about whether I was taking drugs or drinking. I'm not that kind of parent, Charlie. I will always care about what you're doing with your life."

Something I said hit a nerve with her because she took

the time to process my words and think about them. "Your mum did drugs?"

I nodded. "Yeah. Coke mainly, but she didn't discriminate when she was desperate."

She narrowed her eyes at me. "Did you ever do drugs?"

"Yes."

"What? When?"

"After I left you and your mum, I started on the coke. I did it for about a year, and it almost killed me."

"As in you almost overdosed on it?"

"No. I was taking so much of the shit that it brought out my violent side. I was getting into fights almost every night, taking on anyone who pissed me off. If I hadn't kicked my habit, I would have ended up killing myself in a fight."

"So, what, now you just drink? No drugs anymore?"

"Yeah. I haven't touched anything besides alcohol since then."

She was quiet for a beat before blurting out, "I've smoked pot, but I haven't tried anything else."

Fucking hell. I was definitely not ready for this conversation. But, I had to be. And I had to keep my fucking cool or else I knew she'd walk. At least she wasn't arguing with me anymore. "You still smoking it?"

"My boyfriend smokes, so sometimes I do it with him. But I don't really love it. Usually it just makes me feel sick. I'd rather drink."

I inhaled sharply. "Your boyfriend?" I should have been prepared for that. Charlie was a beautiful girl, so I really should have expected a boyfriend to be kicking around. The fact she'd chosen a fucking stoner didn't impress me, though.

"Yeah, Jamie."

"How long you been with him?"

"About seven months. Mum and Dad hate him, but he's amazing."

No shit her mother hated him. I did too, and I didn't even know the little fucker.

"What makes him so amazing?"

A defensive look crossed her face, and I guessed that came from always having to defend him to her family. "He's the one who gave me the money to catch the bus here, and he's always there for me when I fight with Mum."

"He works?"

"No. I guess his family gives him money or something."

Or something. I bet the little shit was either dealing or stealing stuff. Jesus, it just reminded me how young and naïve Charlie was.

My phone buzzed with a text, and I quickly checked it.

Tenille: Everything going okay there?
Me: Yeah. She's okay.
Tenille: Keep me in the loop. This is doing my head in.
Me: Will do.

Shoving my phone back in my pocket, I said, "Look, I know you're gonna drink at your age. I don't like it, but I get it. But don't do it here, okay? And quit the smokes. That shit'll kill you eventually."

I wasn't sure how I'd managed to do it, but all the fight had left her. She didn't argue with me, but she didn't let me have the last word. "We've all gotta die from something, Aiden."

I pointed my finger at her. "Not in the house."

She bent and picked her drink up off the floor. Passing it to me, she said, "Now go. I'm gonna watch some reality TV and I'm pretty sure you'd hate it."

I took the drink and left her to it. I figured I'd won half

the battle for now. The fact she was still talking to me was the biggest win of it all, but hell, I felt like I'd been to war and back with her today. My respect for Tenille leapt. If this was what she dealt with day in, day out, I had mad fucking respect for her. Which reminded me that I needed to find an ice-skating rink. I was going to take King's suggestion and do stuff with her that she loved, in order to win her over.

CHAPTER 13

Monroe

As I sat and watched Bree ice skate on Tuesday night, I wished I'd taken it up when I was a kid. She seemed to really love it, and it looked like so much fun. Hell, maybe I should take lessons myself. It'd kill two birds with one stone—fun and exercise. There were plenty of adults out on the rink taking a class, many of them older than me. Bree was about fifteen minutes into her lesson, and I'd spent that time watching both her and a man who had to be at least sixty. He moved like he was my age. If he could do it, surely I could.

A waitress interrupted me when she delivered my order of hot chips to the table where I sat in the tiny café at the rink. The heating in there coaxed me in. I'd rather watch Bree from the warmth than sit on the bleachers and freeze.

"Thanks," I said as she placed the bowl of chips in front of me.

"Just let me know if you want anything else, love. I'm

serving hot food for another half hour and then closing down the kitchen."

"Will do." I wouldn't want anything else, though. God, I shouldn't even be having these chips. I'd hit the gym at lunchtime, so I was probably undoing all that work. *Story of my life.*

As I watched her walk away, I caught a glimpse of a guy entering the café—the kind of glimpse that made me keep looking. I did a double take when I realised it was Hyde. What the hell was he doing at an ice-skating rink? He didn't strike me as the type of man to skate.

Oh, God, my belly started doing somersaults. And all I'd done was look at the man. I needed to get myself under control. But damn, these kinds of somersaults weren't common for me. Why, why, why did *he* have to cause them?

He took a few steps into the café before turning to look out at the rink. I watched intently as his gaze stayed pinned there and his mouth curled up into a smile. He wasn't here to skate; he was here with someone.

I looked away and focused on my chips and Facebook. Anything to take my attention off him and those muscles of his that made me want to do dirty things with him. Not to mention that ass. Fuck, I wondered if his cock was pierced.

Stop it, Monroe.

Enough.

He is not the man for you.

A girl could daydream, though, right?

Scrolling through my Facebook newsfeed, I discovered my sister had started another online marketing course that day. Savannah was a twenty-nine-year-old uni dropout who had quit her teaching degree about a year ago after coming home from two months of overseas travel and declaring teaching wasn't for her. She'd decided to try internet marketing instead, and was convinced she'd make her fortune in that field. Our father was concerned about this change in direction, and that she was throwing money away by buying a multitude of online training courses, but Mum told him to let her be. Mum believed that everyone eventually found their calling in life, some just found it later than others. Dad didn't agree, but he'd let it go for now. This new course had to be, by my count, her sixth one this year. I kinda believed the same as Mum—Savannah would find herself eventually.

"This seat taken?"

My head snapped up at the sound of Hyde's deep, gravelly voice. Oh dear Lord. Mother of all things holy. This man had it all going on. Especially when he flashed that smile at me that he was currently flashing.

"It's all yours," I said against my better judgement. But really, it'd be weird if I told him to find a different table to sit at. The café was tiny and there were only about four other spare seats.

He pulled the chair out and folded his huge body onto it, his long legs stretched out in front of him and his arms crossed over his chest. "I figured you'd say no after that tongue lashing you gave me the other day."

"Trust me, I wanted to." The words fell out of my mouth before I could censor them.

His lips twitched. "I like a woman who's honest."

"Yeah, well I'm not sharing my chips with you, so don't ask for any."

This time a smile spread out across his face. "Message received loud and clear, sugar." He uncrossed his arms and leant towards me. "You should probably know, though, that you've got tomato sauce on your face." Taking hold of my jaw, his thumb swiped the sauce from under my lip. He then placed his thumb in his mouth and sucked the sauce from it while I sat mesmerised by his moves. The man made cleaning my face look sexy as hell. I wanted to squirt sauce all over my face after that.

"Thanks," I said, but it came out like a bloody croak. What the hell was happening to me? I didn't get nervous around men, but Hyde made me act all kinds of weird.

His smile turned into a grin, but he didn't say anything else. He simply lounged back in his seat and crossed his arms again.

I ate a few more chips in silence and tried to focus all my attention on Bree, but just having Hyde sitting next to me made that difficult. As much as I avoided looking at him, I could smell him and sense his presence. And he smelt so bloody good with whatever scent he was wearing. Damn him.

"Who are you here with?" he asked, giving me a reason to turn back to him.

I found him watching me closely, which I both loved and hated all at the same time. "My friend's daughter, Bree. You?"

"My daughter."

Colour me shocked. That was the most unexpected thing to come out of his mouth. I hadn't picked him for being a father, and certainly not one who spent Tuesday nights taking his kid ice skating. But I loved that he did. "How old is she?"

"Sixteen."

"Oh God, you must be in hell. Bree's fifteen and she's more of a handful than she's ever been. How are you even managing to look so cool and calm? I mean, we've spoken a few times now and besides being a bit of an asshole the last time I saw you, you didn't seem run down or beaten to a pulp by your kid." God, I was fucking rambling. Would someone take a shoe and shove it in my mouth to shut me the hell up?

He chuckled, and that surprised me too. Hyde always seemed so intense and serious. I had to admit, I liked this side of him. A lot. "She lives in Melbourne with her mother, so she hasn't had the opportunity to beat me to a pulp yet. I'm sure it's coming, though. We've already gone two rounds today."

"Any bloodshed?"

"Only mine so far."

I laughed. "When did she arrive?"

"Three days ago."

"Oh man, strap on some combat gear. You're in for a wild ride."

"Yeah, I figured that after the first day."

"How long have you got her for?" It wasn't school holidays, so I wondered if she'd moved in with him.

"Her mother will be here tomorrow, but I'm not convinced Charlie wants to go home with her."

"Her name's Charlie? I love that."

"It's short for Charlotte."

An insistent tap on the window of the café drew our attention. It was Hyde's daughter. He promptly pushed his chair out and went outside to her where they engaged in a short conversation before making their way to the skate hire counter.

Charlie was a stunning girl with the same dark hair that Hyde had and a beautiful face I was sure the boys flocked to. I wondered how much stress she caused her father where boys were concerned. I remembered how much hell I'd given mine when I was a teenager. He swore half his grey hairs were from that time in my life. I'd had a new boyfriend every couple of months until I found one I really liked in my last year of school and had kept him for almost the entire year. My father hadn't been excited about him and it had caused us numerous fights.

Hyde helped Charlie exchange skates and waited until she was back out on the rink before he came inside again. He ordered a drink and then joined me at the table.

After drinking some of his coffee, he said, "You got kids, Monroe?"

"No, not yet."

"You want them?"

I nodded. My heart actually hurt at the thought of not having kids. "Yes," I said quietly. This conversation had turned personal, fast. Another thing I hadn't expected from him, but that was probably my bias against bikers. "I want a big family. Five kids. Maybe. Or three, at least. I guess it depends on my partner and what he wants. And whether those three have driven me insane before I can go for another one." Why the hell was I sharing all this with him? It was like my mouth had a mind of its own and just kept going.

His lips twitched. It seemed to be a regular occurrence, but then again, I was babbling a little, so I could understand his amusement. Please God, let me shut up. "You've put some thought into this. But you haven't found a father yet?"

I sighed. "Sadly, no. I'm flat out finding a man who likes meat, let alone one who wants to settle down and have kids."

He frowned. "Meat? Who the fuck doesn't like meat?"

"Right?! My thoughts exactly." He was tall *and* he liked meat. *And* he smelt heavenly. I died a little on the inside. He wasn't the man for me, but fuck, he was beginning to tick a lot of boxes.

He leant back in his seat, stretched his legs in front of him and reached his arms back so he could cradle the back of his head with his hands. Good Lord, did the man not know how sexy that move was when he did it? It was like having your favourite food laid out on a banquet in front of you and being on a nil-by-freaking-mouth diet.

"I guess there's always IVF or some other shit you could try if you can't find a guy who likes meat," he said, his mouth curving into more of a grin.

I pursed my lips in mock annoyance with him. "You're

finding this meat thing hilarious, aren't you? I'm telling you, it's a serious thing to look for in a man."

Still grinning. "I have no doubt. Tell me, what else are you looking for? Someone who flosses regularly? Or maybe someone who gets their tax in on time every year?"

I lifted a brow. "Flossing is very important. And honestly, I hadn't thought of the tax thing. I may need to add it to my list."

He laughed, and my belly fluttered at the sound. It was like a deep rumble of sexy goodness that I wanted to provoke over and over from him. "Ah, the mysterious list you mentioned the other night."

"I did?" God, I didn't remember that. What else had I said to him?

He shifted so he was leaning forward, his body and face closer to me. Dropping his voice to a low gravel, he said, "Yeah, you said I ticked two items off it. I had no idea what the fuck you were talking about, but it's making sense now." He paused for a beat before adding, "I'm guessing the fact I like meat gets me another tick."

Okay, it was time for me to woman up. Hyde had me on all kinds of edge just by being in the same room as me. No man ever did that to me. I was the woman who could flirt with anyone and never get tongue-tied. And yet, Hyde was making me question my ability to even engage in adult conversation.

I leant forward, resting my elbows on my knees and putting my cleavage on full display for him. Hitting him with the sexiest smile I could muster up, I said, "Three ticks don't make a list, tiger. You're gonna have to do better than that."

"I'm not looking to hit a list, sugar. But I will tell you, that vibrator of yours could learn a thing or two from me."

Fuck.

Hyde-1. Monroe-0.

"Roe, I hurt my ankle." Bree's voice cut through the heat between Hyde and me, which was the saviour I needed right then. If not for her, I'd be sliding fast into dangerous territory, contemplating letting a biker show me a thing or two. Or three or four. Hell, why stop at four? *Jesus.*

I stood. "Here," I said, motioning for her to come to me," Sit down, honey. What did you do to it?"

She limped my way, her skates in her hands. "One of the assholes out on the rink pushed off the wall, straight into me, and I twisted my ankle as I fell."

"Little shit," I muttered as I crouched to take a look at her ankle. I had not even one ounce of an idea as to what I was looking for, but it didn't appear to be swelling, so I figured that was a good thing.

"You can still walk on it?" Hyde asked.

Bree nodded. "Yeah, but it hurts really bad."

He shifted to sit on the edge of his seat so he was closer to her. After taking a good look at her ankle, he said, "It doesn't look crooked or swollen. Is it numb at all?"

She pressed on her ankle in a few spots. "No."

He stood. "Good. I'll get you some ice. Wait here."

As we watched him go, Bree said, "He's hot, Roe. Do you know him or did you just meet him here?"

I stopped drooling over his ass and turned to face her. This checking-out-guys side to her was new. Well, at least the sharing it with me was new. Her mother would have had a fit if she knew Bree was checking out a man old enough to be her father, but I figured it was a natural progression in a girl's life. I didn't want her to feel like she couldn't talk to me about guys, so I ran with it. "I've met him a few times now, but I don't really know him. And yeah, he's hot as sin, but definitely not my type."

She hit me with a look of shock. "You're kidding, right?

Like, why is he not your type? What doesn't he have that you're looking for?"

"Bree, baby, he's the bad boy your mama will warn you about when you get a little older. Bad boys are okay to fool around with, but you don't date them."

"So all your life you've dated the good guys? Is that working for you?"

I narrowed my eyes at her. "When did you become so sassy?" Honestly, I loved her sass, just not when it was directed at me.

A smile spread across her face. "Just pointing out something you may want to consider. You know, kinda like you do *all the time* for me."

I returned her smile. "Smartass," I muttered. "And while I haven't met the man of my dreams yet, I'm not sure a guy like Hyde would fit that bill."

Her smile morphed into a smug grin. "Don't judge a book by its cover, Roe."

I poked my tongue at her. "Shut up, missy. And stop throwing all the shit at me that your mother and I have been throwing at you all your life. That's good advice, but sometimes you just need to ignore it."

She laughed, but her laughter quickly died as she gripped her leg. "God, this hurts. I want to go back out there and run into that kid who ran into me. He should be hurting too."

Hyde returned with ice, and positioned Bree's leg up on the chair. He placed the ice on her ankle and said, "You'll probably wanna get her one of those compression bandages and keep her foot elevated."

"And see the doctor, I'm guessing." My first aid knowledge was going to need a major brush up if I was ever blessed with children.

"Yeah," he agreed. I loved that he didn't make fun of the fact I had zero awareness of how to treat this. He was just like bam, bam, bam, do this, do that, and all will be good. Hyde seemed like a take-charge kinda guy, and that right there made me like him more.

Bree glanced up at Hyde with a look of appreciation. "Thank you for all your help."

"No worries." He grabbed a spare seat from the table behind us and sat. "It's a good sign that it's not swelling. I'd say it's a minor sprain only."

"God, I hope so. I do not want to have to get a boot or anything like that," Bree said. At my smile, she pulled a face and added, "Those things are not hot, Roe. No guy is gonna check me out while I'm wearing a boot."

I held up my hands in defence. "Point taken, but I'm not sure I agree with you. I think you could milk a boot for a long time. Guys like to help pretty girls."

Hyde seemed amused by our conversation, but he didn't get involved. And a moment later when his daughter came off the rink, he left us to help her.

I watched him with her for a few minutes. He had to be one of the most attentive fathers I'd ever come across. Where some dads would be itching to get out of here, Hyde seemed intent on taking his time with his daughter. It was like he savoured every minute. I guessed that was perhaps because she lived in another city and he maybe didn't get much time with her. Whatever it was, I loved it. And bloody hell if that didn't annoy me a little. I didn't need any more reasons to like him.

CHAPTER 14

Hyde

It had been three days since Charlie showed up on my doorstep. I wasn't sure if we'd progressed far in our relationship, but the fact she'd agreed for me to take her ice skating had to be a good thing. Tenille had told me that ice skating was the one thing Charlie loved to do the most, and watching her out there on the rink blew me away. She was fucking good at it. It killed me that I'd missed out on all the steps she'd had to take to get to this point in her life. I wouldn't miss any more.

"Do you know them?"

I followed Charlie's gaze to Monroe and Bree. "Not really."

She'd just taken her skates off and tied the laces together before sliding her shoes on. "What does that mean?"

"I've met Monroe a few times, but we don't really know

each other." I watched as Monroe bent to pick up Bree's skates, and spent a good few moments appreciating her ass. She had curves in all the right places, and my hand itched to touch that ass.

"You call her by her surname?"

"No, it's her name."

"Cool name. I've never heard it before."

Monroe put her arm around Bree's waist in an effort to help her walk, and I had the sudden urge to ensure they made it out to their car safely. Turning to Charlie, I said, "You ready to go?"

She nodded and grabbed her stuff. "Yeah."

I headed in Monroe's direction, meeting her just as she started struggling with Bree's bag as well as the other stuff she carried. Reaching for it, I said, "Here, let me take it."

She hit me with a look of relief and passed me the bag. "Thank you."

Charlie and I followed Monroe and Bree out to Monroe's car. It was pitch-black outside, which pissed me off. The skating rink owner should have made sure the outside lights were switched on. I'd be having words with them about that.

I lit the torch up on my phone and angled it in the direction we walked. Monroe stopped when she came to a red Mazda. "This is us," she said as she unlocked the car and walked Bree around to help her into the passenger side.

My attention caught on one of her back windows. Moving to it, I confirmed what I thought and said, "Someone's smashed your window."

Her head popped up and she eyed me with disbelief. "Motherfucker."

My thoughts, too. I dialled a number and put my phone to my ear. When the call was answered, I said, "I'm gonna text you an address. Can you send Roach over to replace a car window for me?"

"Sure thing, man."

"Appreciate it." I ended the call and texted him the address and car details. It wasn't until she spoke that I realised Monroe had moved so she stood next to me.

"Ah, you know I'm quite capable of organising stuff on my own, right?" She sounded pissy. Kinda like she sounded the night I'd asked her to move her car out of Nitro's driveway.

"You'd be waiting for hours if you called someone. My guy'll be here within half an hour."

"Okay, so while I am thankful about that, I'd actually really rather you ask me first before you start organising shit for me."

"I don't see what the problem is here. You needed help, I organised it."

The car park lights turned on, and I took in her widened eyes and her annoyed expression. She was definitely pissed at me, but I failed to understand why. It was a no-brainer that I'd call for Roach when I knew he could get here fast.

She placed her hand on her hip. "What if I'd had someone I knew who could come and do it?"

I frowned. "Do you?"

Exhaling in frustration, she said, "No, but that's not the point! You don't get it, do you?"

Charlie stepped in at that point. "He really doesn't. Aiden sees everything in black and white from what I can work out."

Something Charlie said caused Monroe to falter. Shifting her attention between Charlie and me, she finally settled it on me and said, "I like that."

Jesus this woman confused the fuck out of me sometimes. "What?" She'd just given me hell for doing exactly what Charlie said I did, and now she was telling me she liked it. I wondered if she was this confusing to everyone she met or just to me.

"Aiden. I like your name."

I stared at her for a long quiet moment. No one had called me Aiden in fourteen years. Not until Tenille and Charlie came back into my life. It was a part of me that I'd left behind all those years ago, and it felt strange for someone other than my family to utter it. I did have to admit, though, that it sounded good rolling off her tongue.

Before I had a chance to respond, Charlie's phone lit up with a few texts that came in one after the other, causing her to swear after she read them. "That fucking asshole!"

"Boy troubles?" Monroe asked, completely shifting gears from our conversation to give all her attention to Charlie. How women managed to do that was beyond me.

Charlie met her gaze and nodded. "It's our anniversary today, and he promised me he'd Facetime tonight, but my friend just sent me photos of him drunk at a party. And that's after he blew me off yesterday to hang with his friends instead."

"Oh honey, you need to let him know that he's going to have to up his game or else you're out of there."

"No," I said forcefully. "She needs to end it with him." The little shit needed to be wiped from her memory as far as I was concerned. He was lucky I didn't live in Melbourne.

Monroe gave me a look that even I could decipher as meaning *keep out of this*. Taking Charlie's arm, she pulled her close. "Okay, he's going to call you tomorrow all apologetic. I recommend you be icy to him. Let him know he fucked up. Then he's going to try to make things right. The trick here is to accept his apology, but make it clear that there's no way you'll ever accept this again. You may need to stay icy for a little while, but then again, you don't want to drag that out too long, because then that just makes you bitchy. And no guy is going to put up with bitchy for very long. But girl, what you need to be prepared for is this—if he screws up again, you need to stick to your guns and ditch his ass." At Charlie's look of horror, Monroe raised her brows and added, "Life is too short to put up with shit from a man, honey. There are a lot of other guys out there who would kill to have you by their side. Don't settle for less than the best."

"Or," I said, "you could just tell him where to go now and save a lot of time and effort."

They both stared at me as if I was talking out of my ass and then turned back to each other and ignored what I said. When Bree hobbled around the car to join them, I said, "You wanna get off that ankle and rest it." She also ignored me and started talking boy shit with Monroe and Charlie.

I spent the next half hour checking in with King about club shit that was going down and waiting for Roach while doing my best to drown out the conversation taking place between the three girls. I tried to interrupt at one point to ask Monroe if anything was missing from her car, but she quickly shook her head and continued on with the boy talk.

I caught bits and pieces of what she told Charlie, and while I was on board with the ball-breaking advice she seemed to be giving, I wondered how the hell anyone survived dating her. She'd be hard fucking work with all her demands.

———

Tenille texted me early the next morning. Shit was going down at home with Craig, so she wouldn't make it to Sydney that afternoon. Charlie gave the impression she didn't care, but I saw the disappointment cross her face for a split second when she heard the news. My kid was a fucking pro at acting unaffected by family stuff, but I could see her mask. In the few days she'd been with me, not much had changed between us, but because I knew she hid her real feelings, I tolerated the attitude she still flung at me. Mostly. Every now and then, I pushed back, and it was in those moments when she let me that I knew we'd eventually find each other.

Tenille had organised for Charlie to keep up with her schoolwork via email, and I made sure she was up and getting ready to do it before I left home each day. That morning had been a struggle because she wanted to sleep instead. We'd argued for a good half hour about it. Once I was convinced she'd stay up and get on to it, I left for the clubhouse. King was still hunting the Italian who supposedly had something to do with Jacko's murder, and he'd told me the day before that he wanted me, Devil, and Nitro with him when he paid a visit to Salvatore Ricci, one of Storm's enemies. Salvatore had been out of town for a few days and was scheduled to arrive home in a few hours. King's plan was to catch him when he least suspected it, and he figured that would be when Salvatore made a stop to visit his mistress on his way home.

I was surprised to hear Monroe's voice when I entered the clubhouse. Making my way inside, I found her talking with King who seemed mildly amused by something she said.

His eyes met mine and he grinned. Motioning towards me, he said, "Here he is. You can give him the cash yourself."

She spun around to face me. Closing the distance between us, she thrust an envelope at me. "Here's what I owe you for the car window."

I frowned as I glanced down at the envelope. "You don't owe me anything."

"Yeah, I do. Well, I owe your friend so you can give it to him."

I held the envelope out to her and jerked my chin at it. "He doesn't want your cash, sugar."

She held her hands up and shook her head. "I don't care. I don't take things for free, Aiden."

King's brows lifted and he hit me with a questioning look. "Aiden?" Looking back at Monroe, he added, "You two on a first name basis, *sugar?*"

She looked at him. "We're not on anything. And I really need to get to work." Taking the envelope off me, she forced it into King's hands. "Maybe you can sort this out for me." With that, she stalked out of the clubhouse, leaving me staring after her and King watching me with interest.

"What?" I barked when I turned to him.

Nodding in the direction Monroe left, he said, "You tapping that, brother? 'Cause if you're not, I've gotta get me a piece."

"No, have at it," I barked again. This whole conversation pissed me the fuck off. "But be prepared because she's a fucking handful." As much as I tried to ignore it, the fucking thought of him going anywhere near Monroe irritated me.

His grin grew. "I'll leave her for you. Besides, I've got enough of a handful at home. I don't need any more women trying to break my fucking balls at the moment."

"Jen's still giving you hell?"

His mouth flattened. "When does that woman *not* give me hell? I've slept here for the last few nights so I could get some fucking peace."

I'd never understand their relationship. It wasn't like King to let anyone control him, and yet there he was changing his life because of her.

He passed me the envelope of cash. "The plan for today has changed. Salvatore's trip has been extended a day. I'm gonna take care of some other shit that's come up. I want you and Nitro to visit that guy Fox told you about. He's finally home. Do whatever the fuck it takes to get an address for Marx. I want a fucking face-to-face with the motherfucker."

Marx had been eluding us at every turn, and King was reaching crazy levels of fucked off about it. I nodded. "Will do." I didn't intend to leave that asshole until I had what King needed.

CHAPTER 15

Monroe

"You're not yourself. What's going on?" Tatum asked.

I drank some of my cosmo before turning to face her. "It's Hyde. That's what's going on." Just the thought of the man caused my stomach to swirl with butterflies. And not just the good type of butterflies. There were some seriously confused butterflies in there too.

We were sitting in the pub after work, the night after I spent time with Hyde at the skating rink. I'd seen him that morning to give him the money I owed him, and I hadn't been able to stop thinking about him all day.

"Are you seeing him?" She seemed just as confused as I did.

"No."

"So how's he affecting you? You're not making any sense, Roe. You're usually cool and calm over men, but you seem anything but calm tonight."

I exhaled a long breath. "I'm interested in him, but I don't want to be. He's a biker, and you know how I feel about bikers. And he can be infuriating sometimes with the way he tries to boss me around. I do not need a man in my life who is always trying to take charge of me."

Her lips pulled up slightly at the ends as if trying not to smile. "Wasn't it you who said you wanted a man with some balls to go with his dick? Or something like that? I kinda think you do want someone to boss you around. Just a little bit. And as far as bikers go, don't judge Hyde based on that. Look at Nitro. You didn't like him to begin with, and now you're all about him."

"Well, there's a difference between a man who bosses me around a little and one who does it a lot. Hyde's argued with me over a few things now. Like last night, he was at the skating rink when Bree and I were there, and he walked us out. Someone had smashed one of the windows on my car, and he just took it upon himself to call a friend to come fix it. Without asking me!"

She laughed at that. "Oh, Roe, come on, admit it—deep down you like a man who can take charge. I think you're just fighting your attraction because he's a biker and you're scared that he's different to any guy you've ever dated."

"I don't need a man who will fuck me over, Tatum. I'm not saying Hyde would, but he told me he doesn't have much experience with dating, so I really don't think he's the kind of man interested in settling down and having kids. I don't have time to waste on a guy like that."

"Hang on, when did you discuss dating with him?"

"That night he showed up at my house. I told you about that. I was drunk and said lots of inappropriate things to him. I forget some of it, but I definitely remember discussing his love life with him."

She finished her drink and slid the glass across the bar

before turning her body to me. "Okay, let's go over all this. You are way too anxious about it all. You've let dating become a task you need to do in order to achieve your mission. You need to take a step back, Roe, and breathe, and just have some fun. Take a chance on him if you're that interested in him. See where it goes. Maybe it'll just be some casual sex and fun before you move on to someone else who might end up being the man for you." She shrugged. "There's nothing wrong with having a little fun in your life."

I stared at her. "Umm, since when did Tatum Lee become all about fun?" I had to admit, though, that I loved this new side of her. It was good to see her happy.

Her gaze shifted to look at someone behind me, and her face lit up. Glancing back at me as she slid off her stool, she said, "Since this man." Nitro moved next to her, slid his arm around her waist and pulled her close so he could drop a kiss on her lips.

"Vegas," he murmured in greeting. Still a man of few words.

She looked up at him. "I'm ready to go."

Frowning, I said, "We just got here. You need to stay for at least one more drink with me."

Smiling at me, she shook her head. "No, you've got other things to do. I'll call you tomorrow to check in."

It wasn't until Nitro stepped to the side that I realised what she meant. Hyde stood behind him. His eyes met mine when Nitro moved, darkening as he took me in. Being watched by Hyde was one of the most unnerving things ever. I wasn't sure if I wanted to hide from him or bare my soul.

I tore my attention from Hyde and gave it back to Tatum when she said, "I'll call you tomorrow."

Hyde's presence had pretty much wiped all coherent thought from my mind, so I simply nodded and murmured, "Okay."

As she and Nitro walked away from us, Hyde moved closer. His scent almost hypnotised me, if that were even possible. Looking down at me, he said, "What are you drinking?" The husky tone of his voice was like the final nail in my coffin. He could lead me down the path to sin with that voice.

"A cosmo please."

He turned to the waiting bartender and ordered drinks before shifting his gaze back to me. His body was so damn close it almost pressed against mine. His eyes dropped to my chest. "You weren't made to be subtle, were you, sugar?"

"Can't say that word's in my vocabulary, no." The way he devoured my body told me I'd made the best decision when I'd bought the black dress I wore tonight. Knee-length with a plunging neckline and accentuated with a belt around my waist, it clung to every curve I had. My girls were up and proudly out, just the way I liked them. I mean, if you had it, flaunt it, right? And I'd had the red in my hair touched up that afternoon. It hung in lazy vivid-red curls to just below my breasts. I wasn't sure which part of me he thought wasn't subtle, but I guessed it had something to do with my dress by the way he seemed unable to draw his gaze from my body.

Finally he found his way back up to my face. The heat flashing in his eyes shot a round of lust through my veins. Good God, this man, though. I wondered if he had any idea of the storm he caused within me. "Don't ever add it." If what he said didn't make my legs sway a little, the forceful, gravelly way he said it did.

The bartender placed our drinks on the counter, distracting us from each other. Hyde dropped some cash on the bar, took a mouthful of his whisky and looked back at me while I got down as much of my drink as I could in one mouthful. I needed it. I could stand my ground with any man, but Hyde had a way of catching me off guard.

"You calm down after that thing about owing me money this morning?" And there he went, flipping my feelings about him on their head.

I fixed him with a look that let him know I wasn't impressed. "I didn't have anything to calm down from."

"You seemed all worked up about it."

I drank some more of my cocktail. "I wasn't." But I was getting there now, that was for sure.

He drank some more whisky, keeping his eyes steady on mine. "Okay."

Okay? Oh no he didn't. He didn't get to end a conversation with that bullshit. "Okay? Seriously, you're going to end with that?"

"It seemed pointless to argue."

I finished my drink and placed the empty glass down with some force. Sliding off my stool, I said, "We weren't arguing. I was simply telling you like it was."

"Yeah, I've picked that up about you."

My eyes practically popped out of their sockets. "Picked up what about me?"

"That you like to tell men *like it is*."

"I do not! You just have this way of pushing my buttons. I feel like it's you, not me."

His lips twitched. "Sugar, if I knew which buttons I was pushing, I'd push them some more. I never said I didn't like the way you told me how it was."

I snatched my bag off the bar. I needed a moment to get my thoughts under control. In the space of seconds, I'd switched from wanting him to wanting to smack him to wanting him again. My mind needed a break from the whiplash. I took a step away from the bar and said, "I'll have another cosmo."

Without waiting for his response, I headed in the direction of the ladies' room. I'd almost made it there when a hand slid around my waist, and I was pushed up against the wall in the dark hallway. A hard body pressed against mine as the hand around my waist slid down to settle on my ass and warm breath whispered across my cheek. "My cock likes that attitude of yours. Surprised the fuck outta me, but I can't deny I want more of it."

The proof of his statement ground against me, sparking need all over me. Every inch of my skin blazed with desire. I gripped his shirt with both hands and found his eyes. "You and I weren't made for each other, Hyde."

"I'm not saying we were."

My body went to war with my mind. It fought me kicking and screaming, desperate for what was on offer, but I didn't want to surrender. "So what's the point of starting something?"

He pushed his cock harder against me. "I came here against better judgement tonight. Nitro told me you'd be here and I came because I couldn't, for the fucking life of me, get you out of my head. I want my hands on those curves of yours and my dick as far inside you as you can take it."

I'd never dated a guy or even been with one who spoke as filthy to me as Hyde did, but everything he'd just said did it for me. Especially the bit about my curves. Hell, at this point he could probably start bossing me around, and I'd do whatever he said.

I gripped his shirt harder, pulling it, and him, even closer. "Does that dirty talk always work for you?"

The determined glint in his eyes caused another explosion of need in me. "Can't say I've ever used it before, sugar. Never wanted to fuck a woman who argued with me like you do."

"Fuck," I muttered. I wanted to say yes, so badly, but something held me back. Something I couldn't quite put my finger on.

He bent his head so he could trail kisses along my collarbone. My skin sizzled with heat where his lips touched it. I struggled with the urge to curl my fingers in his hair and hold his head in place. When he was done, he lifted his face and rasped, "Give me one night. I'll show you what you're missing with those vibrators."

I could do one night. Truth be told, I could do with one night of real cock. It had been a long time between drinks. But first I needed to know if he could kiss. There was no point going home with a man who didn't know his way around a set of lips.

I let go of his shirt and reached for the back of his neck. Pulling his face down to mine, my mouth found his. I moaned as his tongue slid inside and he took charge. I knew instantly that Hyde knew his way around a kiss. I also knew that he was going to rock my world. Every part of me fell under his spell as he consumed me. There was no turning back from this.

By the time we were done with the kiss, he'd run his hands over my ass and then up my body to my breasts before finally taking hold of my face. He came up for air and growled, "I hope to fucking God that's a yes."

I smiled. "That's a yes, tiger. Now get me the hell out of here and show me what you can do with that cock of yours."

CHAPTER 16

Hyde

My dick was hard as fuck by the time I got Monroe back to her place. Half of it was due to her efforts at fighting me over this. I was conflicted. I wanted to slam her onto her back and fuck the hell out of her, but there was just something about the way she attempted to run the show that turned me on. I decided to let her think she had a say in it for a little while longer.

As soon as we made it through her front door, she'd grabbed my hand and led me to her bedroom. I'd briefly taken in the colour explosion of artwork, pillows, and other shit in there before she distracted me with a hand to my dick.

Biting her bottom lip, she smiled seductively at me and said, "I'm not ashamed to admit I've been imagining this cock since that night you rescued me from my front yard."

I undid the belt from around her waist. "What kinds of things have you been imagining, sugar?"

Her hips drew my eyes. I couldn't fucking drag my gaze from them. Monroe had an hourglass figure—the kind that gave a man something to hold onto while he pounded into her.

She flicked the button on my jeans and slid the zip down. Reaching into my pants, she wrapped her hand around my dick. With her eyes firmly on mine, she slowly stroked it, her movements very deliberate. "I've been thinking about how it would feel in my hand. How it would taste if I ran my tongue along it, licking the tip and sucking it slowly, my tongue making circles around the tip. Over and fucking over. And I thought about how much I want to take this cock into my mouth and deepthroat you." She brought her face close to mine so she could whisper in my ear, "The thought of your dick hitting my throat gets me so fucking wet."

I groaned, not sure how much longer I would last if she kept this sexy shit up. She had a dirty fucking mouth on her. I made a mental note to make sure I gave her that opportunity one day. She could suck my dick to the back of her throat any fucking time she wanted.

Grabbing a handful of her hair, I pulled her head back so I could dip my mouth to her neck. She moaned, and I growled, "You like a little rough play?"

She kept stroking my dick. "I'm all about the rough play, tiger. I'm hoping you can bring it."

I pulled her hair harder as I nudged her legs apart with my knee. With one hand holding her hair, I reached my other hand to the bottom of her dress. That fucking dress should be made illegal. It hugged every curve of hers and was a fucking hazard to my health.

Her dress was too fitted for what I wanted, so I let go of her hair and gripped the bottom of the dress with both hands. A moment later, I had it off her, and she stood almost naked in front of me.

Dropping my gaze to her tits, I said, "Fuck, red, I don't even know where to start." Cupping her tits, I bent my face to them and sucked a nipple into my mouth. Jesus, I loved tits that were more than a handful, and Monroe had that. Her tits were a gift from fucking God as far as I was concerned. I could dedicate a whole session to them.

"Not sure if you're aware, but you have a way of making a man want to do the filthiest fucking things to you."

A sexy smile spread lazily across her face. "What filthy things are we talking? I'm all for filthy."

I ran my hands down her back and took hold of her ass. Another gift from the big guy. "The kinds of things that will make it hard for you to walk tomorrow."

"Oh God, you're trying to kill me, aren't you?"

"Just trying to fuck you, sugar."

Her lips parted mine and her tongue slid in. She kissed me like I imagined she would fuck me—thoroughly and deeply—while her hand remained around my dick, stroking me, getting me closer to my release.

When she finished kissing me, I said, "Take off your bra and panties."

"You don't want to?"

"No, I want to watch you do it."

She let my dick go and slid her hands down her body until she reached her panties. Slowly hooking her fingers over them, she slipped them off, all the while keeping her eyes firmly on mine.

Fuck, she gave me a show. I took hold of my dick and jerked off while watching her remove her bra in the same way. It was hot as hell. But not half as hot as when she reached her hand down to her pussy and ran a finger in circles over her clit.

She turned me on so damn much that I knew I couldn't last much longer. I fucking wanted to drag this out all night long. Wanted to command her to fuck herself with her fingers while I watched. Hell, I wanted to ask her for a fucking lap dance, but a man had to be realistic. My dick was hard as steel for her. I fucking needed to be inside that sweet cunt of hers as soon as possible.

As I watched her finger herself, I rasped, "You've got two minutes left, sugar, and then I'm getting in that pussy of yours."

I removed my clothes while I continued to watch her. I then located a condom and slid it on. When I was ready for her, I ordered, "I want you on your hands and knees on the bed, ass in the air."

She shook her head at me, her fingers still working that pussy. "No, you're not fucking me in the ass. That shit's reserved for men who stick around."

"Wasn't planning on it. I just want your ass in my view while I fuck you."

"Well, I was thinking—"

Jesus, this was not the time for her to argue with me. I snaked my hand around her waist and pulled her body to mine. "When I tell you how I want to fuck you, you don't argue with me," I growled.

Her eyes flashed with heat. Gripping my arms, she said forcefully, "I want to watch your face while you do it."

I jerked my head at the bed. "Get on your back."

Her lips curled up in a smile, and she did what I said.

I positioned myself on top of her. I then ran my finger along her pussy to see how ready she was for me. She was wet as fuck.

Holding her gaze, I growled, "Stop thinking and start fucking, sugar."

Not giving her a moment to argue with me, I thrust inside of her. Sweet fucking Jesus, her cunt wrapped around my dick like it was made for it. When her arms and legs gripped me, and a long, satisfied moan tore from her mouth, I pulled out and slammed into her again.

"Fuck, I like your kind of filthy," she said in a hot-as-hell tone. "Don't stop now."

"Wasn't planning on it."

"Thank God."

I got serious then. If she was down with me fucking her the way I wanted to, I'd take her up on that. I pounded into her over and over, not giving either of us a second to catch our breath. Our fucking turned into a violent, demanding need we both had.

I grunted through her nails digging into my skin and scratching lines down my back.

She pushed me to give it to her harder.

Every minute of being with her drove me towards a climax like I'd never achieved. When I finally came—and fuck knew how I managed to last as long as I did—I thrust into her with so much force her head almost rammed into the headboard.

I roared out my release as she gripped me tighter, nails piercing my skin, and screamed out her own.

"Fuck, you weren't kidding when you said you liked my kind of filthy, were you?" I said after I rolled off her.

She made one of her sexy noises and curled against my body, her arm over my chest, leg over mine. "No, I wasn't. I like being fucked exactly the way you did it."

I stretched an arm over her shoulder. Usually, I had no desire to hang around and talk after I fucked a woman. But with Monroe, I couldn't get enough of her. "I'll bring my filthy anytime you want it."

Another sexy moan fell from her lips as she stretched her body in one of the most arousing moves I'd ever seen. She ended up half on top of me with her leg hooked around mine, tits pressed against my chest, and her hand curved around my neck. Those full lips of hers captured mine in a long kiss before she said, "I think you should bring it right now. And when I say bring it, I mean give me every-fucking-thing."

I reached for her leg and gripped her thigh. Pulling it, I slid it up my body, spreading her wide to give me access to her cunt. My finger was on her clit a moment later, and I ran lazy circles over it. My eyes remained firmly on her face. I wanted to watch as she took the pleasure I gave. She didn't disappoint. As I built her bliss, her eyes fluttered closed and she bit her lip while giving me more of those sexy-as-fuck sounds that got me off.

"Fuck, Monroe, any man ever told how fucking hot your mouth is? You keep making those sounds and I'll blow before I get back inside you."

She opened her eyes as a smile spread across her face. "Slow down, tiger. We've gotta get you hard again."

I slapped her ass. "I need to get rid of this condom first. But I'm telling you now that my dick will be hard before you can get on your knees and lick my balls."

She moved off me so I could leave the bed. I made my way into the bathroom and disposed of the condom. She met me in the doorway as I turned to leave.

Hand to my chest, she said, "I think we should move this into the shower." At the arch of my brow, she added, "I have a thing for clean sex. Don't get me wrong, I fucking love sex anyway I can get it, but there's just something about a man who smells amazing. It gets me off like you wouldn't believe."

I cupped one of her tits and tweaked the nipple. "If water and soap get you off more than I did in that bed, I'm all for the fucking shower."

She grinned and moved past me towards the shower. I trailed my gaze down her body, lingering on her ass.

Monroe's curves were to fucking die for, and that ass was something else.

She snapped me out of my trance. "You gonna stand there staring at my ass all night?"

I closed the distance between us with two determined strides. "You keep it up, and that sass will get you fucked harder than you can take," I growled, forcing her into the shower.

She dragged her bottom lip between her teeth. "I'm really fucking hoping so."

My gaze caught on the colourful assortment of sex toys she had in her shower. "Fuck, red, you weren't kidding about the vibrators, were you?" There were at least seven different vibrators, dildos, and bullets in her shower. On top of that, she had a handle and footrest set-up. The only thing I was surprised not to see was a dildo suctioned to the wall.

"I don't kid about sex. I'm dedicated to it in ways you can't even imagine."

"I don't want to imagine. I want first-hand fucking experience. Get your ass over to that wall and your foot up on that rest." I needed those legs of hers spread and my fingers in that pussy.

She did as I said while I grabbed the soap. My dick hardened at the sight of her gripping the handle, leg up, ready for me. Jesus, it would be fucking hard to walk away from her when we were done. If I didn't have to get home to Charlie, I'd spend the night between Monroe's thighs.

"Cleaning myself off you is a fucking shame, sugar," I said as I soaped up her pussy.

Her back arched as I ran my hand through her folds. "Yeah, but you'll be back there soon."

I cleaned every inch of her, taking my sweet time with her tits, ass, and pussy. When I was done, she turned and took the soap from me. A few moments later, she'd lathered my chest and had shifted her attention to my cock.

Wrapping one hand around it, she kissed me before saying, "I want to suck you off, but I also want you to come inside me again. It's a real fucking dilemma, because I'm not sure if you've got two more in you tonight."

A phone rang in another room, breaking into our conversation. "You need to get that?" she asked.

"It's not mine."

She frowned. "Well, it's definitely not mine."

The ring tone was the Sesame Street theme song, and it sure as shit wasn't coming from my phone. If it wasn't hers either, we had a problem. I placed a finger to her mouth, indicating she should be quiet. "Wait here. I'll go take care of this."

She nodded, and I stepped out of the shower, wrapping a towel around my waist as I moved silently towards the ringing phone. I would fucking cut the balls off whoever had broken into her house. However, as soon as I entered her bedroom where the sound was coming from, I realised we didn't have an intruder. It was my fucking phone ringing.

I snatched it up off the floor where I'd dropped it in my jeans. Charlie's face grinned at me from the phone. "You changed the ring tone on my phone?" I muttered, answering the call.

"Yeah, you like?"

What I did like was the smile I heard in her voice. That, I would have paid good money for. "What's up? You okay?" She'd told me she would be all right at home on her own, but my fatherly instinct had kicked into high gear. I shouldn't have fucking left her.

"Settle down, I'm good. No need to stress. I'm calling because Mum arrived about an hour ago and she's wondering what time you're coming home." Her voice dropped as she added, "I think she wants us to have a family dinner or some shit, but I'm good if you're staying out all night."

I held the phone away from my ear for a moment to look at the time. Just after nine. "I'll be there in about half an hour."

"Oh, okay." She sounded surprised. "I'll tell her."

We ended the call and I bent to reach for my jeans.

"It was yours after all?" Monroe said from behind.

I turned to find her standing naked in front of me. Fuck. My dick ached to fuck her, but the desire to get home to Charlie—to not let her down—won out. "Sorry, sugar, I've gotta get home to my kid."

A smile flickered across her face and she came to me. Her hands looped around my neck and she kissed me. It was long. Deep. And fuck if it didn't stir more need in my gut. "I like that about you."

When she dropped her arms and took a step back, I let my towel go and put my jeans on. "Yeah, well kids come first."

Her eyes dropped to my dick. "They do, but there's something to be said for a man who walks away from sex with a hard-on he'll have to take care of himself, for his child. Unfortunately I've met many who wouldn't."

I grabbed my shirt and the towel off the floor. After passing her the towel, I put my shirt on and then snaked my arm around her waist. Dropping a kiss to her lips, I said, "This needs to be continued."

"No, this was only one night, tiger."

My lips brushed her ear as I rasped, "Your pussy is, right now, begging you to fuck me again. I'm gonna give her what she wants."

"My pussy doesn't need you worrying about her. She can find cock elsewhere."

I tightened my hold on her, pulling her body hard against

mine. "You can fight me on a lot of shit, Monroe, but not this. This is the one fight I win. I'll be calling you and you'll be answering that call. And we are going to get clean as fuck in that shower of yours and then I'm going to fuck you harder and longer than you've ever been fucked in your life."

Our eyes met when I let her go. Hers were wide. She didn't argue with me, didn't say another word. She simply watched me collect my keys off the bedside table and exit the room.

Monroe might have thought we weren't made for each other, and hell we probably weren't. But we were sure as shit made to fuck each other.

CHAPTER 17

Hyde

I scrubbed my face and stared at Tenille as she slammed cupboards and drawers in my kitchen. She was pissed off with me, but I had no fucking idea why. And she'd hardly said a word to me since I'd arrived home, so there were no clues there.

"Tee, what the fuck's going on?" I finally asked. Charlotte had hightailed it out of the kitchen five minutes ago after an argument with her mother, so I was making it my mission to figure this out.

She slammed the container she held down and met my gaze. "You came to me! *You!* It wasn't my choice for us to come back into each other's lives."

My temper spiked. I fucking hated the way she fought with me when I didn't know shit about why she was angry. She'd done it when we were together, and it seemed old habits died hard. I took a deep breath. "You're not making any sense. How about you back the fuck up and start from the beginning here. Why are you so pissed at me? I mean, I came home twenty minutes ago and we've hardly said a word to each other. How the fuck have I managed to get you so worked up in that time?"

Her eyes widened. "You never did understand women, Aiden, and it appears you still don't." She rested her hands on the counter as she glared at me. "How do you think it makes me feel when the man I loved for so long—the man who I just found out didn't really die years ago, who just showed back up in my life, telling me he wants to be there for me now—comes home the first night I'm in his new home, having just been with another woman? You think that makes me feel good?"

Fuck.

I raked my fingers through my hair, unsure of the best way forward here. Moving around the counter, I reached for her, but she slapped my hand away, so I stopped and said. "Tee, I didn't know you were coming here tonight. Last I heard, you were dealing with shit in Melbourne with Craig."

She blinked a few times, and I wondered if she was about to cry. She didn't, though. "I left him," she blurted out.

I was surprised, but relieved. As far as I was concerned, Craig wasn't good enough for her. He didn't love her the way she should be loved. "What happened?"

She dropped her gaze and fussed with the food she had on the counter. She'd bought a roast chicken and had filled plates with meat and salad for dinner. "He's been coming home drunk for months, and he's always fighting lately. I've had enough."

"Fighting?"

"Yeah. I don't know where or with who, but he comes home beaten and bloody some nights. Others, he turns up with ripped and blood-soaked shirts."

Sully had told me about the drinking, but I didn't know about the fighting. "What did he say about all that?"

She stared at me silently for a long while before admitting, "He told me not to ask questions about things that didn't concern me. About things I didn't really want to know." Her voice cracked. "And when I pushed him on it, he hit me and told me it was all my fault."

I clenched my fists. I wanted to knock him the fuck out. I wanted to make him bleed myself. Putting my hand out, I demanded, "Give me your phone."

Her forehead crinkled. "Why?"

My body tensed the longer this took. "Tenille, give me your phone. I want a word with that motherfucker."

"No. He's never hit me before. This was just a one-off thing. You don't need to get involved."

I drew in a long breath and let it out slowly, willing myself to get my shit under control. I wasn't the same man Tenille had married anymore. She wasn't acquainted with my violent side, and I didn't want her to get fucking acquainted with it.

Needing a moment, and a whole lot of the one thing that had a shot at calming me, I stalked to the cupboard where I kept my whisky. Grabbing it out, I poured a mouthful into a glass and downed it. Not even close to enough, I poured another mouthful and knocked it back too.

Moving to where she stood, I said, "Where's your phone? I'm not going to ask again."

She responded to my forceful tone and pulled her phone from her back pocket. "What are you going to say to him?"

I took the phone. "What's your password?"

"I asked you a question."

Another deep breath. "Your password, Tenille?"

She rattled off four digits, which I keyed into her phone. I then scrolled through her contact list to find Craig's number, all the while, ignoring her tirade about what an asshole I could be.

Craig answered on the fourth ring. "Where the fuck are you, Tenille?"

I saw red.

"This isn't Tenille." If a voice could commit murder, Craig would be dead.

"What do *you* want?" he spat back.

I squeezed the phone. "I want you to know that *I* know what you did. And I want you to also know that in my world, a man doesn't hit his wife and get away with it."

"So, what? I should watch my back or some shit? You're gonna come get me?"

"I don't come *get* people, Craig, but I do take care of them," I said far more quietly than I was feeling. A hurricane of violent thoughts raged inside me. In my mind, I'd already hurt him a million different ways. Some of them, the kinds of ways a person didn't survive.

Silence for a beat. And then—"Put my wife on the fucking phone, asshole."

"If memory serves me correctly, I never divorced Tenille. And I sure as fuck didn't die. Which makes her still *my* wife."

Silence again. "Fuck you!"

The phone went dead, and my eyes met Tenille's. Confusion lay there. "Oh God." Her hand flew to her mouth. "This is a fucking mess, Aiden."

I nodded. "Yeah. But if you want to leave Craig, there's your answer."

"That's not an answer! It doesn't matter if we aren't technically married, we were together for a long time, and we have a lot of shit to work out."

Why did women have to make everything so damn hard? In my mind, it was a no-brainer. She wasn't happy. She wanted to leave Craig. They were never legally married. Fuck up solved.

"So what's the plan now?"

She stared at me with a broken expression. "I don't know."

"Stay here for a bit. Figure shit out." I refrained from telling her to never go back to Craig, but God help him if she did. I'd never take my eyes off him again.

"Yeah, maybe." She seemed anything but certain, but this was still fresh. Tomorrow things might be a little clearer.

"And Tee?" At her questioning look, I softened my voice a little and said, "I'm sorry about coming home like that."

She nodded. "I shouldn't have lost it with you."

It killed me that she had to navigate this new relationship with me. That I'd brought this on us. But there was no way back, only forward.

Changing the subject, I said, "Have you and Charlie figured stuff out?"

"Yeah, we had a good talk. But if I'm gonna be staying here for a bit, you need to be prepared for lots of arguments between us."

I could only imagine. Charlie had inherited her parents' temper. "I'll deal."

"Mum!" Charlie called out.

"What?"

"Come here."

"No, you come here if you want me."

She went quiet for a moment before yelling, "God, why do you have to be such a pain?" She stomped out to the kitchen, glaring at her mother. "I need to know which lipstick looks better on me." She held up two options.

Jesus, all that for lipstick.

Tenille pointed at one of the lipsticks. "That one. Why?"

"I'm Facetiming with Jamie tonight. I need to look my best."

I scowled. "I thought that little shit was in the doghouse."

She gave me an unimpressed look. "We moved past that."

"What happened to leaving him out in the cold for a while like Monroe said?"

Tenille's eyes hit mine. "Monroe?"

"She's cool, Mum."

Tenille's brows arched and her body snapped straight. Something was going on here, but again, I had no fucking idea. "Who is she?"

Charlie frowned at Tenille's sharp tone. "She was at skating last night with her friend's daughter."

"So she's not your woman?" Her icy gaze penetrated mine. Fuck, she ran hot and cold.

Before I could answer, Charlie said, "They're not together. They hardly know each other."

Monroe wasn't my woman, but Tenille didn't need to know anything further about our relationship. The last fucking thing I needed right now was to revisit the fact I'd come home straight from fucking another woman. That conversation hadn't gone so well the first time; I could guess where it would lead if mentioned again. A man didn't need to issue any invitations to break the peace in his own home.

CHAPTER 18

Monroe

"You're walking like you've been thoroughly fucked. Is there something you're not telling me?" Tatum said on Friday night. We'd skipped drinks at the pub after work because Nitro had asked her to lay low due to some club stuff going on. She'd arrived at my place about an hour and a half ago carrying a bottle of Jäger and cans of Red Bull. Jäger wasn't her favourite drink, but she'd recently started doing Jägerbombs with me because I loved them so much.

I made us another round of drinks. I'd lost count, but it was probably our sixth round. Passing her glass, I said, "That's because I *have* been thoroughly fucked this week. And can I just say, I'm pretty fucking sure it was the best sex I've ever had."

She looked at me over the rim of her glass. "Fuck me, you slept with Hyde?"

I sagged against the kitchen counter where we sat. The

thought of sex with him made me swoon. I'd hardly thought about anything else over the last two days. "I did."

"And?"

The breath whooshed out of me as images of fucking him ran through my mind like a video—a video I'd been watching like a crack addict since Wednesday night. "Sister, the man knows what the hell he's doing."

She laughed and drank some of her Jäger. "Are you going to go back for more?"

"I don't know. He tried to boss me into saying yes to more, but I'm not sure I want to go down that road."

"Why not? If it was that good, I'm surprised you haven't already called him. You don't usually say no to good sex. Plus, you told me you're sick of one-night stands."

"I want more than casual sex with a guy, Tatum, and I think that's all Hyde is offering. Honestly, why would I put myself in the situation where I get attached to him when he's not interested in getting attached to me?"

She rested her elbows on the counter. "Do you like him enough to want something more?"

It was a question I'd been going over and over in my mind. One I wasn't sure I wanted to answer. But this was Tatum and I told her everything. "I feel like I have a love-hate relationship with him. He's too damn bossy for me most of the time, but then he will say or do something that impresses the hell out of me. He seems like a good dad, and I think that says a lot about a person." I sighed. "Yeah, I like him. But it doesn't mean much if there's no hope of anything happening with him, you know?"

"I understand what you're saying. But you know what? Sometimes we don't know what we want until it's given to us. You're pretty hard not to love, Roe. Hyde might just change his mind once he gets to know you."

A loud knock sounded from the front door, followed by, "Roe! Let me in, I've got shit I neeeeed to discuss!"

It was Savannah. I'd never seen her so excited when I let her in. She practically bounced on the spot.

"I just met the father of my babies!" She exclaimed. I was almost sure she was about to pee her pants from the happiness radiating off her.

I followed her into the kitchen where Tatum and I were set up with drinks and nibblies at the kitchen bar. "Who? And where? You want a drink?"

She madly nodded and motioned with her hand for a drink. "Yes, I need all the drinks to celebrate." Sliding onto one of the spare stools, she continued, "We met on the train coming home from work. I practically poked his eye out with my umbrella. I said sorry and just about fainted when I realised how good-looking he is. He's a fucking suit! I've been fantasizing about him ripping his tie off and tying me up with it ever since I had to say goodbye to him."

I handed her a drink. "So, what, you guys spent the ride home talking? He asked for your number? You've got a dinner date this weekend? I need to know everything." I was heavily invested in this story already. Any love story was worthy of my attention. Because, love... who the fuck didn't *love* love?

"Yes, yes, yes! To all of that!" My sister was a die-hard romantic like me. "I'm gonna need your help picking a dress to wear. And will you do my make-up? Say yes or otherwise I might just stab you at this point."

I laughed. She seemed so worked up about needing my help. "I'll do it, babe. We can go shopping for a new dress tomorrow morning if you want. I haven't got any plans for the weekend yet."

She collapsed against me with relief, hugging me. "Yes! That sounds perfect."

"What's his name?" Tatum asked.

Savannah's face lit up again. "It's the absolute perfect name ever. Theo."

Tatum's lips curled at the ends, and I knew she was trying not to laugh at Savannah. She loved her, but she also wasn't all about the dramatics that my sister was well known for. The extent of Tatum's ability to handle drama and over-the-top behaviour was with me. And I was sure that was only because she loved me so much.

"I love it," I said.

Tatum finished her drink and shoved the empty glass across the counter at me. "Yeah, it's a cool name," she agreed. Although she wasn't a fan of Savannah's excessive excitement, she always threw her support Savannah's way.

Savannah's smile could have lit my house. "It really is."

My phone vibrated on the counter. Checking it, I found my mother calling. "Put the kettle on. I'm about five minutes away."

"Huh?" I wasn't aware she was coming over, but the way she said it was like I should be expecting her.

"To hear about Savannah's new man! She rang me and told me to come over."

I slid off my stool and made my way to the kettle. Flicking it on, I said, "You should have gotten Dad to drive you so you could have a drink with us. Tatum's here, too."

"He's driving. Pour me a drink instead."

I grinned. I loved having my family around me. "Done." I ended the call and announced to the girls, "Mum's on her way. It's time to get serious here. We've got a lot of celebrating to do. Tatum's found the perfect cake for her wedding. And her man's on total board with it. Sav's found herself a suit. And I've had the best sex of my life."

"I promise we'll get to the cake, Tatum, but Roe, you need to spill about this sex."

"It was with a biker," Tatum said with a mischievous glint in her eyes.

"No!" Savannah said, shocked. "I thought you were all about the steady, stable guys."

She was right. I'd been so vocal over the years about always steering clear of bad boys. The longest relationship I'd had was with the kind of guy you didn't bring home to your parents. It had ended badly with him cheating on me and lying to me about almost everything. It took me a long time to recover my self-esteem after that. And I'd put on a lot of weight in the process. I'd sworn I'd never date a guy like him again.

"Sav, if you saw this guy, you'd know why I slept with him. It was just sex. It's not like I'm dating him."

Tatum made a weird noise and raised her brows. "Don't believe her, Sav. I predict she's going to be all over this guy soon."

"We're here!" Mum announced from the front door. She had a key to my place and let herself in.

Dad followed her into the kitchen. "You girls had dinner yet?"

I shook my head. "No, we've just been eating cheese and dips. You hungry?"

"How about I go and grab some pizzas?"

"Sounds good to me," I said. "But before you go, I need the light changed in the hallway. It's too high for me. Can you do it?"

"It can't wait?"

"It's so dark without the light. I'm concerned Mum might trip. Her eyesight is so bad these days."

"Yeah, okay, good idea. I'll grab your ladder from the garage."

"I'll be fine," Mum said. She hated any fuss about her

eyesight or anything to do with her getting older. My mother liked to pretend she was still forty. I couldn't blame her; I figured I'd take after her in that respect.

"It'll take me five minutes," Dad said as he turned to head into the garage. I loved the way my dad adored my mother. He'd do anything for her.

"Okay," Mum said, clapping her hands together while looking at Savannah, "tell me everything."

We spent the next twenty minutes going over Savannah's man, Tatum's cake, and my sex. Dad left during the middle of our conversation. And then Mum shared some news with us.

"Your father and I are going to buy a caravan and travel around Australia. It probably won't be happening for another six months, but we're getting organised for it now."

My eyes widened with happiness. "That's awesome!" They'd been talking about seeing more of Australia, and I'd been encouraging the idea. I was a huge fan of parents spending their kids' inheritance—I wanted my parents to enjoy their retirement.

"Best news!" Savannah said. "Make us some more drinks, Roe. This definitely calls for cheers." She left us to put some music on, and a few moments later my home came alive with beats and laughter.

It was about ten minutes later that my phone rang. I didn't recognise the number. Usually when someone called who I didn't know, I let it go to voicemail, but the alcohol buzzing in my system caused me to be a little playful. "I'm only interested if you're tall, hot and know how to use what God blessed you with."

Silence for a beat. And then a deep voice rumbled down the line. "And let me guess, if I like meat, that's a bonus."

Hyde.

I threw the last of my drink down my throat. "Always a

bonus, tiger." I squeezed my legs together. This was the call he'd promised me, and I still hadn't decided what I was going to do. I needed to fob him off to give myself some more time. But damn if just the sound of his voice wasn't sending my core into a state of need.

"How about you open your front door and let me in?"

Fuck.

He was here.

Fark.

"I'm kinda in the middle of family stuff." Jesus, worst excuse ever. But fuck, I could hardly think straight.

"I can hear. Sounds like a party. Open the door, Monroe. I'll make it worth your while."

Oh. Good. Fucking. God.

Hyde making promises like that was dangerous. And that bossy tone of his that usually pissed me off? It wasn't pissing me off this time.

"Who is it?" Tatum asked, but she knew. She could tell from my reaction who it was.

I moved the phone away from my mouth a little so I could answer her. "Hyde."

Mum's eyes sparkled. "Hot-sex Hyde?"

Fuck me.

Shoot me now.

He had to come over when my family was here.

"Yeah, Mum, hot-sex Hyde."

"Monroe." Hyde's voice sounded from the phone. He didn't say anything but my name, and yet I knew from his forceful tone the words he wasn't saying. He was bossing me without even fucking bossing me.

"Can you come back later? Or tomorrow?" I knew what his answer would be, so I was just wasting my breath.

"No."

I tried to ignore the look of pure expectation and excitement flashing in my mother's eyes. "Fine," I muttered and stabbed at my phone to end the call. Jabbing my finger at Mum, I ordered, "Stay here."

She grinned, and I knew I had zero chance of holding her back. Groaning, I headed to the front door.

I opened it to find Hyde gripping the top of the doorjamb with both hands, staring down at me with the kind of look that could only be described as carnal. Before I could gather my wits, he dropped his arms, scooped me around the waist and pulled me outside. After he had yanked the door closed, he forced me up against the brick wall and ground himself against me.

"Been thinking about you, sugar," he rasped against my ear. "We need to make a plan to get you back in that shower of yours."

My breathing sped up and butterflies took over my stomach. I placed my hand against his chest in a half-hearted attempt to push him away. That attempt failed. Mostly because I really didn't want him anywhere but up against me. "Fair warning, my mother's inside and she will probably open this door any minute."

His heated gaze met mine. "Noted." He settled his hand on my ass. "What time will this party of yours finish?"

"I don't know." I wanted to run inside and kick everyone out right now.

We stood in silence for a few moments, eyes searching each other's. It was like he was trying to work something out in his mind. Finally, he bent and claimed my lips in a kiss that revealed his desire for me. It was raw. Rough. Demanding. He was letting me know he wouldn't be taking no for an answer.

Before he'd finished with me, my mother opened my front door and said, "Oh. My."

I tried to end the kiss, but Hyde made a growly noise and

pressed himself harder against me, his fingers digging into my ass as he held me in place. When he finally came up for air, he set me straight. "When I'm kissing you, you don't get to end it."

A sigh sounded from my mother. I barely heard it, though. Hyde commanded every ounce of my attention. I was fucking putty in his hands.

He let me go and turned to face Mum. "Jesus, there's no mistaking you're Monroe's mother." His tone made it clear he said this in the best way, and I guessed by the way my mother responded that he was looking at her with an appreciative gaze.

She flashed him a huge smile, her eyes dropping to take in his impressive body. "So, you're hot-sex Hyde."

He glanced at me with an amused smirk. "Hot-sex Hyde?"

I returned his smirk. "Come on, you've gotta admit it was pretty hot."

My mother inserted herself smack bang in the middle of the conversation. "From everything I heard, it was hot as hell."

Hyde dropped his head for a beat before looking back up at me with a slight shake of his head. I loved the smile on his face. "Can't say I've ever come across a woman who shares everything with her mother."

I threw caution to the wind. Hell, what woman wouldn't when a man like Hyde was watching them with that smile? "Welcome to the family. You wanna come in and meet my sister, too? She also knows how good you are in bed."

My mother's excitement spiked. "Yes, come in. Sav will love you."

He kept his gaze on me. "I take it Sav's your sister?"

"Yes, Savannah." I nodded at Mum. "And Mum is Angela."

Taking a step away from me, he gestured towards Mum. "Lead the way."

This thing with Hyde was taking a new turn. I'd expected him to take Mum's invitation as his cue to leave. I hadn't thought he'd want to stick around and get cosy with my family. And yet, there he was—following my mother inside my house as if it was the only place he wanted to be.

CHAPTER 19

Monroe

I had to give Hyde full points. He was handling my mother and sister like a pro. They'd grilled him for the past hour on everything from his thoughts on shower sex to his family, to life as a biker. He'd somehow managed to satisfy their curiosity without really giving them solid answers. I figured his muscles and voice had them under the kind of spell that allowed him to get away with not giving them the sort of information they were actually looking for.

My father watched the conversation silently. I knew he'd be picking apart everything Hyde said and did. Dad didn't take it easy on any guy I dated, and it seemed he was more wary of Hyde than he'd been of any man I'd brought home.

As Savannah shared a funny story from something that happened to her during the week, Hyde leant close to me and said, "Any chance we can move this party along to the part where everyone goes home?"

"You really think we've got any hope of getting my mother to leave? You've won her over. She's here for the long haul."

His eyes searched mine. "You're not shitting me, are you?"

I grinned. "No. I think it's safe to say you've probably never met a woman like Angela Lee."

"You'd be right there. You girls always share such personal information with each other?"

"Oh, you have no idea. My mother likes sex as much as I do, and she likes talking about it just as much."

"What are you two discussing?" Mum demanded to know. She was way past her alcohol limit for the night and was veering into smashed territory.

"I think this party is over, Mum."

"Yeah, me too," Tatum said. I could always count on her to take my back.

Mum pouted. "We were just getting to know Hyde."

Dad stood and motioned for Mum to follow suit. "Plenty of time for that, Angela."

I packed up some pizza for them to take home and did my best to get them all out the door. I was as desperate to be alone with Hyde as he was. Dad, however, had other plans.

As he and Mum made it to the front door, he turned and looked at Hyde. The way he looked at him told me that whatever he was about to say wasn't going to lead to anything good. "What's your surname, Hyde?"

"Dad," I warned, but I knew it was futile. He'd been hanging for this conversation since he arrived back with pizza. I was surprised he managed to wait this long for it.

Hyde's gaze remained steady on Dad. "McVeigh."

"Your mother named you Hyde?"

"No."

Dad planted his feet wide and crossed his arms. "You this cagey with everyone?"

Oh good Lord.

"Colin—" Mum started, in the same warning tone I'd used, but Hyde cut her off.

"Yeah, it's a practice I've learnt over the years so that people can't fuck me over. You and I get to know each other better, it'll be a different story."

Dad took that in. He seemed less than impressed, but my father wasn't stupid. He knew when to push the point and when to back off. "You start spending time with my daughter, we're going to be revisiting that a lot sooner than you might think."

Hyde surprised me when he nodded and said, "Agreed."

Dad grunted in response but didn't say anything else. The two of them simply stood there sizing each other up. It was a waste of time in my opinion, and I wasn't even sure why Hyde bothered. It wasn't like he and I were pursuing anything other than hot sex.

It took my family another ten minutes to leave. After I had closed the front door behind them, Hyde spun me around and pinned me against it. Not wasting a second, he reached for the bottom of my shirt and slipped a hand under. "I like your family, sugar, but the last hour was fucking painful. My dick is so damn hard for you that we're gonna have to skip getting clean in the shower."

I pressed myself against him, desperate for the same thing. "I'm on board with that." Gripping his shirt, I pushed it up and over his head. Dropping it to the floor, I let my eyes fall to his chest. "Seriously, it's a sin how hot you are." Placing my hands on his muscles, I said, "This is like perfection."

A growl rumbled from deep inside him right before his lips came to mine. Kissing me with force, he took my breath away. No man had ever kissed me the way Hyde did. I felt his kisses deep in my toes; they reached every nerve ending I had and scorched me with their heat.

Remembering his earlier declaration that when he kissed me I didn't get to end it, I wrapped my arms around him and kissed him back until I was panting for breath.

By the time he'd had his fill, he'd removed all my clothes except my bra and panties. When he was done with my mouth, he moved down my body slowly until he found my breasts. Another growl came from him. I would never get enough of the hot-as-fuck noises he made. He was the kind of man who made it clear the effect I had on him and how much he liked it.

Threading my fingers through his hair, I arched my back and said, "I really like what you're doing—like, *really* like it —but I'm so ready to have that mouth of yours on my pussy."

Another sexy growl from him. He then angled his head so he could find my eyes. With hands still firmly on my breasts, he watched me while taking my nipple into his mouth. After sucking it for a moment, he asked, "How wet are you for me?"

He drove me insane by dragging this out. Taking hold of his face, I pulled his mouth back up to mine and kissed him. "You need to stop making me wait for you and find out for yourself how wet I am."

His eyes darkened and he spun me around to face the door. Before I had a chance to keep up with him, he had my hands flat against the door above my head, my legs spread and my body pressed against the door. Grinding himself against my ass, he rasped, "I'm in control here, sugar. *You* do what I say. Not the other way around. And I'll taste your cunt when I'm ready."

I bit my lip and closed my eyes for a beat, enjoying the

way his bossiness made my whole body tingle with excitement. *A man who took charge during sex. Finally.*

His hands gripped my waist and he crouched behind me. Hooking his fingers over the top of my panties, he ripped them down. I stepped out of them and waited with anticipation for his next move. I assumed it would be to finally give my pussy the attention she needed, but he had other ideas.

Standing, he unhooked my bra and removed it. Turning me back around, our eyes met again, his full of heat. Unzipping his jeans, he said, "I want your hand around my cock."

The man was talking my language.

I reached into his pants and did as he'd ordered. Hyde's cock was fucking huge. The biggest I'd ever had. The only thing that would have improved it was a piercing. But he was so damn talented at using it, that I'd even deal with no piercing if he was my man.

His eyes closed as he dropped his head back while I pumped him. "Fuck, Monroe, you can do that any day of the week you want to."

I opened my mouth to reply, but his phone rang.

Worst timing ever. His phone had a habit of interrupting me getting what I wanted.

"Fuck," he muttered, reaching into his back pocket for his phone. Checking caller ID, he gave me an apologetic look. "I've gotta get this."

I nodded and let his dick go, but his free hand moved straight to mine and held it in place, letting me know I should keep going. With his eyes firmly on mine, he answered the phone. "King, what's up?"

They had a short conversation. I couldn't follow it because they seemed to talk in the shortest sentences known to mankind, sprinkled with a good dose of grunts in between. I would never understand how men could get their point across with so few words, but Hyde ended the call with a clear understanding of what he had to do.

"I've gotta go, so this is gonna be quick," he said, surprising me. I'd figured we were done for the night. I was all down for quick; I just needed cock.

He grabbed a condom from his wallet. Once he had it in place, he spun me again so my back was to him. He thrust inside me a moment later, hard enough that I ended up slammed against the door.

Holding my hips firmly, he pounded into me with a determination I loved. Hyde took charge and made shit happen, and I was one happy woman with his style of fucking. There was no talking, no fumbling, and no hesitation. He went after what he wanted, and he did it with a relentless force that had so far delivered a mind-blowing orgasm.

Even today, when he had to do it quickly, he didn't disappoint. And again, by the time he was finished, I wasn't sure my legs would be able to hold me up for much longer.

After he came, his body rested against mine for a minute, his hands moving around to cup my breasts. "Jesus, Roe, this pussy of yours gets me off like nothing else." He trailed kisses down the back of my neck and along my shoulder, his teeth nipping my skin as he went.

Roe.

I loved the sound of that coming from him. I wasn't sure why it made me feel so good, and I reminded myself not to get attached. But damn, it felt personal. It felt like we'd taken a step beyond where we were before he fucked me. And while I liked that, it was probably just that my nickname had fallen from his lips in the heat of the moment.

Pulling out of me, he let his hands roam down my body from my breasts to my hips to my ass. I turned to find him reaching for his shirt. He picked my clothes up too and passed them to me. Again, his gesture made me feel good.

Stop it, Monroe.

It's just sex.

Dropping a kiss on my lips, he said, "I'll get rid of this condom."

I dressed while he was gone, and headed back into my kitchen to find a drink. I needed one after that. After I'd let my feelings start wandering to places they shouldn't.

He met me in the kitchen, his hands all over me again. With one last kiss, he said, "I'll call you."

I drank some of my drink, my tummy alive with butterflies. "We need to stop this now, Hyde."

"No."

All my mixed emotions about him collided. Irrational anger resulted. "Why do you always get to decide things?"

"Why are you fighting this?"

"What is *this*?" I threw back.

"It's exactly what you like, sugar. Dirty fucking sex."

"That's what *you* want."

"You don't?"

"I told you last time this was a one-time thing. I don't want casual sex."

His eyes narrowed at me. "You want more?"

And there was the rub. "I don't know what I want."

He raked his fingers through his hair. "You're making this hard to follow."

"Okay, let's forget what I want for a minute. You told me you don't date, so we're an incompatible match anyway."

He stepped closer to me, his hand curling around my neck. "You need to stop overthinking this. And stop figuring that you have me worked out." He kissed me one last time. "Like I said, I'll call."

I stood in shock as he walked out. Yet again, he'd told me how things were going to go down between us, and I'd let him. And he still hadn't confirmed he wanted more than sex.

His vague "stop figuring you have me worked out" was such bullshit. It gave me nothing more than I already had. And fuck, I still wasn't sure what *I* wanted.

But really, I *was* sure.

I wanted a whole lot more sex with Hyde. I just didn't want to admit that I also wanted to spend more time with him.

CHAPTER 20

Hyde

Monroe was distracting me and she wasn't even anywhere near me. I couldn't get her out of my head. And that was a dangerous distraction to have when Storm was in the middle of shit.

Salvatore Ricci had turned out to be a dead end. He didn't have anything to do with Jacko's death and had proved it to us. That left us with a few other options, but getting to the bottom of it all was proving hard to do. King's call tonight had been in regards to the guy Fox had put us onto. He'd been found dead with a message delivered to King afterwards.

"You've taken what's mine, now I will take what's yours." King's wild eyes came to mine as he waved the piece of paper sent to him in a box with the guy's head. "What the fuck does this even mean?"

I had no idea either. It made no sense to me that this

guy's head had been sent to us. We'd had nothing to do with him until recently. And it made even less sense as to what King had supposedly taken from whoever was behind all this.

Bronze stepped forward. King had called him, Devil, Nitro, Kick and me in to deal with this. "You definitely don't know this guy?" He indicated to the head in the box. "Not even from years ago?"

King scrubbed his face. "I'm almost one-hundred-fucking-percent sure I've never had anything to do with him."

"And he gave you no leads when you saw him?"

Nitro shook his head. "Nothing. Hyde made sure he was in enough pain to speak if he had anything worth sharing, but he didn't."

Bronze nodded. "I don't need specifics." It was the warning he often gave us when we were about to cross one of his self-imposed boundaries. I didn't know why he bothered. Simply working with us the way he did crossed enough lines to ensure his imprisonment if his colleagues ever discovered his corruption.

"I want to know everything about him," King said to Bronze, indicating he wanted Bronze to look into him.

Bronze exhaled a frustrated breath. "I'm stretched, King. You've got me investigating three other guys. I'm trying to get through a huge workload at work, and I'm trying to evade Ryland, which is starting to prove difficult. Something's gotta give if you want me to look into this."

King frowned. "Why the fuck is Ryland on you?"

Bronze shrugged. "Got no fucking idea. I've either searched something or asked the wrong person something, and it's triggered his interest in me. He's been sniffing around for days, asking me all kinds of shit about Storm. I need to lay low."

King met my gaze again. "We need to deal with Ryland."

"Take him out of the equation?" I asked to confirm I'd understood where he was going with this.

Bronze held his hand up. "No. Let me look into him."

"What will that achieve?" I asked, not following.

"There'll be some dirt there. I just need to find it and then use it to get him to back off."

This whole fucking situation was doing my head in. I'd had little sleep this week. That, on top of dealing with this shit, caused me to lose my patience with Bronze. "I'm about fucking done with pussy-fucking-footing around this, Bronze. I say we remove Ryland once and for all. And as for these three other Italians, why the fuck are we being so damn careful with them? Just fucking eliminate all of them."

"Fuck, Hyde," Devil said, "Who twisted your panties today?"

I shot daggers at him. "It's starting to feel like Storm has lost their edge. We need to mark our fucking territory and make it clear again that you don't fuck with us."

"Yeah, but we can't just go fucking pissing over whoever we want," Nitro warned. "That shit will give us more issues than we have now."

I needed a fucking drink. "Fuck it," I muttered, and turned to head into the clubhouse bar.

"Where the fuck are you going?" King demanded.

"I'm getting a drink. Maybe when I get back you assholes will have come to your senses."

I stalked out of the office and down the hallway to the bar, ignoring the shit they called out to me as I went. The minute I hit the bar, I decided it wasn't the best idea. Being Friday night, members packed the room, and they were loud as fuck. A headache had kicked in while listening to everything King said, which meant the combination of music blaring from the speakers and drunken antics was like walking into hell.

Kree watched me with a wary eye. Smart woman. "Whisky?"

I nodded. "Why are you here? I didn't think you worked nights anymore."

"I don't usually, but we were short staffed, so I came in." She poured my drink and handed it to me. "Why do you look like you could murder someone?"

I poured some of the whisky down my throat. "Because I could."

An argument broke out between two club members next to me at the bar. Within moments, fists were involved, and the few empty glasses on the bar top went flying, smashing onto the ground.

"For fuck's sake!" I roared and moved to break them apart. I managed to do that, but in the process, ended up with a fist in my eye. That infuriated me more than I already was, and I retaliated with a fist to his fucking face, knocking him to the floor.

I glared at him as I picked up my drink. "Next time you wanna fight, take that shit outside." I downed the rest of my whisky and shoved the empty glass at Kree. "I'll have another," I barked.

She arched a brow. "You want to try that again?"

"Not particularly."

"I'm not making you another until you speak to me like a civil human being, Hyde."

Fucking hell. "Make me a fucking drink, Kree, or else you and I are gonna have words about your employment here."

"Hyde." King's ominous voice came from behind me.

I faced him, shoulders squared. "Have you come to your senses?"

Distaste clung to his words when he ordered, "My office. Now."

We watched each other, silently waging war. This wasn't

an unusual occurrence for us. One minute united, the next going to battle with each other. It never lasted long, but over the last few months, tensions had simmered to boiling point. I did my best to reel my shit in, but when my mind snapped like it had tonight, my efforts were futile.

When I didn't budge, he repeated himself in the quiet, menacing voice that signalled he'd also reached his limit. I managed to come to my senses enough to heed his warning. When we arrived at his office, he kicked everyone out and closed the door behind us.

"If you were anyone else, I'd tell you to get the fuck out of the clubhouse for the way you spoke to Kree."

"You're fucking joking, right?"

"No."

"Who the fuck is Kree to you, King? I've watched the way you are with her. I've never seen you like it with any other woman here."

"That's not fucking important here. Your—"

I cut him off. "You've never cared about this shit before. Why the change all of a sudden?"

"Fuck!" He slammed his hand down on the desk and then paced the width of the office in silence for a few moments. Finally, he stopped and looked at me. The torment I saw in his eyes was enough to make me stop. Something else was going on here.

"What?"

"The club is in danger, and I can't fucking figure out who is behind it. I can't fucking stop it. And I can't fucking make sure everyone is safe." He paused for a moment. I'd never seen King in this state before. He lived and breathed power, not this bewilderment. "The only thing I seem to have any control over at the moment is the club." He jabbed a finger in the air at me. "I fucking need you behind me, brother. Not pissing all over club members and staff. Not losing that fucking temper of yours all the damn time. Go home, get yourself together, and when I see you next, I don't wanna see any of this bullshit. It's done. I'm not fucking putting up with it anymore."

He was right. I was smart enough to acknowledge that.

I nodded, but said nothing. There wasn't anything to say to that. King wasn't looking for promises; he never was. The only thing he was interested in were actions that produced results.

"Go home. Bronze is looking into Ryland and the other guy for us. There's nothing else to do here tonight." With that, he exited the office, his shoulders tense with the burden he carried.

Fuck.

Letting King down wasn't something I wanted to do. And I'd done plenty of it over the years. I hadn't cared enough, though. Life had just been something to get through. Until now. Now, I had reasons to do better. To be better.

I stopped at the bar before I left. Kree was busy so I waited for her. When she was free, I said, "I was an asshole. I'm sorry."

Her eyes searched mine. I had the distinct impression she was assessing my honesty. Finally, she nodded and said, "Apology accepted. Don't do it again, Hyde. I've put up with enough shit from men in my life. I won't accept it anymore."

"Understood."

I respected the hell out of a woman who stood her ground. If she'd told me to go fuck myself, I would have understood. Now that I'd calmed down I would have. Not earlier, though. No, earlier my temper owned me. And that scared the everloving fuck out of me. It reminded me that I really was my mother's son.

CHAPTER 21

Hyde

I cracked an eye open and instantly regretted the whisky I'd drunk when I got home last night. My head throbbed and I felt like shit. The headache was intensified by the yelling coming from another room. Tenille and Charlie were going at it.

Checking my irritation, I headed out to the kitchen where they stood arguing. "What the fuck's going on?" I asked.

Two heads snapped around to face me, and they both yelled something about the other. I held up my hand. "How about you take turns? I've got a headache and can only focus on one at a time."

It took them a good five fucking minutes to tell me they were fighting over Charlie getting her hair done. She wanted a colour that was apparently out of Tenille's budget.

Desperate to end the yelling, I cut in. "I'll pay for it."

Charlie's eyes widened with surprise. Tenille's darkened with anger. Neither reaction was what I'd expected.

"You're fucking kidding me," Tenille started in on me. "You're just going to come back into our lives and play the fun dad who gives her everything she wants?"

"Jesus, Tee, that wasn't my intention." Where the fuck did women come up with these ideas?

"Regardless of whether I could afford it or not, Charlie knows that until she brings her grades back up and stops smoking and drinking, I'm not paying for her to get balayage."

"Balay-the-fuck-what?"

Charlie groaned impatiently. "Balayage. It's a colouring technique." To her mother she said, "You're so hypocritical! You drink your gin like its water, but you have a whole other set of rules for me."

"That's because it's my job to have rules for you." Tenille's voice grew louder. Blinking, I took a good look at her. She looked like shit—tired and drained.

"What's in your plans for the day?" I asked her.

That question really pissed her off. "Don't change the conversation!"

I reached for my bottle of whisky and poured some into a glass. "Wasn't trying to. I figured maybe you should take a day and go out. Do something by yourself."

Tenille's hand slammed down onto her waist as she glared at me. "You're trying to get rid of me?"

"Fuck, tone that shit down, woman." Her voice had turned into a screech that hurt my head. "No one's trying to get rid of anyone. I'm suggesting, though, that we could all do with a break from each other."

"You've hardly been home, Aiden. I don't know what the fuck you need a break from."

I swallowed all the whisky in my glass, hoping to fuck I

could control my rising temper. "Tenille," I said, deathly calm, "walk away from this conversation, pick up your bag and remove yourself from this house for at least half the day. When you get back, we will resume this discussion and come to an agreement on Charlie's hair." How the fuck hair colour could cause a problem like this was beyond me.

"Ugh," Charlie whinged before stomping off to her bedroom. "I wanted to get it done today!"

Tenille picked up her handbag. Dropping her gaze to the bottle of whisky, she said, "You're turning into your mother, Aiden. Something you swore you never wanted to do."

The front door slammed after her a few moments later as her words settled deep in my bones. They cut like a mother-fucker because she was right—I had sworn I wouldn't become my mother. A mean drunk. And yet, I was fast becoming exactly that.

Fuck.

I shoved the whisky back in the cupboard and dumped my empty glass in the sink. Walking faster than my headache preferred, I made my way to Charlie's room where I found her with earphones in on her bed.

Glancing at me, she pulled an earbud out and muttered, "What do you want?"

"You need to cut your mother some slack. And you need to realise that her rules are there for a reason. And for fuck's sake, you're old enough to know that parents do the shit they don't want their kids to do. Drinking doesn't make her a hypocrite."

She looked at me with shock. This was the first time I'd been so blunt with her. I'd been fucking tiptoeing around her, not wanting to chance pushing her away. But the time had come for me to step up to the plate and parent her. And she could try to push me away all she liked. I wouldn't stand for it. I was in her life now whether she wanted me or not.

"You don't understand, Aiden. She's turned into such a bitch this last year. I don't know what's going on with her, but she hates everything I say and do. Nothing is good enough for her."

"Ever stop to think about shit from her perspective? For her to leave Craig, I'm guessing they've had a lot of problems."

"Dad does a lot for Mum, but she's never happy with him either. They fight so much. The only time she seems happy is when Gibson comes over."

I ignored the fact she called Craig dad and zeroed in on the way she spat Gibson's name out. "You don't like him, do you?"

Her face darkened. "No. He's a creeper. He's always watching me, asking me about how school is and about my friends and my sport. I mean, why does he even care about that stuff?"

My fists clenched by my side. I hated that Tenille had let him into their lives. "Do me a favour and stay away from him."

"I thought you two were close when you were younger?"

"Why would you think that?"

She shrugged. "I don't know. He talks about you a lot. He's always reminding Mum of things you guys did with his son."

Tenille had said something similar. It made no sense to me. I'd always thought Gibson cared about me, but he'd shown his true colours the day he threatened to kill my family and me. "When was the last time you saw him?"

"Not for a couple of weeks. I think he's been overseas." She huffed out a breath. "God, can we stop talking about this and start talking about my hair? You need to talk Mum around."

"I'll talk to her when she's calmed down, but I'm gonna need to see some respect coming from you towards her."

She slumped against the wall. "I'll try. I just hope she tries too. I'm sick of her making me feel like shit."

I decided it might be a good idea to keep them apart for the day, to give each a chance at getting their head together. "You ever been on a motorbike?"

Her eyes sparked with interest and she sat forward. "No."

"You wanna go for a ride?"

She was off the bed in a flash. "Hell yes!"

If I'd realised she'd be this excited about something that meant we'd be spending time together, I would have suggested it sooner. Jerking my head towards the front of the house, I said, "Get your ass outside. And Charlie?"

"Yeah?" She was already halfway across her bedroom.

"No more talk of hair today. I take you out on my bike, we're gonna discuss everything else that has been happening in your life."

Slowing, she met my gaze. She understood my meaning. I could tell by the way she looked at me with a little hesitation. Today would mark a change in our relationship. I'd be asking for more from her from here on out.

"Okay."

With one word, she made my fucking day. The headache pounding in my head cleared, and hope stirred deep in my gut. My kid and I were finding our way back to each other.

CHAPTER 22

Hyde

Holding my phone to my ear, I watched Monroe in her front yard from where I'd parked my bike outside her house. Sully was on the other end, but I had trouble focusing on what he said as Monroe proved again what a distraction she'd become in my life.

"Are you listening to what I'm saying, Aiden?"

I wasn't listening to a damn word he said because the only thing I could focus on was the fact another man had his arm around Monroe. *And I didn't fucking like it.*

"No, I missed it."

Monroe laughed as the guy standing next to her with his arm around her shoulders said something to her. The smile on his face irritated the fuck out of me. Fox was with them, laughing too.

Who was the motherfucker with Monroe?

Sully's voice boomed from my phone. "I said I'm heading

down to Melbourne today to check on Craig like you asked. He's been in Perth but is back now. I'm not sure how long for, though. I'll check in with you when I have more information." I'd asked him to investigate what Craig was up to that caused him to come home beaten up.

I gripped the phone harder when the guy with Monroe squeezed her closer to him for a moment. "Sounds good."

With that, I ended the call and gave my full attention to the asshole with Monroe. Committing his face to memory, I vowed to find out who he was. I also vowed to get Monroe on the same page as me. I was done with letting her fight this thing between us.

Her gaze turned to me as I walked towards her. She hit me with a sexy smile. At least she hadn't given that to the motherfucker.

"Hyde," Fox greeted me.

I nodded at him. "Fox."

"I didn't know you were bringing your sexy ass over today," Monroe said, her voice all smoky and breathy, hitting me right in the dick. "I thought you were gonna call," she added, a hint of playfulness creeping in to her voice too.

"I decided not to take a chance on you ignoring my call."

Her head dropped to the side, eyes full of heat. "You *really* think I would have ignored your call?"

"Right," Fox cut in, "That's our cue to leave you two alone." He indicated for the asshole with his arm *still* draped over Monroe's shoulders to leave.

"Thanks for everything, Fox. I'm excited about our plans. I just hope I can find a way to pull them off," Monroe said.

The asshole said something to her that I couldn't hear before following Fox out of her yard. I watched silently, tracking their movements. They couldn't leave soon enough as far as I was concerned.

Monroe slid her arm around my waist and pressed her

body against mine. "It's good to see you, but I really wish you'd called first."

Hardly paying attention to what she said, I growled, "Who was that?" I couldn't keep the demanding tone from my voice even if I'd tried. I needed to know who he was and what the fuck he was to her.

Her eyes narrowed. "What does that mean? If we were dating, I'd say you sounded jealous."

"Answer my question, sugar. Who the fuck was that?"

She let me go and took a step back. "Whoa, tiger, steady on there. That was Leo, Fox's cousin and a friend of mine. What's going on here?"

With a determined stride, I closed the short distance between us and took hold of her by the waist. "What's going on here is that I didn't like his hands on you."

Her eyes widened and she planted her palms on my chest. Trying to push out of my hold, she said, "I don't live my life making sure to only do things you like."

I tightened my hold, not letting her move a fucking inch. "I never said you had to, but I would like to know what that asshole means to you."

"He's not an asshole, Hyde. He's a good friend. That's all."

"Looked like more than that to me."

"You *are* jealous."

I ignored that. "You sleep with your friends, Roe?"

She smacked my chest. Still trying to move out of my embrace. Still failing, because there was no way in hell I was letting her go. "Oh my God, you did not just say that to me! We've made no promises to each other, so who I sleep with is none of your business."

"I'm making it my business. And I'm telling you now, I don't want another man's hands on you."

"Well, sorry to burst your bubble, but the only man who

gets to dictate that kind of shit to me is the man I'm dating. And seems as though you and I aren't dating, you get zero say in whose hands are on me." She hit my chest again and added, "Now let me go." Her eyes were full of that fierce energy I loved in a woman.

"How about you and I start dating?"

She stopped trying to escape my hold. "You don't do dating."

"I don't *do* dating because I haven't found a woman I wanted to date."

"Oh, but now you have? Or is this just because you got your dick in a twist when you saw me with another guy? I'm not down with a man fucking me around, Hyde. If you only want me when you think someone else has me, you can walk away right now."

"Jesus, woman, are you always this fucking difficult?"

Her mouth fell open. "Are you always this fucking insulting?"

"I don't date women just to keep other men from them. I can't stop thinking about you, Monroe. You're there when I wake up, and you're still there when I go to bed at night. And in between, you're every-fucking-where. Hell, I'm even thinking about you when I should be focusing on club business." I pulled her even closer to me and growled, "I just about lost my fucking shit when I saw that asshole's hands on you. That's never happened in my life."

She stared at me for a long few moments before muttering, "God damn you have a way of saying stuff that makes me wanna drop my panties and fuck you on the spot." Slapping my chest again, she added, "Stop doing that! A woman needs some control in a relationship."

My lips twitched. She had a way of amusing the hell out of me. "I'll take that as a yes, then?"

She pointed a finger at me, in the way that let me know

she was about to lay down some rules. "Yes, but I'm not sure about this possessiveness you've got going on. It's kinda hot, but at the same time, I don't like being told what to do."

My lips grazed her cheek on their way to her ear. "Sugar, stop trying to boss me. I fucking boss *you*. And as far as that possessiveness goes, we're good unless I turn up here again to find someone's hands on you. That happens, all fucking bets are off. I don't share what's mine."

She didn't say anything, but I was sure I heard a moan fall from her lips.

Not wasting any time, I smacked her ass and said, "Now, I want you inside, naked. We're about to get wet."

Her upper body angled backwards and her eyes found mine. "See, that's why I said before that I wished you'd called me first. It's that time of the month for me where I don't share a shower with anyone. And before you tell me I can suck your dick instead, I'm not in the mood for that either."

My lips twitched again. "And here I was thinking you thought about dick 24/7."

"Oh, I do. I just have a few days a month where I don't want one anywhere near me."

"How many more days we talking about here?"

"I think I'd like to keep you hanging. I'm not going to tell you."

"You have no idea how much you keep me hanging. Get inside and we'll find other ways to pass the time."

Fuck, I just wanted to be with her. At this point, I didn't care if that meant I was inside her or not. So long as we were in the same room. Being with Monroe felt good. And I hadn't felt good like this in a long fucking time.

CHAPTER 23

Monroe

Hyde's arm hooked around my waist and he pulled my body to his. Sunday mornings had never felt so good.

He'd showed up last night waving his possessive flag all over the place marking his territory, making me fall for him more, even though I tried hard not to fall for that shit. But damn, knowing a man wanted me that much was always going to cause me to fall.

There was no sex to be had because I had my period, but he'd sat through reruns of *Friends* with me, helped me cook spaghetti for dinner, ordered me to stay on the couch getting my *Friends* fix while he cleaned up the kitchen after dinner, and then stayed the night. While he hadn't been able to keep his hands and mouth off me, he hadn't tried to force anything more. In my book, that shit earnt him a fucking medal.

I placed my hand over his. "Morning, tiger."

His leg curved over mine, pressing his erection against my

ass. Having my period sucked. All I wanted was Hyde inside me, but I wasn't a woman who ever had sex on her period.

"Fuck, Roe, I need your hand around my dick," he said as he nuzzled my neck.

"I told you I don't do dicks when I'm on my period."

He groaned and ground himself harder against me. "Fuck, woman, you're a savage."

I decided to play with him a little longer. The truth was, though, that I wanted his dick as much as he wanted me to have it, so I wouldn't be able to drag this out for too long. "I'm down with watching you take matters into your own hands." I made sure to push my ass back against his dick.

While he kept grinding against me, one of his hands moved its way up my body to cup my breast. Tweaking my nipple, he rasped, "You wanna tease me with that ass of yours, you're gonna end up on your back so I can fuck your tits."

Desire exploded through me. Fucking my tits sounded like heaven. I teased him some more, making sure to really rub myself against him hard.

He didn't fail me. Before I knew what was happening, he had me on my back, his knees either side of my body as he knelt over me. Grabbing my hand, he wrapped it around his cock. Eyes to mine, he ordered, "First your hand, then your tits. Next time you wanna tease me, think twice, sugar."

I licked my lips as I pumped his cock. "I've decided that teasing you is fun. And that you are changing my mind about dicks at period time."

A deep, guttural groan came from him while I got him off. "As in you want my dick deep in your cunt instead of between your tits?"

Hyde had a way with filthy words. They got me hot, even during the time of the month when nothing usually got me hot. But no way was I into what he suggested. I squeezed his dick harder as I moved my hand up and down it. "No. There's no pussy for you today, but I'm definitely into this tit sex."

He stopped what I was doing so he could position his dick between my breasts. I squashed them together and held them there so he could focus on fucking them.

The visual of his cock pumping between my breasts, his body driving him towards his release, and the erotic grunts coming from him turned me on far too much. I was going to be left with a need I couldn't begin to fulfil.

"Fuck," I muttered while I kept my tits pressed together. "I'm so fucking horny right now."

He kept thrusting his dick between my breasts. "I can take care of that for you."

"Yeah. No." I was still being stubborn. Maybe one day, if we were together for a long time, I'd be into period sex with him, but not yet.

"Christ," he growled. "This is gonna be fast."

He only managed two more thrusts before he came. Holding his dick while he directed the cum onto my breasts, he met my gaze and said, "Your tits and my cock need a standing date."

"I'm on board with that. Especially because you're gonna cook me breakfast while I take a shower."

His lips curled up at the ends. "Really?"

"Yes, really. You wanna shoot your jizz all over me, you're in charge of making food while I clean that shit up."

"You fucking love that shit, sugar."

"That may be the case, but I also love food. Almost as much... no, some days, more.... No, scrap that, I always love dick more, but right now I am starving, so you need to feed me if you've got hope of ever getting inside me again."

He chuckled, and I had to say, I loved that sound coming

from him. Moving off me, he said, "You got bacon and eggs in your fridge?"

"I've got eggs. No bacon. How about scrambled eggs?" I really was hungry, but I also wanted to see how domestic he was.

"Fuck that, we need bacon. I'll go grab some while you're in the shower."

A man after my own heart. I grinned. "Thank God you love meat."

He chuckled again. "I always did have that going for me."

Yes.

Yes, he did.

The man could cook. Good God, could he cook. I hadn't had bacon and eggs that good in a long time. And then he'd cleaned the kitchen again. Without me even asking. He'd taken charge and ordered me to put my feet up while he cleaned. What man did that?

"How long have you lived on your own?" I asked from the kitchen table where I sat watching him clean.

"Fourteen years."

"Were you always this domestic? Or did that just come from all those years by yourself?"

"Always. My mother didn't lift a finger most of her life, so I learnt pretty fucking fast that if I didn't cook and clean, I'd be hungry and living in filth."

My heart squeezed at the thought of any child going through that. I'd been blessed with my family. "How old were you when you figured that out?"

His eyes met mine, and I saw the pain there. "Seven."

He went back to loading my dishwasher while I sat in silence wondering about his life. Now that we were doing the dating thing, I wanted to know everything there was to know about him. But I wasn't convinced Hyde was the kind of man to share that kind of information easily. I decided to push him a little.

"Are you close to your parents?"

He was bent over the dishwasher, and I saw his body tense at that question. Surprising me, he glanced up and said, "I never knew my father. My mother died when I was twenty-one. She and I were never close."

I'd figured he wouldn't be close to them if they treated him like that as a seven-year-old, but I always held out hope that people could change. Mostly, though, they didn't.

"I love that you've chosen to parent your daughter differently."

He straightened, his body still tense. By the look on his face, I decided I must have said something wrong. "Charlie's only just come back into my life. My fault, not her mother's. But yeah, I would never raise a child the way I was raised."

I frowned. "You haven't had anything to do with her until now?"

"I was there for the first two years of her life. Shit got in the way of that until just recently." He watched me closely. It felt like he was trying to judge my reaction.

I stood and walked to him. "Something you need to know about me, Hyde, is that if you're in my life, I don't judge you."

His eyes searched mine for a beat and then he nodded. "Good. I judge myself enough for everyone."

I knew he was being honest with me. It was right there in his body language and his voice. I realised then just how much Hyde carried his pain with him, and I wondered what he'd been through in life to cause that anguish. I hoped in time he would share it with me so I could help him through it.

He kissed me before smacking my ass—something he seemed to like to do—and saying, "Yesterday you told Fox you were excited about some plans but not sure you could pull them off. What plans are these?"

Figuring that changing the subject was his way of dealing with whatever he had going on, I ran with it instead of forcing him to talk about something he didn't want to. "I want to convert some of the space in my shop so I can add another room and bring in someone to do waxing. There's a dress shop a few doors down from me that is flat out, so I figure between the women I have coming in and her customers, there're enough women to target for waxing. But, I don't really have the cash to pay someone to do the work, so I'm gonna have to get creative to make it happen. Fox had some ideas. Now I just have to go through them and see what I can do."

Someone knocked on my front door just as I finished telling him about my plans. When Savannah called out my name, I said, "Shit, I forgot she was coming over." She was here to tell me all about her big date the previous night.

"That's your sister?"

"Yeah. Sorry, but we already had plans to go out for lunch today."

"Let her in. I'll grab my stuff and get out of here."

I gripped his shirt as he turned to go into the bedroom. "We need to discuss you taking me on a date."

"As in out to dinner?"

Honestly, the man had no idea. It had clearly been too long since he'd dated a woman. And it was clearly my responsibility to teach him what he needed to do. "Yeah, as in out to dinner. If I'm gonna do this with you, you're gonna have to earn it."

Those lips of his twitched again. I seemed to amuse him a lot. "Noted. I'll pick you up for dinner tomorrow night."

I was free tomorrow night, but there was no way I was allowing him to dictate terms to me. I liked to start a relationship the way I intended it to go on. Him always making the decisions was not the way I saw our relationship going.

Shaking my head, I said, "Tomorrow's no good for me. How about Tuesday night?"

Full points to him for not even blinking an eye. "I'll pick you up at seven."

I smiled and pulled his face down for a kiss, ignoring the fact my sister's knocking had grown louder. "I can't wait to see where you take me." The first date was everything in my opinion. It set the course for the future. I had high hopes of Hyde rocking my world on a date, just as much as he did in bed.

CHAPTER 24

Hyde

"I'm just saying I think it might be wise to choose our battles," I said to Tenille late Tuesday afternoon. We were discussing Charlie and the fact Tenille felt like she was out of control.

"So you're the expert now, are you? A week or so of parenting and you know everything?" We'd been going over this for a good half hour, and I didn't see the end in sight.

I raked my fingers through my hair. "No, but I'm not a fucking idiot, Tee. I've been watching you two fight and listening to what she's saying about it all, and I think that you fighting every damn battle is just pushing her further away."

"Oh, so you think I should just let her smoke and drink and give me attitude, do you? Not to mention cutting class and letting her grades slip." I saw where Charlie got her attitude. It rolled off Tenille in waves.

"I'm suggesting you work on a couple of those things at a time. Pick the most important one, say her grades, and go to war with her about that. The rest, tread carefully. Have you seen her smoking or drinking since you got here?"

"No."

I nodded. "She and I had a talk about it. I told her not to do it in the house. I figure I can't control what goes on outside the house, so why fight her on it?"

"You're delusional, Aiden, if you think that by simply telling her not to do it here will stop her."

"I know it won't stop her doing it. But I'm hoping that by not alienating her completely, I'm keeping the communication going between us. And that by giving her some room to figure shit out on her own, she will come to respect me and want to show me she can make better choices."

My phone buzzed with a text. My dick stirred at the thought of it being from Monroe. We'd been exchanging dirty messages all day.

Monroe: You know how I didn't want dick the other day?
Me: Yeah.
Monroe: I'm over that. Just so you know.
Me: Thank fuck.
Monroe: I want it every way I can have it tonight.
Me: Ass?
Monroe: Steady on, tiger. A man's gotta prove himself first.

Tenille cut in, "Are you just going to ignore me now? Your woman's got all your attention, has she?" She spat her words out like they tasted awful. I imagined they did, and I hated that I'd caused her to feel this way. I needed to fix whatever issue we had here.

"Tee," I started, but the sound of glass smashing outside distracted me. Placing my phone down on the counter, I said, "Hold that thought. I'll be back."

Jogging outside, I discovered that some kids were playing ball on the road and had smashed one of my neighbour's windows. He was already outside dealing with it, and waved me off, letting me know he had it under control.

By the time I got back inside, Tenille had my phone in her hands and had scrolled my messages with Monroe. She looked at me with a level of hurt I'd never seen coming. "I thought you didn't really know Monroe."

"Fuck," I muttered. Yet another conversation I wasn't prepared for. Scrubbing my face, I said, "I didn't when you asked. Now I do."

She shoved my phone at me. "So you coming back to us wasn't you wanting me back?"

I frowned. "You're married, Tee. While I'm not a fan of Craig's, it was never my intention to break up your family when I came back."

"Do you still love me?" she demanded.

"It's been fourteen years. I never thought I could come back, so I had to find a way to move on."

"So that's a no, then?"

"I'll always love you, but I'm not *in* love with you, no. You can't stand there and tell me you're in love with me. You moved on years ago." Christ, this was a fucked-up mess.

Her breaths came hard and fast while she stared at me. She seemed lost, and I tried to figure out how to deal with that, but I was out of my fucking depth here. "I did move on, but you coming back has stirred so many feelings in me that I never knew were buried. I only moved on because I thought you were dead. Not because I stopped loving you."

"You're telling me you don't love Craig?"

"I don't know anymore. My thinking is all screwed up."

"Where is he?"

"He's working. Splitting his time between Melbourne and Perth."

"No, I mean why isn't he here? Why isn't he fighting for you to go home?" She'd hardly heard from him as far as I knew.

She wrapped her arms around herself like she was trying to warm up, even though it wasn't a cold day. "I don't know," she said quietly.

I moved to her and pulled her into my arms. Tenille would always be the woman I'd loved first and the mother of my child. I'd never stop loving her, but there was no way back to each other as far as I was concerned. However, my guilt at what I'd put her through over the years ate me alive. Some days I was sure it would consume me. They were the days I hit the whisky the hardest. If I had any chance at defeating my mother's genes in me, I had to find a way past this guilt.

"I've got a guy looking into what's going on with him," I told her.

She jerked out of my hold. "What? Why would you do that?"

"To help you find some answers as to what the fuck's going on in your marriage."

"That's none of your concern, Aiden," she snapped.

"Is there something going on here I don't know about, Tee?" She seemed cagey all of a sudden. Like she wanted me far away from her marriage and all the shit going on with it.

"No." But she'd shut down completely on me, so I had to wonder the truth of the matter. As she turned to leave the kitchen, she threw out, "And Charlie isn't getting that hair colour. If you say yes, there will be hell to pay." She stalked towards her bedroom, leaving me clueless as to what the hell was going on.

Grabbing my phone, I tried to call Sully, but he didn't answer. I hadn't heard from him since he arrived in Melbourne a few days ago. That concerned me; Sully always stayed in contact. I sent a text to Bronze asking him to look into it for me. If anything had happened to him down there, I was hoping the cops would know.

After I had texted Bronze, I shot Monroe another text.

Me: What kind of proof are we talking?

She came straight back.

Monroe: Ever considered getting your dick pierced?

    Me: That's how a man proves himself to you?

    Monroe: No. I was just throwing that out there for your consideration. Proof = time getting shit right.

    Me: Noted. I'll be there soon.

    Monroe: If you come early, we could fit a quickie in. Just sayin'.

Well that was a fucking no-brainer. Ten minutes later I was on my way to her house.

CHAPTER 25

Monroe

I sat at the table across from Hyde and did my best not to show my disappointment. For our first date, he'd brought me to a pub for dinner. And because there was some huge soccer or football or what-the-fuck-ever game on that night, the pub was rowdy and full of assholes, one who had already spilt beer all down my dress.

He'd started the night out well by turning up to my house early and fucking me senseless. I'd thought at that point it wouldn't matter how the rest of the date went, but this pub proved me wrong.

We'd just finished eating—the food was the worst, but I didn't tell him that—and he'd asked me more about the plans I had for my shop. However his phone kept sounding with text messages, which distracted him a little.

"Everything okay?" I asked. I loved my phone as much as the next person, but I never put it on the table during dinner with someone. I kept reminding myself that he had a daughter, so that was probably why he kept checking the messages.

He placed the phone down and gave me his attention. "Sorry, sugar, it's my family. We're dealing with some issues at the moment."

After we had discussed his parents the other day, I hadn't realised he had any other family members. I loved that he opened up like this. "How many brothers and sisters do you have?"

His forehead wrinkled in a frown. "Huh? None."

"Oh, I just assumed you meant siblings when you said family." He must have meant cousins or some other extended family.

"No, it's my ex and my kid."

His ex? He referred to her as his family still. I kinda liked that—because in this day and age of messy breakups it was refreshing to hear a man call his ex-wife family still—while at the same time experiencing a stab of jealousy in my chest.

Not wanting to get into a discussion about his ex, I decided to focus on his daughter. In my experience with dating divorced men, talking about their ex never went well. "How's Charlie going with her skating?"

The tension that had crept across his face while taking those text messages settled and he smiled. "I haven't had a chance to take her again, but she went on her own the other day. She came home in a good mood, so I figure we need to get her there as much as possible."

"So she and her mum are still here?" I recalled him mentioning that Charlie's mother was coming to get her, but that he wasn't sure Charlie would want to go.

"Yeah." He didn't offer any further information, and I didn't push.

"Well, at least you get to spend more time with her. Have you guys done much since she's been here?"

"I took her on a ride the other day. First time on a bike for her. She seemed to love it. Other than that, we're taking it slowly, getting to know each other after never really being in each other's life."

I drank some of the cosmo he'd bought me. "I remember when I was sixteen. I gave my parents hell. It's a miracle we all survived that."

"I'm figuring that out pretty fucking fast. We're in the middle of World War III at the moment because of some baly hair colour shit that her mother doesn't want her to have. You'd think Charlie's life was crashing down around her with the way she's carrying on."

My ovaries exploded a little while listening to Hyde talk about his daughter. And him trying to say balayage and trying to keep up with what his daughter wanted only helped that explosion along.

While I'd been playing it cool, trying not to bombard him with questions about his life, I suddenly couldn't contain myself any longer. It wasn't how I usually operated, and I figured it would soon shed some light on whether Hyde really was ready to date me or not. "You guys had Charlie young. I'm figuring you for about thirty-five or so."

"Thirty-six."

I smiled. "You just earnt points for not asking me how old I am. But FYI, I'm thirty-one. When's your birthday?" If there was one thing I was anal about, it was keeping track of the birthdays of those in my life. I liked to make sure their days were special.

His eyes darkened. "May seven, but I don't ever celebrate it."

"Why not?"

He reached for the whisky in front of him. He'd ordered a drink earlier but hadn't actually drunk any of it, which seemed odd. However, at that question, he drank half the glass.

"We never celebrated it when I was growing up, so I've continued that tradition." It was like he had to rip those words from his soul. The pain in them sat heavy between us, and I knew this wasn't a conversation I should continue. Not tonight.

"Okay, so changing the subject a little, why did you decide to join Storm?" I'd always wondered what made men choose the biker life.

He drained his glass of whisky and sat forward, resting his elbows on the table. "Let's talk about you, sugar. You always been a tattoo artist?"

I would rather he'd answered my question, but I got the distinct impression Hyde didn't share personal stuff easily. I could be patient; I just hoped it wouldn't take him long to open up to me. "Yeah, and I'd always wanted my own shop, so I bought it three years ago when the previous owner put it on the market for cheap."

"That—"

He was cut off when another asshole spilt some of his drink on me as he walked by our table. Drunkenly stumbling along, he grinned at me and said, "Sorry about that, baby." He stopped and let his gaze drop to my chest, whistling low as he did so. "Damn, you shouldn't be allowed out in public. Those tits—"

Hyde shoved his chair back and stood, towering over the asshole. His anger oozed from every pore, scaring me a little. "You need to keep your eyes and your fucking mouth closed when you walk past my woman." He didn't bellow his order, but rather it came out in a low, murderous tone that anyone would have trouble misunderstanding.

The asshole held his hands up defensively, backing away

from Hyde. "Sorry, dude, it's just hard not to notice a beautiful woman when I see one."

Hyde hissed. It looked like he was about to go to battle. "Back the fuck up and stop fucking talking."

The guy nodded madly and was turning to leave when a friend of his joined us. "What's going on, Kenny?"

Kenny, the asshole who spilt his drink, tried to pull his friend away. "Nothing. It's all good, man."

His friend shrugged out of his hold and eyed Hyde. "I'm not fucking intimidated by some biker asshole. You think you can come in here and threaten us just because he looked at your slut the wrong way?"

Hyde's fist connected with the friend's cheek, causing him to stumble back. Without giving him a chance to recover and walk away from the situation, Hyde kept going, punching him over and over.

I jumped to my feet and yelled, "Hyde! Stop it! He's not worth it."

My requests for him to stop were futile. The other guy fought back, turning this into a bloody and violent fight. I'd seen plenty of fights in my life, but Hyde took it to a whole new level. It wasn't until security got involved, three of them yanking Hyde from the fight, that it calmed down. By then, they were both covered in blood, and I was so done with this night it wasn't funny.

I didn't wait around for him to deal with security. I picked up my clutch and stalked outside in search of a taxi. Fucking bikers. I knew they were bad news, so why the fuck did I let my guard down and let one in? As far as I was concerned, this was the first date from hell, and I wasn't convinced there would be another date for us.

CHAPTER 26

Hyde

Fuck.

I'd managed to fuck this night right up. I'd thought bringing Monroe to a fucking pub on game night was the worst mistake I could have made. That was during dinner when I saw the disappointment sitting on her face. Turned out I was wrong. The worst mistake I could have made was letting some motherfucker get to me when he couldn't keep his eyes off her.

Jealousy wasn't something I was used to. Hell, this was the first time in my life I'd ever experienced it. Seeing another man even glance sideways at Monroe caused a nuclear reaction in my fucking head. I'd fought like fuck not to react to the asshole who mentioned her tits, but when his friend referred to her as a slut, I saw fucking red.

And then I'd lost my shit.

And my woman.

After cleaning myself up, I headed over to her house. She stood in front of me now, at her front door, a bewildered look on her face.

"I don't want to talk to you tonight," she said as she pulled her sexy dark-red robe around her. It was distracting as hell because it barely covered her thighs and revealed enough cleavage to get me hard, but now wasn't the time to be distracted, so I kept my eyes off her body.

"I fucked up, Roe."

"You think?"

I shoved my fingers through my hair. *Fuck.* "Let me in so we can talk."

"I told you that I didn't want to talk tonight. I need some space to figure out how I'm thinking."

I didn't know much about women, but I knew giving her that space would lead nowhere good. "No."

Her eyes bulged. "You're kidding me, right? You screw up and then you refuse to give me some space to process what I saw tonight?"

"Fuck, I'm sorry you saw that, sugar. I let that asshole get to me when I should have just told him to fuck off and left it at that."

"Tell me something, Hyde. Is that standard behaviour for you? Because if fighting is something you do a lot of, I'm not interested in going any further with this."

I clenched my jaw. "Not usually." There was no point bringing up my past, because it was exactly that—the past, not the present.

"So does not usually mean you do it sometimes?"

"It means that sometimes it's called for."

"Often it's not. Just so you know."

I was a fan of Monroe's attitude but not when it came flying at me like this. This just pissed me off. "There are some things you don't know about that do require my fists.

Let's just leave it at that. All you need to know is that I don't usually get them out in this kind of situation."

She fell silent for a moment. When she crossed her arms over her chest, I knew she was shutting down on me. "I'm getting the drift. You should go. There's no way you're getting in my pants tonight."

Fuck, didn't she understand? This wasn't even about getting my dick wet. This was me, trying to make things right.

Frustration filled me, and I tried to force the point. Stepping one foot inside her house, I pushed my way in and had her up against the wall before she could open that pretty mouth of hers and argue with me. "We need to get one thing straight here. I didn't come over to fuck you. I came to apologise and tell you I would do better next time. I'm far from fucking perfect, though, so if you're looking for perfection, you're right—this should end now."

I'd caged her in with my arms against the wall either side of her, my body flush against hers. I'd expected her to fight me, but she didn't. Instead, her breathing picked up and she said, "I'm not looking for perfect. I'm just looking for a man who isn't going to lose his shit like that all the time." Her voice dropped to almost a whisper when she added, "You scared me tonight, Hyde."

Regret was a vicious bitch, one I was well acquainted with. Seemed I spent half my fucking life with her on my back. She swooped in and reminded me what a fuck-up I was. The difference this time? I had a reason not to sit with that regret and drink my way through it.

I cupped Monroe's cheek. "I'm sorry, red. I can't take it back, but I can sure as fuck vow never to do it again."

The hesitation I saw in her eyes told me she wasn't quite sure. Her words confirmed it. "How do you even know you can make that promise? I watched you tonight. You lost yourself in that fight. It was like the violence consumed you. I don't want you to make promises you can't keep. That's even worse than not making a promise."

She was dead fucking right. How the hell could I promise her that when I couldn't get a grip on my temper? But fuck, I didn't want to lose her. I needed her light to help me through my dark. I'd figure this shit out so she never needed to be exposed to it again. "I've only got my honesty to give you. I will make this right. You will never be scared of me again."

"I wasn't scared *of* you," she whispered. "I was scared *for* you. And for the guy you were fighting. I've never felt afraid of you, but I really thought you could have killed that guy tonight. That's what I was scared of."

"So what are you telling me here, Roe? Are you walking away from this before we even get it started?" I'd fight her tooth and nail, but first I needed to know where we stood.

"I'm saying what I said when you first got here—I don't want to talk about it tonight. I want you to give me the space to think it over."

Out of everything that had gone on, I realised that if I didn't give her that space, the rest wouldn't matter. She needed to know up-front that I'd not force myself on her when she needed time out.

I nodded and dropped my arms. "You've got tonight. After that, you let me back in here,"—I placed my hand against her chest—"so we can talk this out."

On the way home, I grasped how important this thing with Monroe was to me. I'd never looked for another woman after Tenille. Had never wanted the complication again. Had never wanted to put a woman's life at risk like Tenille's had been just by being married to me. But leaving Monroe's house that night, without knowing where we stood, caused my chest to constrict in ways it never had. This wasn't love—

not yet—but it meant something to me. Something I wanted to fight for.

———

I spent the next day taking care of club business. King and I had managed to move past our issues. I'd been making an effort not to lose my temper with any club members, and he'd been distracted by shit going on with Jen. He'd also been walking around in a mood due to Bronze finding no dirt on Ryland yet. He also hadn't found anything useful on the guy whose head had been delivered as a warning.

King sent me out early to clean up a mess one of our clients had gotten themselves in. The cleaning side of our business had ticked along quietly over the years, but King had ramped it up over the last month due to our drug income dropping. The club was bleeding cash, so he took on almost any cleaning job sent our way these days. He'd been more picky until recently, which concerned me. Who the fuck knew whether these new clients could keep their mouths closed about what we did for them? The last fucking thing we needed was one of them singing to the cops.

I arrived back at the club around four that afternoon to find King in his office having a heated discussion with Bronze. Something about an attack King planned that Bronze was against.

"You do that and you'll have the feds crawling over you like you never imagined they could," Bronze warned.

The vein in King's neck pulsed. He was worked up more than usual. "I'm sick of sitting here doing fucking nothing, Bronze. Ryland's had my hands tied for far too long, and Marx has evaded me because of it. I need to get out there and slit throats and cut some fucking balls off. Anything to make people talk and tell me where the hell Marx is and who's behind it all."

"Jesus, King, stop fucking talking," Bronze muttered. "I don't want to fucking know this shit." He was exhausted. The dark circles under his eyes and the way his shoulders slumped told that story.

I stepped in. "Whose throats are we slitting?"

Bronze held up his hands. "I'm leaving. Don't call me when the feds throw you in jail." He didn't wait for King's response, just simply walked away from the conversation. King didn't try to stop him either, which told me he was serious about his plans.

"Bronze ruled out one of the three Italians we've been looking at. That leaves two. I'm done with quietly investigating them. I want you to take one team of members to one of them, while I take another team to the other one. If we have to slit their men's throats in order to make them talk, so fucking be it. This happens tomorrow. By the end of the day we'll know which one it is."

"And Marx?"

"He'll be out of business once we know who's controlling him."

I rubbed the back of my neck as the tension crept in. "Fuck, King, I'm not sure that Bronze isn't right about this."

King scowled. "Last week you would have been all over this plan. What's changed?"

"Last week I let my mood dictate my actions. This week I'm trying like fuck not to do that." I'd failed so far, but a man could only try. And this shit King suggested could fuck the club right up if we weren't careful. "We go out there and cause a blood bath like you're suggesting, that's a lot of potential enemies we're creating. Those crazy fucking Italians have some loyal supporters."

"You think we can't handle ourselves, brother?" King had

a god complex some days. On others, he managed to lock it down. Today was not one of those days.

"Have we been handling ourselves, King? You tell me. From my perspective, it feels like we've lost some of our edge because of Ryland. He's too close to us for you to even consider this attack. Bronze isn't shitting you when he says the feds will be all over us if we do this."

"So we just sit with our hands tied, holding our balls, and allow one man to decide what we can and can't fucking do? Fuck that. We're in the middle of a fucking war here, Hyde. We don't run from war. We stand and we fucking fight to the bitter end."

I pushed my anger away. I needed to get my point across without my temper getting in the way. "We stand this time? It might *be* the bitter end."

King stood with his hands clenched by his side, with an expression on his face I knew to mean he'd already made up his mind. "Tomorrow, Hyde. We get this done."

CHAPTER 27

Monroe

I relaxed into my comfy chair in my office, both hands wrapped around a hot mug of coffee, and let the stress of the day leave my body. It was just after five on Wednesday night, and Fox had two more clients to finish up with. One, he was almost done with, the other waited patiently for him. He had one of the best reputations in Sydney, so people were always happy to wait for him. I was certain that if he ever left me, my business would go downhill fast.

I'd spent the day going over everything that happened with Hyde the night before. My heart warred with my head yet again, and while I felt uncertain about what to do, I knew deep in my gut exactly what I would do.

I'd keep seeing him. He'd worked his way that far into my heart already. But he'd have to step his game up, that was for sure.

Paperwork called my name that afternoon, but the front

door bell tinkling dragged me back out to the front of the shop. I slowed when I saw Hyde standing near the front counter holding a tape measure.

Closing the distance between us, I nodded at the tape measure and said, "What's that for, tiger?"

He didn't miss my intent when I called him tiger. It was my way of letting him know I'd softened my stance since last night. We'd talk it over later, but for now, we could move forward knowing where we stood.

Jerking his chin, he said, "I've come to measure the space you want converted for this waxing room of yours."

Surprise flooded me. I hadn't seen that coming. Placing my hand on my hip, I cocked my head to the side. "You're good with a hammer and nails?"

A sexy grin spread across his face. "I'm good with my hands, full stop. Anything you need doing, I've got it covered."

"Mmm, the cost of the building supplies is a little out of my reach at the moment, but I'd be happy to put your hands to work in other ways."

His arm slid around my waist so he could pull me close. "I've got contacts in the building industry. How about you let me worry about the cost for now?"

"No, I don't ever let men pay my way."

"I figured that already. That's why I said for now. When you've got cash coming in from the waxing business, you can pay me back then."

Every independent gene of mine wanted to say no, but the businesswoman in me knew this was a good deal. My independent side tried to win the argument, but she lost badly. That could also have had something to do with the horny side of me wanting Hyde spending time working in my shop. Possibly with his shirt off. Definitely with those arms of his on display.

"Okay, yes." I pointed my finger at him. "But you agree to take my money, without argument, when the time comes, or I'm taking that yes back."

He chuckled and dropped a kiss to my lips. "Deal."

"And Hyde?"

"Yeah."

"We're going to talk about last night. Preferably tonight if you're free."

His mouth brushed my ear when he said, "You trying to boss me, sugar?"

"Damn right I am."

His eyes met mine, and I couldn't miss the earnestness there. "Tonight is blocked off for you."

The fact he took this so seriously made me feel like I'd made the right decision. "Good. If you're lucky, I'll cook you dinner."

Lines formed around his eyes as he smiled. That smile morphed into a cheeky grin when he said, "I like a woman who knows her place is in the kitchen."

I smacked his chest. "You did not just say that to me!"

Laughing he said, "Calm down, red, I was just fucking with you."

"You better have been. It's gonna be a long night for you on my couch taking care of the hard-on I give you if you weren't."

"Sounds like any night I don't spend with you," he murmured as he let me go. "Now tell me where you want this room built."

I'd been with Hyde for approximately two hours, and he'd managed to drive me almost to the point of not being able to hold myself back. No, scratch that. I'd been with him for *exactly* two hours and eleven minutes, and I was way past the point of not holding myself back.

We'd made it to my place after I closed up at the shop, and after putting steak in the microwave to defrost, I'd practically thrown myself at him. My intent for the night had been to talk to him first and then have sex, but the man was skilled at messing with my thoughts. Just by existing. It was maddening.

He dragged his mouth from mine and took hold of my arms that were around his neck. Pulling me off him, he said, "We need to talk first, sugar."

My eyes widened. "You're shitting me, aren't you?"

His lips twitched. "I wish I was, but I'm not. I want nothing more than to fuck you right now, but it's important to me that we discuss how you feel about last night."

"Stop it."

He frowned. "Stop what?"

"Stop saying all the right things. I was so mad at you last night, and I wanna keep feeling entitled to that, but you're making it hard for that to happen."

He continued to frown. "You wanna keep feeling mad at me?"

Ugh. Why couldn't men just read women's minds? Like, seriously, it would make life a whole lot easier. "No, but I feel so conflicted about you that it would be easier for me to feel like I was right to be mad." I waved my hand at him. "You coming here and saying stuff like that, about it being important to you to talk about how *I* feel, well that makes it hard for me to hold onto those feelings of being right." I mean, how often was it that a man actually wanted to discuss how I felt about the shit he'd done? Most men I dated wanted to move past their fuck-ups as fast as possible.

"You *were* right to feel mad, Roe. There're no two ways about that. I don't want to take that from you. But I do want to know you can move on from it. I'm not a fan of shit being thrown in my face later on in a relationship. We need to deal with this now and then never let it be rehashed in retaliation for something else."

And that right there made me fall for him a little more. He may not have dated in years, but he certainly knew how to do relationships.

"I can move on from it, Hyde. I wasn't sure last night because it had just happened, so I appreciated that you gave me the space I asked for."

"You're sure now?"

"I'm still concerned about your temper, but you said you would work on that, and I believe you. I'm not the kind of woman to hold a grudge so this won't be thrown in your face every time we have an argument. And I know you'll always fight for what you believe in. I just don't want you to lose your temper over something like a guy checking out my tits or a guy calling me names."

"I do fight for what I believe in, but I need you to understand exactly what that means." The way he said that raised red flags, but he was right—I did need to know what I was dealing with here.

"Okay, tell me."

He watched me with an intensity that showed how serious he was about this conversation. "There will be days I come home from club work with black eyes or broken ribs or bloody clothes. That, I can't change. Not even for you. I won't talk about that shit with you and I won't ever discuss club business with you. We need to settle that before we even begin something. If you can live with that, I'll work on my temper and do everything in my power not to knock the fuck out of any asshole who comes near you."

I wasn't dumb; I knew how bikers worked. What he said didn't surprise me. What *did* surprise me, though, was my willingness to accept it. I couldn't deny it—I wanted Hyde in my life. He desired me for exactly who I was, and he never made me feel like I needed to change myself for him, even when some of the things I said and did frustrated him. To find a man like that was everything as far as I was concerned. The rest could be worked on, but you could never change whether someone wanted you for you. They either did or they didn't.

I placed my hand against his chest. "I can live with that."

He watched me quietly for another few moments. I couldn't read his thoughts, so I wasn't sure what he would say or do next.

Finally he wrapped his hand around my wrist and moved it to his ass. "Now you can get back to blowing my mind with that mouth of yours."

CHAPTER 28

Hyde

I stared at the bottle of whisky on my kitchen counter. I'd been staring at it for the last five minutes. My body screamed for it, but my head told me if I had any chance at getting my shit together, I needed to empty the bottle down the sink. Memories of my mother drinking at six in the morning flashed in my mind. Her passed out on the couch in the afternoons when I'd come home from school. Her yelling at anyone who tried to help her. It was like a goddam assault with these fucking memories. They punched me in the gut and told me I'd become her.

I was an addict and a mean one at that.

Unscrewing the lid, I picked up the bottle and drained it down the sink. My hand shook a little, but I ignored that. I wasn't a fucking alcoholic. I could live without this shit.

"You kicking your habit?"

I glanced up to find Charlie standing in the kitchen doorway. Her eyes were firmly on the bottle I held. There was no point denying I had a problem. She was a smart kid. "Yeah."

She came closer, her eyes lifting to mine. "Good."

We were like two fucking peas in a pod. Both unable to say anything else, but there was a tension or an emotion or some shit surrounding us that I knew we both felt by the way we silently watched the bottle empty.

My heart raced in my chest. I had to kick this fucking habit, if not for myself, for her. Screwing up my relationship with her the way my mother had with me was not something I wanted to do.

When every last drop had trickled from the bottle, I threw it in the bin. She nodded slowly when I found her eyes again. She then broke through the tension when she said, "That shit'll kill you eventually." They were the words I'd said to her about smoking.

I inhaled sharply and then let the breath out. "Yeah, it will," I agreed. Not wanting to talk about this any longer, I said, "You want some eggs for breakfast?"

She sat on one of the stools at the counter. "We got any bacon left?"

We.

It fucking melted my cold heart. I'd lived my life without her in it for so long and hadn't thought a moment like this would ever happen. My resolve to kick the whisky to the kerb strengthened.

Pulling the bacon from the fridge, I said, "Yeah. You want cheese in your eggs?" I'd watched her scrambling some eggs, and she'd loaded cheese and chives in there. "And chives?"

If I hadn't been watching her so intently, I would have missed the look that ran across her face for a split second. She hadn't expected me to know that. She didn't acknowledge it, though. "And onion, please."

That was possibly the first time she'd used her manners

willingly with me. I'd pulled her up on it repeatedly, and she usually rolled her eyes and added a please or a thank you.

I reached for an onion. "You got it, sweetheart."

She sat watching me in silence while I cooked. It wasn't until I placed her eggs and bacon in front of her and pulled up the stool next to her that she said, "What time did you get in last night?"

Charlie had been here for almost two weeks and not once had she asked anything about my whereabouts. I always made sure to know what she had planned for each day, but she didn't seem to care about anything I did. This was another first for her.

I poured sauce on my plate. "I just came home about an hour ago." I'd stayed at Monroe's after we'd cleared the air. She'd kept me awake until just after three. When I'd left her, she'd complained that she probably wouldn't be able to walk today. Knowing my woman would think about me every minute of the day when she tried to walk or sit or do anything made me one happy asshole.

"So you're seeing Monroe now?"

"Yeah."

"I liked her."

I glanced her way. "Her advice pay off with that little shit you're dating?"

She rolled her eyes. "Why do you hate on him so much?"

"I don't trust him."

"You don't even know him."

I put my cutlery down and turned my body so I could face her. "A man doesn't need to know a boy to see him for what he is, Charlie. You forget that I've been where he is now. I met your mother when I was sixteen and chased the shit out of her trying to get in her pants."

Her eyes widened. "Oh God, I don't need to know about your sex life with Mum."

I hid the smile that provoked. "What I'm trying to say is that I know all the sixteen-year-old-male tricks. I know he's trying to get in your pants, and I don't fucking trust him not to hurt you."

She sat with that for a beat and then said, "So you and Mum were together from sixteen?"

I frowned. "She never told you about us?"

"Not really. All she ever really said was that you guys got married at nineteen and had me ten months later. I tried to ask her stuff, but she always got sad whenever I mentioned you, so eventually I kinda stopped asking."

I smiled as the memories came back. "I'd always seen your mum around school. She was the chick who used to tell teachers to fuck off, the girl who smoked down the back of the school, the one who the boys all wanted a shot at. She never looked twice at me until the day I involved myself in an argument she was having with one of the school bullies. She'd stood up for the kid he was roughing up. I knew she didn't have a chance in hell of winning against him, so I stepped in and helped. Of course, that pissed her off, that I took over, but she at least knew my name after that."

Charlie had stopped eating, too, and rested her elbows on the counter, chin in hands. She appeared to be enjoying this conversation. "You beat that bully up, didn't you?"

I chuckled. "Not fully, but I had to show him that messing with Tenille was a bad idea."

"So how long after that did you two get together?"

"She kept me hanging for a good month or so. Your mother was smart. By the time she finally said yes to a date with me, I was like a fucking puppy following her everywhere."

"I can't even imagine that about you."

"Oh, you better fucking believe it. Tenille fucking owned me."

She pushed off the counter and sat ramrod straight on her stool. "How could you leave her, then?" The question fell from her lips softly, almost as if she was scared to ask it.

This was the question I'd prepared for over the years. I'd lain awake countless nights unable to sleep, imagining having Charlie back in my life. I'd pictured our reunion, and this question had played in my mind like a broken record. But sitting face-to-face with my daughter and trying to express my reasons was far different from doing it in my mind.

"I'm not sure you'll ever be able to understand this, but I did it to protect you both. I got myself into some bad shit and threats were made against our family." I didn't want to get into too many of the details with her. Hell, I didn't want her to know that this shit went on in the world, but I had to give her something to help her grasp it.

She sat in silence, and I held my breath waiting for her response. Finally, she ran her fingers through her hair and said, "You're right. I'm not sure I'll ever understand that. Mostly because—does that stuff really happen in real life or just in the movies? But, I know you're a biker, and I'm not clueless, so I know you're into bad shit." She paused. "I still don't get how you could leave Mum if she *owned* you, though. And you left me, too." Her voice wobbled on that last bit, fucking slaying me.

"Fuck, Charlie, adult shit doesn't make sense half the fucking time. When you love someone the way I love you guys, you do anything to keep them safe. I'd rather you both be sad than dead." When she didn't say anything to that, I added, "I'll always regret what happened back then. If I could take it all back and be the father you needed while you grew up, I would. But life doesn't give you a second go at shit, so here we are, stuck with my choices in life. You'll never know how happy I am to have you in my life again. I just hope you'll give me a chance to show you that I can be a father."

"It's weird for me because I already have a dad."

She still referred to Craig as Dad, and rationally I understood that, but the possessive side of me fucking hated it. I figured she would always call him that, and I'd always be Aiden to her. I just had to find a way to make peace with that and allow her to have us in her life however *she* needed. Not how I needed.

I nodded. "I'll always be grateful to him for what he's done for you." That, at least, was true. "But you need to know that I'm not going anywhere. I don't care how long it takes you to accept me. I won't be leaving again."

She took a deep breath and then exhaled. This had to be a lot for her to process. "Okay."

"Okay?"

She picked up her cutlery. "Yeah, okay, I get it. You're not gonna stop bossing me around. But just so you know, it's hard enough having two parents telling me what to do. If I've gotta put up with you, too, I'm gonna need something in return. Like balayage or some shit."

"Yeah, good try, sweetheart. You think I don't value my balls? Your mother would fucking kill me if I paid for that."

"Ugh. Well, you're gonna have to come up with something. I'm not down with having three of you all over my shit unless I get stuff out of it."

My kid was the fucking shit. I couldn't have asked for a better one.

"What the fuck is balayage anyway? It's a weird fucking name to call a hair colour."

She rolled her eyes at me. "Oh, Aiden, you have so much to learn."

CHAPTER 29

Hyde

I arrived at the club an hour later with the intent to talk King out of the plan he had for the day. Turned out his plan had already been altered. In a way none of us saw coming.

Marx had stumbled into the clubhouse an hour or so before me, almost unconscious. He'd taken a severe beating before he arrived and had lost consciousness soon after arriving. Our doctor was with him while King paced his office.

"Did you get anything out of him before he passed out?" I asked.

"No. He was delirious and raving about wanting to die. Nothing I said seemed to get through. The only thing I made out was that he was Marx."

"You think that whoever did this to him is the guy he's been working for?"

"Wouldn't surprise me, brother."

"Where does this leave us today?"

King stopped pacing. "I'm putting everything on hold until I can get Marx to talk." His phone rang, and after checking caller ID, he said, "What's up, Kick?"

From what I could follow, Kick was at the hospital with Evie, and it didn't sound good. King confirmed this when the call ended. "Evie's blood pressure has gone through the roof, so the doctors are considering delivering the baby today. He's staying with her."

"I'll drop by and check in with him later."

"Thanks." His voice was tight. I knew he'd prefer Kick on deck, but King would never ask that of him in this situation. It was one of the things I respected the most about King—he always put family first.

The doctor knocked on the office door, and King motioned for him to enter. Closing the door behind him, he said, "Your guy took a bad beating, but he's only suffering from broken ribs and a broken nose. He's in a great deal of pain, though, so I've given him something for that. If you want to talk to him, now's your chance, because he'll sleep most of the day with those drugs."

King nodded. "Thanks, Doc."

Not wasting a second, King and I made our way to where Marx rested. His swollen eyes came to us, and he grimaced in pain.

"You able to fucking talk now?" King demanded.

Marx's face was a wreck of bruises, cuts, and dried blood. His body didn't look much better. I took some fucking delight in that.

"Yeah," he croaked out.

"Took some fucking balls to show up here. Either that or you figured you were good as dead already, so you had nothing to lose. What the fuck's going on?" King asked.

Marx's throat must have been dry because he tried to swallow a few times.

King bent over him, a look of menace on his face. "You want some water, motherfucker?"

Marx nodded, barely, but got his message across.

King stayed bent over him, his gaze taking in Marx's body. I couldn't be sure, but I'd have bet that he wanted to inflict more pain on Marx.

He proved me right when he snapped back to a standing position, his crazy eyes seeking mine, and barked, "Jesus, get him some fucking water before I fucking kill him!" Looking back at Marx, he added, "And you'd better start fucking singing for your supper or else the pain you're in will hit a whole new level that I can guarantee you won't fucking like."

Fear bled from Marx, and he squirmed in the bed where we had him. He blinked rapidly a few times. There was no escape for him. He'd come to us, and King would make him regret that decision if he didn't give us what we wanted.

After I had given him some water, he mumbled, "I'll tell you whatever you want to know."

My phone sounded with a call, but I ignored it. Whoever it was could wait.

King pulled up a chair next to the bed and sat. "Who the fuck do you work for?"

Marx pulled a face. "That's the one thing I don't know."

King was up and out of that chair faster than Marx could blink. "Don't fucking lie to me!" he roared.

Marx shrunk from him. "I'm not! I honestly don't know who he is. We never met."

King gripped Marx's chin and squeezed hard, raining a new round of pain down on him. "Tell. Me."

Marx thrashed on the bed, legs and arms trying to fight King. I quickly stepped in and held his legs down while King threatened him again. "You don't start talking now, I'm gonna start removing body parts."

"He sent different people each time," Marx managed to

get out between deep gasps for air. "We met in different places, too. There was no pattern to it." He gasped again when King tightened his grip. "I swear! He told me I would never know because that wasn't how he worked. No one knew who he was."

That made King stop. Letting Marx's chin go, he demanded, "How did he make first contact with you? How the fuck did he know you? And what did he offer you?"

Marx nodded madly, tears streaming down his face. "I'll tell you! I swear I'll tell you everything." Another gasp for air and then—"I don't know how he found me, but the first time I heard from him, he called me. Well, I don't think it was him. I think it was his main guy."

"What the fuck do you mean by his main guy?" I asked, ignoring another call coming from my phone in my pocket.

"I met a lot of different men, but there was this one guy who seemed to be in charge. He was the one I always spoke with on the phone. And then they sent others to drop off drugs and collect cash."

King planted his feet wide and settled his arms across his chest. "How do you know the one on the phone wasn't the man you were working for?"

"By what he said."

"Fuck, spit it out, Marx. What did he say?" I asked.

"He always told me that his boss would be happy with my work." He paused. "Until today."

"What did you do today?" I asked. King remained eerily silent while he took everything in.

My phone rang again. I ignored it, again. We'd be done here soon enough; I'd check it then.

"I dropped off cash to one of their men early this morning, and I followed him, trying to get to the boss. They must have been following him, too, because I didn't get far before they got to me."

King dropped his arms. "So they left you for dead. How the fuck did you get here?"

Marx shook his head slightly. "They didn't leave me there. They brought me here. Opened their car door and dumped me out the front as they drove by."

King's eyes met mine, and I knew we had the same thought. "I'm on it," I called out over my shoulder as I exited the room.

I jogged down the hallway to the room where we ran surveillance. Finding Nitro there, I said, "We need to pull footage of the front of the club from just over an hour ago."

"What are we looking for?"

"The car that dumped Marx out the front."

He whistled low. "Surely they're smarter than that."

"You'd think so, but we need that number plate either way."

Ten minutes later, I had Bronze on the phone. I'd given him the number plate to run. And then I asked, "Any word on Sully yet?"

"Nothing. I'm still looking," he said, causing my gut to tighten.

"Thanks, Bronze." I ended the call and tried to push thoughts of what had happened to Sully from my mind. I wasn't ready to admit my gut feel for the matter. Not yet. I still held hope that he'd show up.

I noticed the missed calls I'd had were from Charlie and was about to call her back when King entered the surveillance room, distracting me.

"Bronze on to it?" he asked.

Both Nitro's gaze and mine dropped to King's hands. Blood covered them. "Fuck, King," I muttered, meeting his eyes again. "What did you do?" Surely he hadn't killed Marx. I was convinced there was more information to get out of him still.

The murderous energy surrounding him filled the tiny room. There was no mistaking how wired he was for death. "He's still breathing if that's what you want to know."

Nitro's brows raised. "You just had a little fun with him?"

"Let's just say that he won't be walking anywhere in a hurry."

"You cut his foot off?" I asked.

King scowled. "Fuck, Hyde, I'm not that fucking stupid." King's mouth twisted into the kind of smile that let you know he derived great—possibly, insane—pleasure from whatever he did. "I broke his leg so he couldn't go anywhere."

"Good move," Devil said from the doorway. "That asshole deserves it."

My phone rang yet again. This time I answered it. "Monroe. I'm in the middle of something. You okay?"

Monroe's voice filtered down the line. It was filled with concern. "I hate to be the bearer of bad news, but Charlie's just been taken to hospital by ambulance. She fell at your place and hurt her arm."

Fuck. I'd ignored Charlie's calls.

Every fatherly instinct I possessed kicked in. "Which hospital? And where's Tenille?"

"Calm down, tiger. She's okay. I don't know where Tenille is. Charlie said she tried to call you, but you didn't answer, so in the end she called Bree. And Bree called me."

She gave me all the details and told me she was on her way there, putting my mind at ease a little.

King narrowed his eyes at me. "Everything okay, brother?"

I blew out a long breath. "No. My kid's in the hospital."

He jerked his chin at me. "Go see her."

"You good here?" Not that I wouldn't go to Charlie

straight away, but I needed to know where we were with the club.

He nodded. "Yeah. I'm gonna wait for Bronze to get back to me and then make plans from there. We'll be sitting tight until then."

Five minutes later, I was on my way to the hospital. My gut churned with worry for Charlie. I knew it was an overreaction, because a broken bone, if that's what it was, could be fixed. But I hadn't answered her calls, and I was pissed off at myself for putting her in a situation where neither parent was there for her.

CHAPTER 30

Monroe

It wasn't often I met a woman I took an instant dislike to, but Hyde's ex-wife was one of those women. I'd been at the hospital with Hyde for almost two hours before Tenille showed up. She hadn't liked the fact I was there with him and had spent the half hour since glaring at me. But besides that, there was something about her that I couldn't warm to. And it wasn't just because she was Hyde's ex.

Hyde was pissed at her. I could tell he was fighting like crazy not to lose his shit at her, which, full points to him, but I wouldn't even blame him if he did.

Raking his fingers through his hair, he barked, "You left her alone when she needed you? When she was sick?"

Tenille turned her glare to him. "That doesn't even have anything to do with Charlie's fall," she snapped.

His face contorted with anger. "She told you she felt sick,

223

really fucking sick, and still, you left her alone. What was so fucking important that you had to leave her then, Tee?"

Tenille was right—this had nothing to do with Charlie's fall, which happened because she was running to the bathroom to vomit—but I was with Hyde. What kind of mother would leave her child when she was sick with a raging temperature and had been vomiting? I wasn't up on first aid, but even I knew that level of sickness required attention.

"That is none of your business," Tenille threw back.

Tension coiled itself around Hyde's body, and he took a step towards her. "I'm fucking making it my business."

Oh Lord. He sounded like he could murder her. I felt the need to step in on her behalf, even though I agreed with everything he said.

Reaching for him, I said, "Hyde—"

Tenille's steely gaze snapped back to me. "Take your hand off my husband."

I lifted my brows. "Your husband?"

A smug expression filled her face. "Oh, you didn't know? We're still married."

"Tenille," Hyde warned in a low voice. "Stop trying to fuck with shit that doesn't involve you, and answer my question."

Her words hit their mark, leaving me confused and upset. Surely she was lying. He'd never told me they weren't divorced.

Tenille moved closer to me. "He never told you, did he?" The woman was awful. I could practically see the venom dripping from her lips. How the hell did he marry and have a child with someone like her?

Well, she wouldn't see me crumble. I didn't believe in letting bullies win. "You can try and change the subject as much as you want, but the fact remains—you were a shitty mother this morning. And I think Hyde deserves an answer to his question."

She slapped me. "Fuck you, bitch."

My hand flew to cover my face where she'd left a sting. She was a crazy bitch.

Hyde finally lost his shit. Gripping her bicep tightly, he dragged her away from me, down the hospital hallway. She argued with him every step of the way, but he paid no attention. To think I'd tried to help her earlier when I thought he was about to explode. Good luck to her. As far as I was concerned, she deserved anything he said to her.

I pulled out my phone and sent Tatum a text.

Me: Did you know Hyde is still married? She's fucking insane BTW.

Tatum: No. Where are you?

Me: At the hospital with them. His daughter is sick.

Tatum: She okay?

Me: She's got a vomiting bug and has broken her arm I think. They're doing X-rays now.

Tatum: I've never heard about Hyde's wife. You okay?

Me: IDK. I don't like being lied to. You know that. Honesty is at the top of my list.

Tatum: Hear him out, Roe. I think he's a good guy.

Me: Yeah, we'll see.

Tatum: Sorry, babe, gotta go. Billy's in a mood today.

Me: Love you xx

I didn't have to wait long for Hyde to return. He stalked down the hallway towards me, alone, with a furious look on his face. It softened a little as he came closer, but not much. Tenille had worked her way under his skin.

"Sorry about that," he said.

"Did you figure it out with her?"

"No. She won't tell me what she was doing, and now she's fucked off downstairs."

"Does it really matter what she was doing? I mean, nothing could have been more important than staying with Charlie, so whatever it was doesn't make any difference, right?"

He scrubbed his hand over his face, and for the first time that day, I noticed how exhausted he looked. Or maybe not exhausted, but agitated. Something. He was off, whatever it was.

"You're right. At the end of the day, it doesn't fucking matter. I just can't believe she did that."

I bit my lip as I contemplated the best way to ask my next question. But there was only one way to ask it, so I just blurted it out. "Are you still married?"

He held my gaze and nodded. "Yeah."

My heart splintered in my chest, and I realised just how invested I had become in this relationship. But putting up with dishonesty wasn't something I was willing to do. I'd been burnt by lies before and I wasn't willing to go down that path again.

The busy hospital blurred as I focused solely on Hyde. People swarmed around us in the waiting room, but I saw none of them. All I saw was Hyde staring down at me, with what looked like regret.

Taking a step away from him, I said, "Okay, I'm out. I'm done." The words hurt to say, and I felt shaky on my legs. I just needed to get out of there, to my car, where I could sit and process all of this. And cry. Because, fuck, he'd broken my damn heart with his lie.

He took hold of my arm and stopped my retreat. "It's not what you think."

I snorted and tried to wrestle my arm free of his hold. "Yeah, that's what they all say."

His jaw clenched. "Stop fighting me, Roe, and hear me out." The tone he took with me made it sound like I was in the wrong, not him.

Using force, I yanked my arm free. "Don't you do that! Don't you make out that I'm the bad guy here when you're the one who hasn't been honest!" This situation had worked me up, annoying the fuck out of me. I hated sounding like a fucking harpy.

"Fuck, that's not what I'm trying to do. I'm just trying to get you to listen to what I have to say."

I crossed my arms over my chest. "Fine, say it."

"Tenille and I haven't been together for fourteen years. But we never got divorced."

"Is it over?"

"Yes."

"So why does she think it isn't?"

"Fuck, it's a long story—"

"I've got time."

His phone rang, cutting into our conversation. He checked his caller ID and hit me with another look of regret. "I have to take this."

I nodded and watched his back as he walked away from me. He carried so much on his shoulders. I was sure of it. But he didn't seem to want to share any of it. And as for his marriage, I felt like an idiot for allowing his wife to get me all worked up to the point where I refused to listen to him. I didn't usually act crazy like that, but damn it, my jealousy got the better of me.

Hyde finished his call and came back to me. He opened his mouth to speak, but a doctor interrupted. She wanted to go over Charlie's X-rays with him.

I met his gaze. "I've gotta get to work, so I'll leave you to it."

His eyes searched mine and he nodded. "I'll call you when I'm done here."

"No, I don't want you to worry about me. Just focus on Charlie. I'll talk to you tonight." I stood on my toes and brushed a kiss across his lips and then left him before he could argue.

I really did want him to give all his attention to Charlie. But I also needed some space to get myself under control and my thoughts in check. Tenille had fucked with my head way too much, and I had to find a way to clear that shit out.

CHAPTER 31

Monroe

I didn't hear from Hyde all day. It was almost 10:00 p.m. with still no word. I'd texted him around five to see if he had time to chat, but he hadn't replied. I had then spent the last few hours worried about him. Tatum said something the other day about Nitro wanting her to lay low due to club stuff going on, so I was concerned for his safety. Kinda crazy, knowing that Hyde was more than capable of looking after himself, but you never knew what could happen when someone pulled a gun or some other weapon.

I was about to go to bed when he finally showed up. Yanking the door open, I found him on my doorstep looking anything but okay. Dishevelled accurately described him, from his hair to his clothes to his body language. And he watched me with haunted eyes, causing my worry for him to shoot even higher.

I reached for him. "What's going on?"

He didn't answer me. Instead, he stepped inside, shutting the door with his boot, and pushed me up against the wall. His hands were under the baby-doll I wore within seconds, and a deeply satisfied growl came from him when he cupped my breasts.

I pushed against his chest in an effort to stop him, but I had no shot at that. Hyde was on a mission.

He lifted me so he could carry me into my bedroom. I took the opportunity to ask again, "Hyde, what's going on? You look like shit, and I'm worried about you."

Another growl from him. "Only thing you need to be worried about, sugar, is opening those legs of yours and letting me fuck you."

I was all for sex; he knew that. But I was more for him sharing his load. That didn't have to mean dumping all his problems out in the open, but what I was looking for was some back and forth. If this relationship was going to go anywhere, I wanted us to know we could come home at the end of the day and find some comfort there.

When we reached my bedroom and he deposited me on the floor, I forcefully stopped him from getting his hands all over me again. "The only way you're getting fucked tonight is if you stop for a minute and tell me how you are. I'm not looking for details. I just want you to talk to me and share yourself with me."

His face darkened. "It's been a long fucking day. You want me to share the shit I've got going on in my head?"

"Yes."

He shook his head. "No, you don't. If you knew what was in my head, you'd run a fucking mile, Roe."

"You need to give me a little more credit, Hyde. I may not know exactly what you do when you're out on club work, but I figure it's not rainbows and unicorn type shit. I can see you struggling. Between dealing with your daughter, and your wife, and your club, you've got a lot going on. You don't have to carry that all by yourself."

Silence filled the room while he processed that. This relationship was so new that I had no grasp on what he thought. Not when it came to this kind of stuff. So my veins buzzed with a little apprehension as I wondered what he would say or do next.

"I've been a shitty father. My kid hasn't seen me since she was two. I left her mother and never went back until recently. That enough to make you think twice about me?" It was like he was trying to provoke me. Trying to throw bad shit about himself at me in an effort to push me away.

I moved so my body was flush against his, and I gripped his waist. "You've already told me you aren't perfect, so no that doesn't make me think twice about you. I've seen you with Charlie, and I think you're working hard to make things right."

He hissed, and his muscles under my hand tensed. Curving his hand around my neck, he held me, his fingers digging in to my skin. The small amount of pain that caused coiled desire through me. God, I wanted this man, even if he was a fucked-up mess. "I hurt people, Roe. I fucking inflict pain on them until they give me what I want. I am not a good man," he said through gritted teeth. His fingers pressed harder into my skin, and I decided right then that I was going to hell, because this only heightened my want for him.

"You don't hurt people you love."

"I have."

That should have stopped me, but it didn't. "Who?"

He dropped his head and swore sharply, "Fucking hell." Looking back at me, he yelled, "Everyone! I've fucking hurt everyone I've ever loved!"

I flinched when he yelled, but at least I'd managed to provoke some emotion from him. Up until then, he'd been holding it back even though I sensed it lurking. The room vibrated with his anger. It snaked around us, a menacing evil that threatened to rip us apart. But I refused to let it.

I pushed him and slapped his chest in my frustration. "Why are you doing this? Why are you trying to push me away?"

I hated that he was so hard on himself. The Hyde I knew wasn't a bad person. Why couldn't he see what I saw? Why didn't he know that everyone hurt those they loved?

His hand snapped around my wrist as he snarled, "I'm doing what you asked, red. I'm sharing myself with you."

"No! This isn't sharing. This is you trying to show me all your bad parts at once. That's not how relationships are built."

He yanked my wrist closer to his body while still gripping my neck hard. "This is me showing you what you're getting yourself into," he barked. "Now's the time to walk if you don't think you can handle it."

My own anger flared. Why was he trying to ruin this before it even got started? I pulled my wrist out of his hold and pushed him again. Harder this time so that he stumbled backwards. "What else have you got for me, then? Tell me your worst, and we'll see if I stay," I yelled.

His nostrils flared and his eyes flashed with fury. Before I knew what was happening, he had me around the waist and off my feet while he carried me to the bed. Dumping me on my back, he straddled me, hands pinned either side of my body. He stared down at me with the same level of frustration I felt towards him.

"You're playing with fucking fire, Monroe. I'm trying to tell you that I will hurt you. I will fuck with you. I will fucking rip your heart out and smash it to pieces. And you're not fucking listening. But you need to know that's what I do. I'm a fucking monster." His chest pumped furiously as he struggled for breath while spewing his toxic words all over the place.

Rage and passion collided in the room around us as we both fought for what we wanted. He wanted me gone; wanted to save me from himself. I wanted him to understand I didn't love small. When I let him in my life, I chose to accept all the parts of him and to love them equally. And I loved big as fuck. He couldn't escape it.

I clutched his shirt. "You are *not* a monster. And I'm not fucking going anywhere. Go ahead, hurt me, fuck with me and rip my heart out. That's what love is, Hyde. It's the good with the bad. I can take it. But you better be ready for me to fuck you up, too. Because that's love. The give and take is where the magic is. I want to bleed with you and cry with you and be slayed with you. And then I want to laugh with you and build a future with you and get wet in my shower with you. You made me fall for you. Now you can man the fuck up and show me why I made the right decision."

His breaths came hard and fast as he stared down at me. I thought for sure he'd keep arguing, but he didn't. His lips crushed to mine, and he kissed me like it was the last thing he'd ever get to do on earth. Hyde was an intense man, but this kiss was something else. I could have lost myself in it and happily stayed there forever.

When he finally dragged his mouth from mine, he rasped, "I want you on your hands and knees at the end of this bed, and that ass of yours in the air. And Monroe?"

My fingers squeezed tighter around his shirt. "Yes?"

"I hope you're ready to take everything I've got to give."

I knew he wasn't just talking about how he was going to fuck me. His eyes told me that. I nodded. "I am. And one last thing—I don't want a condom between us anymore. I'm clean."

He pushed up off the bed so he could stand at the end

while I positioned myself where he'd said to. His hands came straight to my ass and ripped my G-string off. He then ran them up my back and around to cup my breasts under my baby-doll.

My back arched, pushing my ass up higher. He groaned at that and moved one hand from my breasts so he could nudge my legs further apart and run his finger through my pussy.

"You're fucking dripping for me, red."

I kept my back arched while I also angled my face up. Everything he did felt so damn good. "That's because you get me so worked up, even when you're bloody arguing with me."

He slid a finger inside me, and I moaned with pleasure. "Next time I won't argue. I'll just fuck it out of you."

I moaned loudly, closing my eyes as he fucked me with his finger. I wasn't even able to form a reply to what he said. It turned me on way too much, but I didn't want to encourage him to not discuss shit with me. God, this relationship was one big fucking contradiction. I wanted all the things I shouldn't.

"You thinking about shit, sugar?"

I wiggled my ass at him. "So what if I am?"

He gripped my hips and pulled me back closer to him. His zip sounded, and he slid his cock along my pussy. "I need your mind on my dick, so stop fucking thinking about anything other than that."

"You have no idea—"

His dick slammed into me, cutting me off. My mind exploded with light as need raced through my veins.

Oh God, yes!

Fuck, this was what sex was about. And the fact he was bare only made it better.

Hyde was a fucking master at it, and I would willingly let him take charge of me in this way any time he wanted.

He wiped every single thought from my mind as he held my hips and pounded into me. I gripped the sheets and took every thrust. We were untamed and savage, desperate for each other.

There was a brutal beauty to the way he fucked me. He took what he wanted with ferocious demand, yet he gave me so much in return. More than anything, he showed me how much he wanted me.

He roared out his release when he came. I wasn't far behind, and as I orgasmed, I collapsed onto my elbows. When he was done, Hyde let my hips go and rubbed his hands over my ass. "You're fucking beautiful, Roe."

The angry intensity was gone from his voice, and in its place was something a little softer. Not that soft was a word to ever be used when describing Hyde, but I felt it from him. I loved that he gave that side of himself to me, even if for only a rare moment here and there.

I pushed myself back up onto my hands and turned to face him. Kneeling, I looped my arms around his neck and kissed him. "You make me feel beautiful."

And there was that intensity back in his gaze. "Good. I never want to make you feel anything but that."

I watched him quietly for a beat. "I can love you if you'll let me, Hyde."

He stilled. "You sure about that?"

My heart beat faster. "I've never been surer of anything."

His lips bruised mine when he stole another kiss from me. "Give me everything, and I'll give it right back to you."

It was in these moments, when he allowed himself to be vulnerable like this, that I caught a glimpse of the man I was falling in love with. I knew he'd battle me every step of the way, knew he'd be difficult and argue with me at all turns, but I believed it would be a battle worth fighting. I believed Hyde was worth loving.

CHAPTER 32

Hyde

I stared at the glass of whisky I'd just had Kree pour. My hands shook as I contemplated drinking it, and my head pounded with a headache far worse than any I'd had in a long time.

"You want water instead?"

I glanced up to find Kree watching me with a knowing look. "No, I fucking want this."

She dropped her voice, but the bar was fairly empty at this time of the morning, so no one would have heard her anyway. "How many days has it been?"

"One." But it felt like a hundred.

"You can do this, Hyde."

How the fuck did she know what I could do? I didn't even fucking know what I could do. At this point, I was ready to throw every last drop of whisky I could find down my throat.

Yesterday had been the kind of day I never wanted to

relive ever again. After I'd made sure Charlie was okay and that Tenille would stay with her, I'd had to get back to help King. The number plate on the car that dumped Marx outside the clubhouse came from a stolen car, so that had been a dead end. After receiving that news, King decided we'd visit the last two Italians on our list. The night had descended into bloodthirsty mayhem while I carried out King's orders. Turned out neither of them was the man we were looking for. All it had done was leave a bloody trail that would possibly have the feds crawling all over us. I'd then gone home to a roaring argument with Tenille who still refused to tell me where she'd been when Charlie fell. The way she fought me told me it was nowhere good. All of that without a fucking ounce of whisky in me.

The saving grace had been when I'd ended my shitty day at Monroe's house. It had been an explosive battle with her to begin with, but she stood up to me and gave me everything I wanted in a woman.

I'd made it through the night without touching the bottle, but this morning was a whole other story.

I stood and shoved the glass back towards Kree. "Throw it away. And don't pour me any more."

She arched her brow. "You're gonna listen to me when I say no?"

"Probably not, but you're gonna stand your ground."

"This is the worst plan. Just so you know."

I was feeling agitated as fuck, so I needed to get out of there before I took it out on her. "Noted," I threw back over my shoulder as I headed outside.

King came through the front door of the clubhouse just before I reached it. Narrowing his eyes at me, he said, "You look like hell. How's your daughter?"

"She's got a broken arm."

"And your ex? Still fucking you around?" He'd drilled me

on my family after I returned from the hospital yesterday, so he knew where I was at with them.

"Yeah."

"Go home and sort it out, brother. I'm waiting to hear from Bronze today. He thinks he may finally have something on Ryland, which would be good fucking timing if he did. Until then, I'm just gonna lay low. We can do without you for a few hours."

I nodded. "Call me if that changes."

As I headed home, I wondered if it was the best move. With Tenille being so damn hard to deal with, and me being this agitated, the situation was just asking for trouble.

———

Charlie glanced up from the kitchen counter where she sat eating a bowl of cereal when I arrived home. Frowning, she said, "I thought you had a busy day on today."

"I thought so, too, but plans changed. Where's your mother?"

"In the shower."

I dropped my keys on the counter and sat with her. "How are you feeling?"

She rolled her eyes. "You already asked me that this morning. I'm fine."

I ignored her attitude. "And I'm gonna keep asking you."

After finishing her cereal, she placed the bowl on the counter. "Yeah, well I'll probably start ignoring you."

"At which point we'll have an issue."

Tenille joined us in the kitchen, her hair wrapped in a towel on her head. "What are you doing home?"

"I figured we had some stuff to go over."

She stiffened. "We don't."

I stood. "Tee, let's start over here. I lost my temper with

you yesterday, but I don't want us to go on like this. I don't want us to be angry with each other."

She crossed her arms over her chest. "I don't either, but I'm feeling like I'm out in the cold here."

I frowned. "How?"

"You've got your new woman, and you'll have Charlie here with you. I'm not going to be a part of it all soon. I just don't want to feel like I have no say."

I glanced between Tenille and Charlie. "What do you mean that I'll have Charlie here with me?"

"She hasn't told you yet?"

I checked my patience, but fuck it was hard with the way she drew this conversation out. "Told me what?"

"I want to come live with you for a while," Charlie blurted out.

"Here? You want to live here, with me?" I wanted to believe what I thought was being said, but I was sure I'd fucked it up somewhere. Charlie hardly knew me.

Tenille dropped her arms. "Yes, with you," she snapped. "She wants to come and live here with you and your girl-friend." I didn't miss the nasty tone she took when she mentioned Monroe.

"Mum," Charlie said, "I never said I wanted to live with Monroe. Why are you being like this?"

Tenille turned on her daughter. "Well, what am I supposed to think? You seem to really like her."

Charlie's chest puffed out like it did when she was about to go to war with her mother, so I stepped in. "Okay, you two, enough." I needed to tread carefully if I didn't want to alienate Tenille. "Look, I'm all for Charlie coming to live here—"

Someone knocked on the front door, interrupting us. Charlie slid off her stool and said, "I'll get it."

I watched her leave before pulling Tenille close. "We need

to discuss this without Charlie in the room. Can you hold off until later?"

She nodded. "Yes."

"We also need to discuss our divorce," I said quietly. Her jealousy over Monroe led me to believe this would be a touchy subject, but it was one I had to bring up. I felt like a complete bastard doing it to her, though.

She blinked rapidly a few times before pulling out of my hold. "I was wondering how long it would take you to mention that."

I raked my fingers through my hair. "Fuck, Tee, this whole situation is screwed up. Have you heard from Craig?"

"He keeps calling me, but he's back driving in Western Australia, so he can't get here."

"Gibson keeps sending him over there?"

A strange look crossed her face at the sound of Gibson's name. I would almost have labelled it as fear. I wondered if I'd caused her to feel that way towards him. Not a bad thing if I had. I wanted her to understand how dangerous he was.

"Yeah, I guess so."

"Have you decided to leave him?"

I fucking hoped she'd say yes, but Charlie came back into the kitchen before she could answer me. And with her was Shane Gibson.

My body tensed, and a murderous urge came over me. I fought hard to contain it. If Charlie hadn't been in the house, I doubt I would have been able to control it.

I reached for Charlie and pulled her behind me. No fucking way was I allowing her near him again. "What the fuck are you doing in my house?"

He kept coming towards me. "Hello, Aiden."

"Stop fucking walking," I barked. "Turn the fuck around and go out the way you came in." I balled my fists by my side.

"That's no way to greet me after all these years, son."

I clenched my jaw. All I wanted to do was take the last few steps to where he stood and take to him with my fists. I wanted to kill the motherfucker, but not while my daughter was in the house. "I'm not your fucking son, Gibson."

He finally came to a stop, not far from where I stood. "You never did understand how I felt about you, did you?"

I'd thought I had. I'd thought he was the best man I could find to be a substitute father when mine had never been there for me. When his son, Brad, had asked me to go away with them on a camping trip when we were twelve, I'd thought all my fucking Christmases had come at once. Not once in my life had I experienced anything like that weekend. And that had just been the beginning. By the time I began working for Gibson, we'd spent five years bonding, and yeah, I'd thought of him like a father. But a few years later, he'd fucking annihilated me worse than my own father ever had. Because giving love and then killing it the way Gibson had was far worse than never giving it in the first place.

"I understand you perfectly, Gibson. You're a twisted motherfucker who uses every person he comes across. You take what's not yours to take and—"

His nostrils flared in anger. He never did like being told truths about himself. "You *were* a son to me, Aiden. And after Brad died, you were the only son I had."

Rage fuelled me to the point of insanity. How dare he say that shit to me. After everything he'd taken from me…. I wanted to rip those fucking words from the air and shove them down his throat, and then I wanted to slit that fucking throat so he could never spew lies like that again.

My chest pumped furiously while I tried to suck air in. Everything he said only made this harder while my anger ratcheted up. "Why the fuck did you threaten to kill me, then?" I roared. "Fathers don't fucking kill their children."

"I had to make you leave, so I could keep you safe from the shit going on with the cops. You would have gone to prison, Aiden."

I jabbed my finger at him. "No! *You* would have gone to prison!"

He nodded. "Yes, but you would have too. I didn't want that for you. I knew you wouldn't leave unless I gave you good reason to, so I threatened your girls. It was all I had."

"Fuck that," I spat. "I don't fucking believe you!" The fury rolled through me, building in my shoulders and demanding an escape through my fists. I inhaled sharply and tried to keep every emotion I felt trapped inside. No fucking way could I allow it to escape while Charlie stood behind me.

"Why do you think you're still breathing? Why do you think our girls are—"

I took a step toward him, unable to hold myself back. The air stilled, and a violent calm came over me. The kind of calm that descended whenever I was about to kill. It was the side of me that craved brutality—the side he'd instilled in me when I was a teenager. Back when he taught me how to hunt and kill. "What did you just call them?" I asked, my voice deathly demanding.

Before he could answer, Tee jumped in, fear splashed all over her. "Stop it! You need to leave, Shane!"

My attention was completely on Gibson, but there was an urgency to Tenille's voice that fractured my focus. She sounded off. Glancing her way, I found her eyes wide and pleading silently with him.

"Tenille, you can't control this," he warned, confusing the hell out of me.

"Control what?" I barked. "What's going on, Tee?"

Everything about her screamed panic as her gaze shifted swiftly between Gibson and me. Ignoring me, she begged him, "Please!"

I finally lost my shit then. I couldn't control it any longer. Picking up the first thing I found on the kitchen counter—a glass—I threw it at the wall. "Somebody better start fucking talking, or else that glass is gonna be a head against the fucking wall!"

I barely heard the gasps that came from Tenille and Charlie. My target was Gibson. All I saw and heard was him.

"Bradley would have loved our girls," Gibson said.

Bradley was his son who had died just before Charlie was born. I had no fucking idea what he had to do with any of this.

My fists clenched repeatedly. "Stop fucking calling them that. They aren't yours."

Tenille sniffed, and I realised she had tears falling down her cheeks. What the fuck was going on?

An evil smile lit his face. "That's where you'd be wrong, son. They *are* mine."

Tenille gasped, her hand flying to her mouth. Her eyes met mine, and what I saw there punched me in the gut.

She took a step away from me, but I snapped my fingers around her wrist, preventing her from going any further. "What did you do, Tee?"

Tears still streaming, she looked at Charlie before looking back at me. "It was a mistake. It meant nothing t—"

"What the fuck did you do?" I roared. The room closed in on me, and I struggled for breath again. I knew that when she uttered her next words, my life would never be the same, but I fucking needed to know.

"Charlie *is* yours," she managed to get out in between sobs. "Not Brad's."

Everything spun out of control as those words fell from her lips. I'd thought my life had been ripped apart fourteen years ago. That had nothing on this. I existed for my child.

She'd kept me going all these years. If I didn't have her, I fucking had nothing.

"Bradley is her father," Gibson said, continuing to tilt my world on its axis.

Charlie gasped again. I turned to her, but it was like time slowed, preventing me from catching her before she ran from the room. If my world hadn't been crumbling around me, and if I was thinking straight, I would have gone after her, but I wasn't. My thoughts weren't even thoughts. The only thing filling my head was a fucking train wreck of memories and questions. And after years of locking it up tight, my heart trampled my mind, taking over with too many fucking emotions.

Gibson's declaration that his son was my daughter's real father sliced right through me, taking all the air from my lungs. I was disoriented as fuck as disbelief and confusion replaced my rage. I stared at Tenille. "You slept with Brad?"

She nodded through her tears. "Yes, but it was over before Charlie was born. I promise."

She promised? As if that made all the difference. "You think I care when it fucking started and when it ended?" I slammed my hand down on the kitchen counter, my anger building again. "All I fucking care about is whether Charlie is mine!"

She flinched. "Aiden, she's yours. I know it!"

My mind connected dots. "*That's* where you went yesterday? To see Gibson?"

The guilt that flashed in her eyes confirmed it, but she didn't answer me. "She looks like you!"

I towered over her. "Get the fuck out of my sight," I snarled. "I can't look at you right now."

If I had to look at her for a minute fucking longer, I would do serious damage to her. Everything inside screamed for me to get her the fuck out of the room. She'd taken every good thing I'd ever given her and trashed it to pieces. Everything I thought I knew, I didn't. I knew fucking nothing. And it turned out, I could trust fucking no one.

Gripping my shirt, she begged, "Aiden, ple—"

"Now, Tenille!" I roared. "I can't guarantee your safety if you don't leave."

She played the smart move and exited the kitchen without another word, which left me alone with the man I'd dreamt of killing for over a decade. I wouldn't do it in my house while Charlie was here, but he sure as fuck wouldn't leave without me delivering a fuckload of pain to him.

My fist connected with his face before he saw it coming. He fell, hitting his head on the chair near him. My boot thudded loudly as I took a step to yank him back up. Holding him by the shirt, I punched him again, sending him flying backwards into the wall. He slumped to the ground, still trying to get his bearings.

I stood over him. "You are going to fucking bleed," I spat at him. "For every-fucking-thing you've ever done to me and my family!"

He kicked his leg out, trying to fight me so he could stand, but I didn't allow the pain his kicks caused to break my determination. I punched him over and over until the skin on his face couldn't be seen through the blood covering it. He kicked and punched at me, too, leaving my face with cuts and bruises. I moved like a machine, though. One he would never beat again.

He fought unconsciousness, his eyes rolling back in his head. I gripped his shirt and shook him. "Don't you fucking pass out yet, motherfucker. We've got a long fucking way to go still." I wouldn't be done with him anytime soon.

He looked at me through thin slits as his lip curled into a sneer. "You kill me, your club will have to live with the consequences," he managed to get out while coughing blood.

"You think I give a fuck about that at this point?" I didn't care. Storm would find a way to deal with any shit that my actions caused.

He opened his mouth to speak again, but I jammed my foot against his face, pushing it sideways against the wall. "Stop fucking talking!"

My phone rang, but I ignored it. I was dealing with something that couldn't fucking wait. However, it kept ringing over and over. It wouldn't fucking stop.

Yanking it from my back pocket, I barked, "I'm in the middle of something! What the fuck do you want?"

"Hyde." It was King. He sounded less than impressed, but I ignored that.

"What?" I snapped, staring down at Gibson.

"You care to alter that?" Still unimpressed.

"Fuck, King, I'm dealing with Gibson."

Silence for a beat. "Where are you?"

"My place."

"Your kid there?"

Fuck.

I dropped my head. "Yeah."

"I'm sending Nitro. Don't fucking kill that motherfucker before he gets there."

He was right, but I wasn't sure I could stop myself. "Make it fucking quick."

I looked down at Gibson after King made the call. He was barely breathing, but he wasn't dead. Not yet. He would be, though. By the time this day ended, he'd take his last breath. I'd fucking make sure of it.

CHAPTER 33

Hyde

"He's all yours," Nitro said once we had Gibson in the old warehouse we used for these kinds of things.

Gibson had regained consciousness. He stared up at me from the cold cement floor where we'd dumped him. He didn't speak, though. I doubted he could, even if he tried. I'd beaten him so badly that his face was unrecognisable, swollen to the point where his eyes and mouth could hardly open.

"How you wanna do this?" Nitro asked.

I jerked my chin. "String him up." I needed to work the anger out of my system with my fists.

Nitro nodded and helped me hoist Gibson up. There was therapy in the rope work involved in this endeavour. I derived great satisfaction from it, and when we stood back to survey him hanging there, ready for me, my skin hummed with anticipation.

King came through the doorway at the end of the warehouse and walked our way. It was just the three of us there. King had called again after we'd left my place, to say he'd meet us if he could escape the feds.

"You ducked Ryland?" Nitro asked.

King nodded, his eyes focused on me. "Yeah."

"What?" I asked him. It seemed like he had something to say.

Regret flashed across his face. That didn't happen often with King. "I was calling you earlier to pass on some information from Bronze."

My gut tightened. "Sully?"

"Yeah." He paused for a beat. "Sorry, brother, but they found him riddled with bullets."

"Fuck!" I roared, turning my face to Gibson who hung by his two arms, his head down. "You did this, didn't you?"

He tried to lift his head, only managing to raise it a fraction. But his nod couldn't be missed.

I took the few strides needed to get to him. Squeezing my fingers around his face, I dug them in until he responded with a cry of pain. "You'll regret that."

He spat at me and mumbled something I couldn't understand. It provoked the beast inside me that I'd somehow kept leashed through all of this. If he thought he'd seen the worst from me already, he had no idea what was coming for him.

I gave his face one last hard squeeze and then punched him in the gut. The world drifted away after that while I took out every ounce of rage, resentment, hatred, and pain on him.

I finally embraced every dark thought I'd ever had. And every unhinged desire for revenge that had stirred deep in my soul. I'd lived with these parts of myself for far too long. They'd wound themselves around my heart, trying to choke any last pieces of good left inside. They'd flowed through my veins, trying to poison me. I'd battled them daily. I'd fought the fuck against this side of me, but not anymore. This shit ended with Gibson. I'd beat him black and fucking blue until I released this toxic shit from my body.

Every blow I delivered took me one step closer to the retribution I craved.

I fucking hungered for it.

Dreamt of it.

Needed it like the air I breathed.

"Fuck!" It roared out of me as I punched him one last time before falling to my knees. My heart pounded as I drew deep breaths.

I rested my hands on my thighs, my back hunching over as the violent high consumed me. I wasn't done with him yet. Not by a long fucking shot.

"He's got a bit more life in him," King said, moving to stand next to me.

I looked up at Gibson. "Yeah." His breaths were shallow, but they were still there. Standing, I pulled my knife from its sheath as I met King's gaze. "He won't soon."

King's own bloodthirsty desires flared in his eyes. He kept them locked tight, though. If I hadn't finished Gibson off in a way that drew blood, he would have. But he knew I needed to do this, because it was what he would have needed, too.

Turning back to Gibson, I ran my eyes over his body, taking in every bruise and wound I'd inflicted. I tasted my revenge before I took it. It felt fucking good. However, it would never be enough, and I knew that. But it would be a start.

I stepped close to him and pressed the tip of the blade to his chest. "You won't ever hurt my family again, motherfuck-er," I said through clenched teeth. "Charlie will be safe from you. And I don't give a flying fuck what you say—she's *my* daughter." I pulled my arm back and then stabbed the knife into his chest with all the force I had in me. *"Mine!"*

I stabbed him repeatedly.

I couldn't stop myself.

Blood oozed from him.

It covered him, soaked through his clothes and dripped to the cement floor creating a grisly red pool that only excited my thirst for his death.

I wanted every drop of his blood down there.

I didn't want to stop carving him up until he ran dry.

The blade sliced through every body part as I stabbed him to death.

The sound of flesh ripping apart was the soundtrack I moved to.

The sight of that gaping flesh and his blood, my reward.

It wasn't until Nitro stepped in and pulled me away that the vicious frenzy ended.

I stared blankly at him as he took the knife from my hand.

I was numb.

Dead inside.

I'd taken his life.

Delivered my revenge.

But betrayal had carved a wound that cut deep that day. And that wasn't something Gibson's death could ever soothe.

CHAPTER 34

Monroe

My heart ached when Hyde came into view. He sat alone at the clubhouse bar, staring at the drink in front of him, his shoulders slumped and his head bowed slightly.

I had no idea what I would say to him. All I knew was that he needed me. Desperately.

Closing the distance between us, I was glad we were alone. It was almost midnight, and there were a few club members still around, but King had cleared the bar when I arrived with Nitro. He'd looked at me with those fierce eyes of his. He hadn't said anything. Had simply let me in and jerked his chin towards the bar. But those eyes had said so much. He hoped I could help his brother in ways he hadn't been able to.

I took the stool next to Hyde, sliding onto it, and placed my handbag on the counter of the bar. My nerves had gotten the best of me on the way over here. I didn't want to screw this up. Didn't want to let him down.

We sat in silence for a while. Him staring at the drink on the counter, next to a full bottle of whisky. Me watching with my heart in my throat.

Finally, he asked, "Why are you here?"

His question slayed me in so many ways. It hurt that he even asked it, but the rational side of me understood it came from a place of such desolation.

"Charlie called me. She told me everything." His daughter had been a wreck on the phone. By the end of the conversation, I'd understood why. She'd also shed so much light for me on why Hyde was the way he was. And then she'd made me believe that she *had* to be his daughter when it became clear the reason for the call was because she wanted me to find him and make sure he was okay. She'd had the shittiest day of her life, and all she cared about at the end of it was that someone made sure her father was all right. That was something Hyde would have done, I was sure of it.

His head dropped further and he muttered, "Fuck." Looking sideways at me, he added, "I'm the worst fucking father, Roe. I haven't even checked on her."

I shook my head and placed my hand on his forearm. "No you're not," I said softly. "She doesn't think you are."

"She fucking should." He inhaled sharply and looked up to the ceiling. "Fuck, I may not even be her fucking father."

The despair blazing from him was unlike any I'd seen in my life. I really was out of my depth here, but I persisted.

"So you'll get a paternity test and find out."

My words triggered his temper. "You say that as if it'll fix everything," he snapped. "It fucking won't." He reached for the glass of whisky, gripping it hard, but not lifting it. All the while, staring at it like it was his long-lost saviour.

Being on the end of Hyde's temper wasn't a fun place to

be. I cut him some slack, though, because he had good reason to be angry.

As I watched him with that glass, the pieces of the puzzle fell into place. He often tasted like whisky, but I hadn't seen him drink it often, so I hadn't put two and two together.

"You going to drink that?"

He glanced at me but didn't give me an answer. Instead, he looked back at the glass, still gripping it hard.

"I asked you a question, Hyde."

He scowled at me. "You can go."

I swallowed my hurt.

He's in pain.

Let it go.

"I'm not going anywhere."

His chest rose as he sucked in a harsh breath. Exhaling it, he muttered, "Your choice, but I'm not in the mood for twenty-fucking-questions. You stay, don't ask me shit."

My face heated as his words hurt me again. "I'm not here to ask twenty questions."

He stared at me with eyes that were dead. His brokenness killed me. "What do you want from me, Monroe? I don't have anything to give you tonight."

I placed my hand against his cheek and nodded. "I know. Just let me be here with you."

He watched me for another few moments before turning back to look at his drink. We went back to sitting in silence, for much longer this time.

I wished he would let his drink go, but he didn't. He kept his hand around the glass the entire time, and I felt every bit of his silent battle. I also felt completely useless, not knowing how to help him through this fight.

So I waited.

I remained quiet.

And I prayed that my presence would be enough for him to win this round.

Finally, he asked, "What the fuck am I gonna do if she's not mine?"

I closed my eyes, forcing my tears away. Now was not the time to cry. Now was the time for strength. When he couldn't be strong enough to get himself through, I'd be strong for him.

I opened my eyes and looked at him. "You'll do what you've always done. You'll get through it."

He lifted the glass. "*She's* the reason I fucking got through."

I stared at the whisky, feeling like he was slipping through my fingers. "So you're gonna empty that bottle, then? Make yourself feel better with all that whisky in you?"

He scowled again. "You got a problem with that?"

I didn't want to fight with him. Not tonight. But I was so deep in this with him that all I could do was fight back. *Fight for him.*

"That whisky isn't going to solve a goddam problem of yours."

He swirled the amber liquid in the glass. "It'll sure as fuck make me feel better."

I gripped his bicep hard, desperate to make him hear me. "Let *me* help you feel better."

His eyes bored into mine. "Don't you fucking get it? Nothing you say can fucking help me feel better."

"I know that, Hyde. But tell me something—how many days has it been since you've had a drink?"

He shifted his gaze from mine and stared straight ahead. "Almost two."

I let his arm go. "I guarantee you that you'll regret taking even a sip."

His jaw clenched, and he slammed the glass down.

Whisky spilt over his hand and the counter. "Fuck!" he roared, pushing himself off the stool.

His eyes found mine, and I sucked in a breath at the torment I saw there. His pain cut right through my heart, and I wondered how we would ever get through this night.

"I'm not my fucking mother, Roe!" He jabbed his finger at the whisky. "I don't want that fucking shit, but my body craves it like nothing else."

He pulled deep breaths in, struggling to get his breathing under control. Grasping the back of his neck, he walked away from me before turning and coming back my way. He paced like this for a good five minutes while I remained silent and waited while he did whatever he needed to do.

The silence was shattered when he stalked back to the bar, picked up the glass and threw it at the wall. He then wrapped his hand around the neck of the whisky bottle and hurled it at the wall, too.

Fire flared in his eyes. Anger and so much pain. "I'm struggling, red. Like I've never fucking struggled. I have no idea how to even come back from the shit that happened today. This fucking pain is pulling me under. And all I wanna do is drink myself into oblivion."

There he was.

I went to him, my heart breaking for him all over again. I gripped his shirt. "You do it one day at a time. You lean on me. You lean on King and Nitro and all your other brothers. But no fucking way do you go near that bottle again. You get your ass to an AA meeting if that's what you need, and you accept there's no shame in asking for whatever help you need." I moved a hand to his chest. "And you start sharing more from here. You don't carry your burdens by yourself anymore. That's what I'm here for."

His eyes searched mine while he listened intently to what I said. Resting his forehead against mine and wrapping his arms around me, he exhaled a long breath. He didn't say anything, but he didn't need to. His arms around me rather than that glass of whisky did all the speaking we needed.

We clung to each other for a long time, foreheads resting together. It was in that quiet space that I felt like we'd taken a huge step forward. There really was beauty to be found in pain.

When he lifted his head to look at me, he said, "Come home with me."

I curved my hands around his neck and nodded. I pulled his face down and brushed my lips over his. I had fallen so deeply for this beautiful, broken man, and I would love him so big until he could find a way back to himself.

CHAPTER 35

Hyde

I ran my hand over Monroe's ass before reaching for her leg and pulling it over my own. "Morning, sugar."

I'd been awake for a good hour or more, but I hadn't wanted to wake her too soon. She needed her sleep after last night. Not waking her had also given me time to get my head together.

I'd woken with a million thoughts. Most of them dark. Many of them about finding the closest bottle of whisky. I had a long road ahead of me to win this battle—the drink, the family shit, my relationship with Monroe—but she'd made me understand I didn't have to do it on my own. And for the first time in my life, I was ready to share that fucking burden.

She angled her head so she could look up at me, hitting me with a smile. "Morning."

"You hungry?"

She rolled so her stomach met mine, her pussy teasing the fuck out of my dick. Reaching her hand around my neck, she pulled my lips to hers and kissed me. "Sorry about the morning breath, but I needed those lips of yours."

I gripped her ass. "Fuck morning breath. Give me back that mouth." When she hesitated, I ordered, "Now, red."

A sexy smile spread across her face, and she gave me what I wanted. Waking up with her was the best fucking way to wake up. When she ended the kiss, she said, "I'm impressed."

"What, with my kissing abilities?"

"No, with your restraint. You've got your hands all over me, your mouth on mine, your dick almost inside me, and yet you're offering me food."

"Jesus, woman, don't tempt me."

She grew quiet. "I know you're doing it because it's the first morning we've woken up together in your home, and your daughter is close. And that impresses the hell out of me."

"How do you know all of that?"

"It's the only explanation that makes sense, because you're not a man to walk away from a sure thing like this."

I struggled against the desire to flip her on her back and fuck the hell out of her. That pussy of hers called to me. But she was right, Charlie being in the house changed things. I dropped my lips to hers and gave her one last kiss before smacking her ass. "Time to move this ass, sugar. You're gonna make me bacon and eggs."

She arched a brow, an amused look crossing her face. "Oh, am I? You're fucking dreaming out loud this morning, tiger."

I chuckled as she rolled off me and watched as she reached for her clothes. I'd never get enough time with my eyes on Monroe's naked body. Her curves drove my dick wilder than it ever had been.

Once we were dressed, she came to me and took my hands in hers. Looking down at my bruised and cut knuckles, she asked softly, "How are you this morning?"

That she didn't ask about my knuckles or my face, but simply accepted that shit had gone down, meant the fucking world to me. "I'm fucking lucky to have you, Roe."

She looked up at me. "Well, yeah..." She paused with a smile before continuing, "But that doesn't tell me how you are."

I slid my arm around her waist and pulled her close. "I know that you know I'm in a dark place, and I'm fucking grateful that you're in the corner with me, fighting for me to be a better man. I'm done with yesterday, and I'm moving forward." I bent my face to hers, and my lips grazed her ear when I murmured, "Thank you."

Her eyes misted with tears. "I'm always here for you."

I wiped away the few tears that escaped. "Don't cry, sugar. We're gonna beat this shit. And we're gonna get that paternity test and prove that Charlie is mine."

She smiled and nodded. "Yes, we are."

We.

I fucking loved it more than I ever thought possible.

Smacking her ass again, I said, "Right, kitchen, now."

She bit her lip. "Umm, is Tenille gonna be out there?"

"Fuck no. I kicked her out yesterday."

Her eyes widened. "Really?"

"Roe, there's something you need to know about me. I'm loyal to a fucking fault, but I'm not a man to be crossed. Tenille will always be the woman I loved first, and it'll take me time to move past that shit, but I had to remove her from my home for her safety more than anything else."

She let out a long breath. It was like she'd been holding it for a long time. "Thank God. I didn't like her. And honestly, I wasn't sure I'd be able to hold my tongue if I saw her again. Maybe even not my hands."

My lips twitched. "Going to battle for your man, huh?"

She fired up. "You fucking bet. No one messes with you and gets away with it."

Fuck.

She really was something else.

We found Charlie in the kitchen a few minutes later, pulling eggs out of the fridge. Guilt flooded me as I watched her. She'd been awake when I'd arrived home last night, and we'd spoken briefly, but the fact I hadn't stayed with her yesterday proved to me that I had a long fucking way to go while learning how to be a good father.

Her gaze met mine and she jerked her chin at me. "This shit ain't gonna cook itself."

Monroe laughed, and I grinned. Fuck, she had to be mine. She'd even started talking like me. "Monroe's ready to get acquainted with our kitchen."

Charlie paused and gave me a look that said I had to be kidding. "*Our* kitchen is a little dirty for Monroe to cook in today. *Someone* didn't clean it up when he came home last night."

My heart thumped in my chest. This was Charlie letting me know we were good. Hell, it was her letting me know we were better than good.

I jabbed my finger at Monroe and then pointed at a stool. "You sit your gorgeous ass there." I then jabbed it at Charlie. "And you get me the bacon and some plates. You can also set the table."

She frowned. "Hate to tell you, but there's no bacon left. I ate it all for dinner last night."

I ignored the guilt that reared its ugly head again. I'd lived with guilt over Charlie for a long time, but she'd signalled that it was time to move on, so I would.

"Scrambled eggs are good," Monroe said, watching Charlie and me with a happy expression.

I rattled off a list of ingredients for Charlie to grab, and a minute later, I started preparing breakfast for my girls. After fourteen years of living on my own, I hadn't thought I'd ever want to live with anyone again. I'd thought wrong. I wanted to move them both in today.

"What are you thinking there, tiger?" Monroe asked while I watched her, contemplating that thought.

Charlie burst out laughing. "Tiger?"

Monroe grinned at her. "Yeah, he's very growly when he's being bossy. Have you noticed that?"

"God, yes! I guess that name kinda suits him."

Monroe looked back at me. "So? Your thoughts?"

I met her gaze as I stopped chopping onions. Placing the knife down, I said, "I'm moving you in, red."

She stared at me, surprised. I couldn't tell if she liked that idea or not, but whether she came willingly or kicking and screaming, I'd make damn sure it happened.

"Really? Just like that?" she finally asked, with the attitude my cock liked.

"Yeah," I growled. "Just like that."

She glanced around the kitchen before looking back at me. "Well, we'd need to get rid of some of these old appliances and stuff. And we'd need to move mine in. I hope you're ready for some colour in this place. And candles. And bras hanging in the shower. And my toys." She frowned a little. "Might have to rethink that last one with Charlie living here, too."

"Geez, you people don't move slowly, do you?" Charlie said.

"Life's too short to move slowly, kiddo," I said.

"Yeah, I guess so."

Monroe turned to her. "Your dad told me you're moving to Sydney. Are you okay with me living here with you guys?"

Charlie thought about that. "Yeah, I'm cool." Looking at me, she said, "But do me a favour, Aiden?"

If I'd thought my heart thumped before, it fucking ricocheted around in my chest at that. We hadn't discussed getting a paternity test yet, but she seemed to accept that I was her father as much as I believed she was my daughter.

I held my cool. I'd figured out teens weren't so much into parents being excited about shit. "Depends what this favour is."

"Don't call me kiddo again. If you must call me something every now and then, you can call me baby. But don't make a habit out of it, okay?"

Fuck.

Did she have any idea that what she'd just said to me was everything?

I jerked my chin at her. "Noted. Now fill the sink with detergent. You've got shit to wash up before we eat."

CHAPTER 36

Hyde

I arrived at the clubhouse around nine that morning. King exited his office as I walked towards it. "Wasn't sure when you'd get in today," he said.

After we'd taken care of Gibson's body yesterday, I'd come back to the clubhouse and gone over some club business with him that couldn't be put off, but he'd left me alone all night once I'd made it clear I didn't want company.

"You let Monroe in last night?"

"Yeah, she called Nitro and asked him to organise it with me."

I nodded. King and I rarely exchanged thanks, but we knew when the other offered it.

"Where are you at with your ex and your daughter?"

"I've organised a paternity test. We'll have the results in five to ten days according to their website. Far as I know, Tenille's gonna stick around in Sydney until they come back."

"You think she's yours?"

"I'm running with that thought, yeah." The alternative had been too fucking painful, so I'd pushed it out of my mind.

Nitro joined us. Looking at King, he asked, "You heard from Kick? They had that baby yet?"

King grinned. "Yeah, had her this morning around five."

"You got a name? Tatum's gonna hound me until I give her one."

"Jesus, Nitro, I never asked, he never said," King muttered. "That woman has you fucking wound around her finger."

Nitro shot him a filthy glare, but Devil interrupted us before he could respond.

"Spoke to Bronze this morning. He wanted me to let you know that he still doesn't have anything on Ryland."

"Why haven't we heard even a whisper from the fucking feds?" I asked. As far as Bronze had led us to believe, that would have been a given after we dealt with the Italians.

"Yeah, that's been on my mind, too," King said.

"We need to keep moving," I said. "Get Marx out there again to keep showing us all the places where he met with those assholes. It's only a matter of time before Ryland shows his face again, so the more we can get done before then, the better." Devil and Nitro had taken Marx out for a few hours yesterday, but hadn't come up with much.

King nodded his agreement. Jerking his chin at me, he said, "You and Nitro take him out. I've gotta take Jen to her ultrasound this morning."

It surprised me that he was so involved in her pregnancy. But that was King—doing shit you never expected from him.

I entered my home late that afternoon after a long fucking day of club work that yielded no results. Morale in the club was dropping with each passing day that we couldn't figure out who the fuck was behind all the shit going on.

I dumped my keys and phone on the kitchen counter and went in search of Charlie. Finding her in the lounge room, I collapsed onto the couch next to her.

"You look like shit," she said.

I glanced her way, doing a double take when I saw her hair. "You coloured your hair?"

She touched it. "Yeah. Do you like it?"

I knew I had to tread carefully with this. Females were fucking touchy about their hair. "It's different."

Her eyes widened. "Different?"

Fuck. By her reaction, I'd screwed that up. "I like it, Charlie."

"You're just saying that now. You hate it."

I scrubbed my face. The long day, coupled with not a drop of fucking whisky, meant my levels of patience were at a low. But I kept a leash on my frustration for her. "I'm not just saying it. I never say shit I don't mean. I just preferred it darker. This blonde thing you've got going is nice."

"Oh God! Nice is the worst possible word to describe hair!"

Fuck, it was worse than different? A teen dictionary would be useful right about now.

"Your mother paid for it, huh?"

"Yeah, she's bribing me into being nice to her after yester-day. For the record, I'm all about bribing."

"What happened to the balay-colour-thing you wanted?"

"*This* is balayage, Aiden. Keep up."

I frowned. "Looks fucking blonde to me."

She rolled her eyes, and I knew this conversation was done.

"I got your text about dinner," she said, confirming I was right about the conversation shifting gears.

"You're good with that?" Monroe had asked us both to dinner at her place that night.

"I don't know…. Did you say her family will be there, too?"

"Yeah."

She grinned. "Okay, I'm in, then."

I narrowed my eyes at her. "What's that grin for?"

"I'm all about watching you handle her family. I hope she's got one of those overprotective dads. You know, kinda like you and the way you are with Jamie."

"Smartass," I muttered. "That little shit hasn't fucked off yet?"

She stood. "Nope."

As she took a step to leave, I grabbed her hand and stopped her. "You okay, baby?"

Looking down at me, she nodded, knowing exactly what I meant. "Kinda. It sucks, though."

She wasn't wrong there. "Yeah, it does. But we're gonna get that test done and it'll prove I'm your dad. And then we're gonna forget about all this shit."

She was silent for a few moments. "I'm sorry Mum did this to you," she said softly.

I stood. "Charlie, I don't want you to think about me in all of this. Not in that way. Let me deal with that."

Her voice wobbled on her next question. "What if you're not my dad?"

There wasn't anything in life quite like watching your child struggle. It broke me in ways I'd never been broken. The urge to protect kicked in fiercely, and I pulled her into my arms. I wanted nothing more than to tell her it wasn't fucking true, that it would all work out. But I knew that wasn't what she was looking for. She needed me to be the strong one here, to be the one she could count on to know what to do if everything turned to shit.

With one arm tightly around her and a hand smoothing her hair, I said, "If we get to that point, we'll deal with it together. I will never walk away from you. Ever. I will be right here, still your dad as far as I'm fucking concerned, ready to be in your life however you'll let me."

She blinked a few times before nodding and resting her head against my chest. She didn't try to move out of my hold, and I didn't give her the option. We held each other for a long time, taking the strength and comfort we both desperately needed. Life sure as shit had a funny way of bringing people together.

CHAPTER 37

Monroe

Dad's eyes bulged. "You're moving in with him?"

I put down the tea towel I held and gave my father a look. "Yes, and I don't want you going on about that all night, okay? I've invited you for dinner so you can all start to get to know him."

"You've just met the man, Monroe. Why on earth would you think it's a good idea to move in with him so soon?"

We'd been going back and forth about Hyde for a good ten minutes while Dad drilled me before he arrived for dinner. Both of us had gotten worked up, but this question calmed me down. I smiled at him and gave him the best answer I had. "Because I just know."

Dad frowned. "You know what?"

"That he's the one."

Dad drew a long breath. I knew it was one of his stalling

moves when he grew frustrated. I hated it when we argued like this, but I wouldn't back down from this disagreement.

Mum placed her hand on Dad's arm as she joined in. She knew he was reaching his breaking point, too. "What makes you so sure, honey?"

"I know you just see his roughness and what he shows the world, but there's a whole other man underneath all that. He's thoughtful, and caring, and giving. He accepts me for who I am and doesn't try to change me. He puts up with my demanding side and doesn't complain. He listens to what I have to say about things. He stands up to me and fights me on the things that are important to him. He admits when he's wrong, and he tries to be a better man. He's a good dad. *And* he gives me the fireworks I've always wanted." There were so many other little things about Hyde that I loved. And I knew there would be a million more things I'd discover along the way. People could think we were moving way too fast, but they didn't know what we already had, and they sure as hell didn't know what was in my heart.

Mum's face lit up while I shared my thoughts. "I like him, Col. I saw the way he made Monroe sparkle. I think you should look for that tonight rather than focusing on Hyde so much. Look at your daughter and see that this man makes her feel good about herself. At the end of the day, it's not whether we like him so much as how he makes Monroe's life better by being in it."

Dad looked at her. "You just quoted your mother, didn't you?"

Mum nodded. "Remember how much my father disliked you when you two first met? That's how you're acting now. Think about that before you give Hyde too much hell tonight."

He shook his head. "You'll be the death of me, woman."

She grinned. "I do my best, darling." I wanted to high five my mother, but a knock at the front door distracted me.

Butterflies swarmed in my belly.

Hyde.

Today had been a write-off at work thanks to him. I'd planned on tackling tax stuff but hadn't been able to concentrate after he'd bossed me into moving in. Not that he really had to do much bossing. I just let him think he did.

His intense gaze captured mine the minute I opened the door. I was surprised to find him on his own.

"Where's Charlie?"

His hand curled around my waist, and he pulled me outside. Drawing me close, he bent so he could speak against my ear. "She asked me to drop her at the service station around the corner, so she could buy some drinks, which means I've got you alone for a good few minutes. I've been thinking about those lips of yours all fucking day."

"I like your thinking." I *really* freaking liked it. I needed this time with him before venturing back inside where my father lay in wait.

He captured my mouth in a kiss that took my breath away. "Fuck, sugar, you make a man wanna dedicate days to you."

Happiness hummed through me. I loved his desire for me. Looping my hands around his neck, I hit him with a sexy smile. "How about dedicating something else to me?"

"Why do I suddenly feel like I need to be careful about what I agree to here?"

"I have no idea."

He ground himself against me. "Okay, hit me, but I'm not saying yes until I know what it is."

I pouted. "You're no fun."

"Spit it out, Roe."

"Well," I started, "I was thinking it could be fun if you got your cock pierced."

He stared at me like I had two heads. "You're fucking shitting me, right?"

"No. The sex would be so good."

"That's easy for you to say when you're not the fucker who has to stick a fucking hole through your dick."

Even though he was grumbling, I knew I had him. It would take me some time to coax him, but he was using the tone that told me he'd do anything for me.

My sister walked up my front path. "Did you just say you're sticking a hole through your dick?" she asked Hyde.

"Fuck no," he said, his eyes firmly on mine still. "Your sister is trying to convince me, though."

"You won't regret it," Savannah said.

Hyde moved away from me so he could look at her. "You've fucked a guy with one?"

Savannah smiled. "No, but Roe has. She told me how good it—"

Hyde cut her off with a growl. "Stop talking. I never want to hear about Monroe fucking another man again."

Savannah's brows lifted. "We've got a possessive one here, I see."

I took a step towards him and patted his chest. "You have no idea, Sav." I caught Charlie coming down the street out of the corner of my eye. "Ooh, I love her hair, Hyde."

"Yeah, just don't mention that it's blonde. She's touchy about that."

I frowned. "That's not blonde. It's balayage."

He shook his head and swore under his breath about fucking women and hair. I ignored him and greeted Charlie, "Hey, girl, I love your hair!"

Her beautiful smile filled her face. "Thanks, Roe."

Putting my arm around her shoulder, I guided her inside,

leaving Hyde with Savannah. "Come in and meet my family. Well, my brother and his wife aren't here. You'll get to meet them another time."

I smiled as I heard Savannah grilling Hyde about me moving in with him. Unlike my father, she'd been excited when I'd told her the news. I loved that she threw a million questions at Hyde, though. He could do with an inquisition from her. It'd keep him on his toes.

"Oh my God," Charlie exclaimed as she looked around my kitchen. "I love your style! These colours are amazing in here."

I glanced at the teals and reds in my kitchen. "Yeah, we're gonna have to add a lot of colour to your dad's house. That white and grey he's got going on is yawn-worthy."

I made all the necessary introductions before saying, "Right, let's get the food on the table and then see if we can all get along." I stared pointedly at Dad as I said this. He nodded, and I breathed a sigh of relief. It didn't mean he'd go easy on Hyde, but it did mean he'd give him a chance.

CHAPTER 38

Hyde

"This is fun," Monroe said a few days later at a last-minute club get-together King had organised at the clubhouse. It was one of his efforts to boost club morale. "I mean, it doesn't beat what I had planned for us today, but it's still fun."

I pulled her close. "What did you have planned, sugar?"

"My mouth around your cock. That kind of thing."

I eyed the exit. "We could find a room. You could still take care of that."

"Stop dreaming, tiger. Tatum just walked in, and I wanna meet Evie and her baby. And Hailee's there, too. I've got secret women's business to get involved in."

I tracked her ass while she made her way to Tatum, only dragging my eyes from her when King interrupted me.

"Just had an interesting call with Billy," he said.

"Tatum's boss?"

He nodded. "He may have some information for us in the

next hour or so."

"About the motherfucker screwing with the club?"

"Yeah." He took a long swig of his beer, shifting his gaze to Jen who'd just exited the room. "Fuck, I told her to stay home," he muttered before stalking towards her. He'd been in a foul mood for days because of her. I was looking forward to her giving birth to that baby and leaving him in peace. But that was months away.

I moved to where Kick and Nitro stood in the corner of the room. Kick could hardly take his eyes off Evie and their baby daughter. I didn't blame him. There was nothing like a newborn and their mother. On top of that, Evie'd had complications with her pregnancy, so I figured he was being extra cautious. Exactly how I'd be if I had more kids.

"Kick!" Evie called out. "Can you come and take Elizabeth for a moment?"

Nitro and I watched in amusement as Kick covered the distance between him and his family in a matter of seconds.

"Wanna place bets on how long it takes him to knock her up again?" Devil asked, joining us.

"You reckon six months?" I suggested.

"If that, brother," he said.

Nitro changed the subject. "Where's King at with Marx? Are we done with him yet?"

Marx hadn't proved useful at all. "As far as I'm concerned, we are. But King hasn't mentioned any decision yet. I'll bring it up with him later."

"We need to get him out of here as soon as possible," Nitro said. "The last fucking thing we need on these premises if the feds raid us is him."

The screech of tyres and a bloodcurdling scream from outside cut through the air. The sound of gunfire followed close behind.

"Fuck," I yelled, my entire body alert. Moving swiftly to

the clubhouse bar exit, I met Monroe's gaze and ordered, "Stay here! Do not come outside!"

I ran the distance of the driveway, searching for the source of the screaming and gunfire. Nitro and Devil were right behind me.

"What the fuck?" I said when we reached the end of the driveway. There was no one in sight.

"Where's King?" Nitro asked.

"Last I knew, he was with Jen."

"I saw them come out here a little while ago," Devil said.

They definitely weren't here now.

My gut churned with apprehension. We'd all heard the sounds. So where the fuck did they come from?

"Hyde!"

King.

We moved further outside the perimeter to look down the road and made a gruesome discovery, one I knew would completely change the path our club was on.

"Fuck me," Nitro swore, echoing my thoughts as we watched King approach.

"Motherfucker," Devil cursed, too.

This shit wasn't happening.

It couldn't be.

King walked our way carrying Jen's limp body. Her blood-soaked clothes hung from her, and I knew from the amount of blood that there was no way her heart, or her baby's, was still beating.

I'd seen my president handle some bad shit. Had watched many times while he allowed his madness to take over. I watched now as that madness circled, claiming him.

It was in the rigid set of his shoulders.

The harsh lines etched into his face.

The savage hollow of his eyes.

King would go on a rampage to avenge these deaths.

I strode towards him, meeting him halfway.

"Who the fuck did this? Did you get a look at them?" I demanded, taking in the blood covering him, trying to figure out if he'd also been shot. *Trying to figure out what the hell was going on.*

He exploded with deranged anger. The veins in his neck strained against his skin, and his lips pulled back, baring his teeth. "I don't know who it was, but they fucking messed with the wrong man."

Blood roared in my ears as I balled my fists. The need for vengeance surged through my veins as I stared at Jen lying in King's arms.

Where the fuck would this end? We now had the blood of a woman and her unborn child on our hands. The body count was adding up too fucking fast.

"Let's move this the fuck off the road." Nitro rounded us up and pulled the clubhouse gate closed behind us.

When we were safely inside the compound, King knelt and placed Jen on the grass. He pressed a hand to her belly and kept it there. His jaw clenched as he looked up at us with cold, hard eyes. He didn't say a word, but we all read his silence. No words were needed.

Our club was in turmoil, and anarchy would follow. It wouldn't matter that the feds were watching, or that picking off enemies could bring new ones. King's wrath would dictate our actions from here on out, and as brothers, we would all stand behind him. We would be ruthless and uncompromising to the bitter end.

"Fuck!" Devil thundered, nostrils flaring. "We're done trying to fucking pander to Ryland. We need to take that fucker out once and for all."

King grunted as he stood. Ignoring Devil, he pulled out his phone and made a call. "Billy. Tell me you fucking have something for me," he barked when Billy answered.

When he ended the call, his eyes met mine. "We have an address."

"For?"

"Someone tied to the motherfucker who did this."

King inhaled sharply, determination filling his face. "This guy wants a war? He's fucking got one."

———

It was a two-storey building we were sent to. In a quiet, unsuspecting suburb full of soccer mums. Dusk had fallen on the busy street as people arrived home from work, There were far too many people around for what we had to do.

King didn't care. He'd pulled fifteen club members from the get-together for this. We roared in on our bikes, not even trying to draw attention away from us.

"You take the back, I'll come in from the front," King said, and I directed members to where he wanted them.

There was no silent entry. We kicked in doors and filed into the house, spreading out as we went. It was a huge place with numerous rooms to check. No furniture, though, so nothing slowed us.

The lower level of the house was clear. Not a person in sight, silence consumed the place. I met King at the bottom of the staircase. He pointed up, and most of us followed him. Devil stayed downstairs with another member to ensure no one came at us while upstairs.

We checked every room methodically and came up with nothing. There was no one in the house. I pulled the curtain across in the last bedroom we checked, to see if anyone was outside.

"It's fucking clear," I said to King who paced the bedroom we stood in with Nitro. The rest of the club members waited outside in the hallway, ready for King's next order.

He slowed and glanced up. Pointing, he said, "Here."

I followed his gaze to an attic ladder.

Nodding, I said, "I'm with you, brother." I signalled to Nitro, letting him know we were going up.

King pulled the ladder down while Nitro moved to the bottom of the ladder, his gun aimed up. I followed King, wondering what the hell we'd find. Hoping like fuck it wasn't a trap.

"Fucking hell," King muttered when he reached the attic. I took the last couple of steps, shocked to shit when I reached the top and discovered what King already had.

"Hello, King. It's been a long time."

No fucking shit it had been a long time.

A woman stood in the empty room watching us.

Ivy.

The fucking love of King's life.

I pointed my gun at her, fully expecting King to as well, but he didn't. Instead, he simply stared at her in silence. Stunned. I'd never seen him lost for words like this.

She didn't acknowledge me, but rather kept her eyes firmly glued to King. She had no weapons; truth be told, she *was* a weapon. To King, anyway. Fuck knew how many ways she could screw with him. I imagined she could wreak more havoc on him than any manmade weapon. "Are you going to say anything?"

He took a step closer to her. She allowed that. Didn't flinch. Didn't appear to be concerned that a gun was pointed at her either.

"You look well," King finally said.

Ivy was a beautiful woman. Stunning, in fact, with her olive skin, long legs, toned body, sultry eyes, and dark hair that fell to her waist. And he was right—she did look well. The last time I'd seen her was over a decade ago when King had walked away from her. He'd broken her back then, and I wasn't sure I'd ever seen someone so ruined by a breakup as she had been.

"Looks can be deceiving," she said.

"What's going on, Ivy? Are you not well?" he demanded, concern lacing his question. He was wound tight, the muscles in his back bunched, his arms locked by his side.

"Nothing that would ever concern you. But I didn't come here to talk to you about that." She was all business with her flat eyes, blank face and cool tone.

She knew we were coming?

"Ivy," King said in a low, warning tone. "I asked you a question."

Her eyes blazed with bitterness. "You gave up that right a long time ago, King."

"Answer me!" he roared, his body coming to life with an urgent ferocity.

Ivy snapped as fast as King did. Hostility radiated from her as she took the last step that closed the distance between them and went head to head with the man she'd once loved and promised forever to. "You don't get to demand answers from me, King, so don't fucking ask them! Now, if you want me to tell you what I know about the shit going down with your club, have Hyde take his gun off me."

"I'm fucking confused here, Ivy. You came here, knowing we'd be here? And what the fuck are you doing in the attic?" I shared all his confusion. Was this a fucking setup?

"Yes, I organised this meeting. This is a house I own. And I waited up here because I didn't want all of your men pointing their guns at me."

King was silent for a few moments. The only sounds coming from him were the heavy breaths he took. He surprised me for the second time since we'd made our way into the attic when he ordered, "Put the gun down, Hyde."

I kept my aim on Ivy. "You sure about that, brother?" It felt like a bad fucking idea to me.

"Yes," he barked.

"Fuck," I muttered as I did what he said.

Ivy watched me for a beat before looking back at King. I kept my eyes fucking cemented to her, watching for any sign that she was about to turn on us.

"There's an attack coming," she finally said. "I don't know when and I don't know how, but I've heard him talk about it for weeks. And it won't be just on your club, it'll be on your families, too. He wants them all dead." She paused. "He wants to wipe everyone and everything you care about off the face of the earth. And I believe he could do it."

Jesus fucking Christ.

King forced out a harsh breath. "Who?" he demanded through clenched teeth. "Who the fuck are you talking about? And why?"

Her eyes bored into his. "My husband. You took what was his, so now he wants to take what is yours."

"Fuck! Tony is the one behind all this?"

Ivy was married to Tony Romano, one of Australia's biggest crime bosses. He lived in Melbourne, which was why he hadn't been on our list of Italians to check into. I only knew this because King had made me track her movements for a few years after he'd left her. Her marriage had tipped him over the edge, and I'd convinced him to stop tracking her.

I stepped forward, anger spiking through me. "What the fuck did King take?"

She turned her face to look at me. "He took me."

"How the fuck did I take you?" King growled.

Her eyes met his again, still blazing with a fierce intensity. "You didn't, but he thinks you did. He thinks I'm leaving him because I never stopped loving you."

EPILOGUE

Hyde

3 months later

Monroe hit me with the sexy look she pulled out when she wanted something. I'd just walked in the door after a long day out on club business. I hadn't even had a chance to put my feet up yet, and I knew she was gonna blast me with requests to do shit around the house. I knew this because it had been going on for almost two weeks while she renovated parts of our house.

I rested my shoulder against the doorjamb and crossed my arms over my chest. "What?"

Her lips twitched as she fought a smile. She fucking knew what she was doing. She also fucking knew I'd cave to her demands. I always did.

She came to me and rubbed her body against mine while

looping her arms around my neck, making real sure to get that sweet pussy of hers against my dick. "It's not so much a what as it is a my-parents-are-coming-for-dinner."

"Fuck, sugar, I was looking forward to a little couch time and then a whole lot of time between your legs." Charlie was away on school camp until tomorrow, so I wanted to make the most of the night. Fuck knew, with all the club shit that had gone down recently, we could do with a night together, just the two of us.

She pulled a face. "Ah, well that was never gonna happen. Charlie came home a day early. She's in her bedroom."

My brows pulled together as I pushed off the doorjamb and straightened, ready to go find her. "She okay?"

Monroe gripped my shirt. "Steady, tiger, she's fine. Two of the teachers fell sick, so the trip ended a day early."

Thank fuck she was okay.

I ran my hand over her hair. "She called you when she got back?"

Monroe's face lit up with a smile. "Yeah," she said softly.

I fucking loved the shit out of the way Monroe and Charlie had bonded. The day we received the paternity test results that confirmed I *was* her father, Monroe celebrated by throwing a party. She made a big fucking deal about Charlie in an effort to make her feel special. Hell, the kid deserved it after everything she'd been through. Once we'd moved all of Charlie's stuff in, they'd decorated our house together and spent hours with each other doing the kind of shit females loved to do.

Bending to kiss her, I murmured, "Our kids are gonna be the luckiest kids on the planet, red. Having you for a mother." I knew she thought of Charlie like a daughter, but I also understood that she wanted her own babies. And I was gonna give them to her when she was ready.

"Oh," she said, remembering something, "Tenille called just before. She'll be here just after lunch tomorrow."

We were navigating shared parenting with Tenille while she and Charlie smoothed out their relationship. Craig had moved to Perth and hadn't kept in touch with either of them. Charlie was disappointed, but I did everything I could to be the father she needed.

"She better not be hours later again. I can't sit and watch Charlie get upset all over again."

She smiled up at me. "I can't wait to see you with a baby. I think it might just melt my heart once and for all."

I smacked her ass. I fucking loved that ass. "You let me know when you're ready to get started on that. But for now, I'm gonna take a shower and get ready to face your dad."

She bit her lip. "Ah, yeah, no."

"No?"

She glanced at the clock on the kitchen wall. The large-as-fuck teal clock that took up half the fucking wall. I'd asked her if she was blind when she asked me to put it up, because surely we didn't need a clock that size in the kitchen. She'd just laughed at me and carried on. I'd put the fucking clock up for her, figuring that at least we'd still be able to read the time when we hit ninety.

Pointing at it, she said, "They'll be here in like two minutes, maybe one. There's no time for you to do anything except get the barbeque ready."

I scrubbed my face. "So let me get this straight. I've been working all day, I'm exhausted, with no pussy in sight, I've no time for a shower or a minute to myself, I have to be nice to your father all night, *and* I'm the sucker who has to fucking cook dinner, too?"

She smiled like the world was running exactly how it should be. "Yes." And then she added, "Because you love me."

She was fucking right about that.

I backed her up against the wall and dropped my lips to hers. After I had kissed her, I said, "I love you like nothing fucking else, woman. But there's gonna be some serious time dedicated to my dick later tonight. Just so you're aware."

"You say that like it's you getting the better end of the deal. I would have thought you'd know by now that if I could dedicate every second of the day to your dick, I would. Especially since you got that piercing."

Another thing I'd caved on for her. My prince albert was never far from her mind. Or her pussy.

"Okay," I said, moving away from her. "You got the meat ready for the barbie?" Fuck knew I needed a moment alone to get my dick under control. Throwing the fucking front door open to her father, sporting a raging hard-on was not on my list of priorities.

She reached for my shirt. "Just one other thing, baby."

I hung my head. She only pulled the baby word out when she *really* wanted something. Looking back up at her, I said, "What?"

"I need another room built in the shop. A little bigger than the waxing room you built. I wanna bring a beautician in, too."

I would give Monroe the fucking world if I could. She'd sure as shit given it to me. "How many more rooms you reckon you could use in the shop?"

She frowned. "Why?"

"I figure I'll build them all at once. That way they're done, and you won't ask to cut in on pussy time again."

The doorbell sounded as she pressed a kiss to my lips and said, "You speak my language, Mr. McVeigh." She turned towards the front of the house. "Will you let them in while I stir the sauce on the stove?"

"You're fucking kidding me, red. My dick is hard for you

right now. I don't need to give your father a reason to bust my balls today." If Colin Lee had been any man other than Monroe's father, I wouldn't have given two shits what he thought of me. But he was, so I did.

She pushed me away. "Okay, go take care of that. I'll hold the fort until you get back."

I grabbed the meat out of the fridge and headed outside to the barbeque. Ten minutes passed, in which time I got myself under control and the meat cooking.

Charlie brought out a plate of chopped onions. As she passed it to me, I took in the expression on her face. It was the one she wore when she had to bring up a conversation she really didn't want to have.

"Spit it out," I said.

"Ugh."

I would never understand teen talk. "Ugh, what?"

She shifted nervously on her feet before finally saying, "Okay, so you know this fishing trip we have planned?"

"Yeah."

"I don't think I can go."

"Don't think or can't?"

She pulled a pained expression. "Don't think, but technically can't."

"So you're telling me you could go, but you're choosing not to? What's the reason?"

"Well there's this guy at school who I really like. I mean, *really*. And he asked me out on a date, but it's for the Saturday night we would have been away. We could do fishing another weekend."

"That little shit from Melbourne is out of the picture finally?"

She rolled her eyes. "Yes."

"Thank fuck for that." It had amazed me that relationship had lasted as long as it did once she'd moved to Sydney.

"So are you cool with changing the weekend for the trip?"

"Yeah, but I'm gonna need something out of it." I'd learnt her negotiating trick and had started using it.

She rolled her eyes again. I fucking hated this eye rolling shit, but Monroe kept telling me it was a phase that all girls went through and that she'd grow out of it. Couldn't fucking happen fast enough as far as I was concerned.

"What do you want?"

"This new kid is gonna have to come for dinner here before your date so that Monroe and I can meet him. I wanna know all the details of where he's taking you for the date. And I want you home by ten on the night of the date. Plus a guarantee that you'll answer your phone should I call you."

"Oh God, you're killing me here. Okay, how about he just comes for like ten minutes before the date so you can meet him? I'll tell you the main place we're going. I mean, I won't know everywhere because there has to be some spontaneity. Home by ten thirty. And no phone call." This was our new style of negotiating—I asked for the world and she tried to bargain me down.

I met her gaze. "Sorry, baby, but on this, there's no negotiating. Those are my terms. Take them or leave them." This was her first real life date since she'd moved in with me. If I could go on it with her, I fucking would.

Her eyes widened. "I thought we had this negotiating thing down pat? Why you gotta go break it?"

"Take it or leave it."

She scowled at me for a moment. "Ugh. You used to be kinda cool when I first came, but now you are turning into such a dad."

I watched her as she stormed off. This wasn't anything unusual for us these days. She'd cool down quickly and be back to try to renegotiate terms. On this one, though, she had Buckley's. We'd be meeting that kid before I allowed him any alone time with my daughter.

She passed Monroe's father on her way inside. My chest tightened when I heard her say, "Maybe you could talk to Dad for me. He's being difficult about me dating."

Dad.

It was the first time she'd called me that. I'd do anything to hear it again.

"Good luck with the dating thing," Colin said, joining me at the barbeque.

I eyed him. "Yeah. Charlie's not gonna like how it all goes down."

"She'll thank you one day. Parenthood is a long game. Some strategies you try don't pay off for decades."

I nodded. "Yeah."

We turned silent for a little while. The only thing Colin and I had in common was Monroe, so conversation with him was difficult.

"Looks like you need a new barbeque," he finally said.

I checked my irritation at that statement. "Had this one for seven years, Col. She doesn't need replacing yet."

"Doesn't hurt to upgrade every now and then."

"I don't upgrade old faithfuls."

He pointed at the wooden trolley. "That wood's seen better days."

"Nothing I can't fix."

He was quiet for a moment. "You always this argumentative, Aiden?" I'd given him my name in the first round of twenty-questions after I'd moved Monroe in. He'd refused to call me by anything else since then.

"Only when people don't listen to what I'm saying."

"Mmm."

We stood in silence while I finished cooking the meat. I

threw the mushrooms and onions on the barbie that Monroe had chopped.

"So you've been going to AA?" he said.

I inhaled a long breath. This wasn't a secret, but I didn't love discussing the fact I struggled with alcohol. "Yeah."

Silence again for a long few minutes.

And then—"How long until you decide to marry my daughter?"

I turned to face him. Hadn't seen that question coming. "I've already decided, Col." I was just waiting for my divorce from Tenille to go through.

"I figured as much. But I need to know when it'll happen so I can start getting the cash ready to pay for it."

Hadn't seen that coming either. "There's no need. I'll pay for it."

He crossed his arms over his chest. "You and I are going to have a problem if you argue with me over that."

"What? Different to the problem we have over me being with your daughter?"

"I have no problem with that anymore. You've proven yourself."

"Jesus, you have a fucking funny way of showing it, then."

Before he could respond to that, Monroe and Charlie interrupted us. I narrowed my eyes at Charlie. She appeared happier than when she'd stomped away from me. I wouldn't have put it past her to try to con Monroe into agreeing to this date. The two of them often took sides against me. What neither of my girls understood was that there were some things I was happy to let them have, but others were a hard no. This was a fucking hell no.

"You finished with the meat?" Monroe asked.

"Yeah. Just about done with the mushrooms and onions, too."

Col passed her the tray of cooked meat and then said to Charlie, "I've got something for you, Charlie."

She smiled at him. Charlie liked Col, and I didn't think it was just because she liked watching him give me a hard time. I had to give the guy credit for taking the time to get to know her. It was still early days, but he was shaping up to be the grandparent she'd never had.

He pulled a photo out of his wallet and passed it to her. I couldn't see what it was, but the way her face broke out into a wide smile told me it was something she loved.

She looked at him hopefully. "Is this what I think it is?

He nodded. "Yes. Don't get too excited. She's an old car, but I figure you and I'll have plenty of time to work on her before you get your licence."

"You bought a car?" Monroe asked, full of surprise.

Col looked at his daughter with the kind of look I watched Charlie with. The one that revealed the unconditional love we felt for our child. "Yes." He glanced at Charlie. "Angela has more photos on her phone if you want to see them."

"Cool," Charlie said, her face full of more excitement than I'd ever seen on her.

They left us to go and look at car photos, and I pulled Monroe close, settling my hand on her ass. "We're getting married, sugar."

She pulled her head back so she could look up at me. "Oh, really? Are we? You just decided that, did you?"

I tightened my hold on her. "No, not just now. I decided that a long fucking time ago, but your father has just given his blessing."

Her eyes widened. "Really?"

"Really." I dipped my face to hers so I could catch her lips in a kiss. When I'd had my fill, I said, "I love you, and I respect your father, but just so you know, no one would have kept me from marrying you. You're the woman who showed me there's good out there when all I fucking saw was bad. I can't do this life without you."

She hit me with a smile that reached every corner of my dark soul. "I can't do it without you, either. I love you, Aiden McVeigh, even if you are the bossiest damn man I have ever met."

ALSO BY NINA LEVINE

Storm MC Series

Storm

Fierce

Blaze

Revive

Slay

Sassy Christmas

Illusive

Command

Havoc

Sydney Storm MC Series

Relent

Nitro's Torment

Devil's Vengeance

Hyde's Absolution

Alpha Bad Boy Series

Standalone Novels

Be The One

Steal My Breath

ABOUT THE AUTHOR

Nina Levine

Dreamer.

Coffee Lover.

Gypsy at heart.

USA Today Bestselling author who writes about alpha men & the women they love.

When I'm not creating with words you will find me planning my next getaway, visiting somewhere new in the world, having a long conversation over coffee and cake with a friend, creating with paper or curled up with a good book and chocolate.

I've been writing since I was twelve. Weaving words together has always been a form of therapy for me especially during my harder times. These days I'm proud that my words help others just as much as they help me.

www.ninalevinebooks.com

38523031R00183

Made in the USA
San Bernardino, CA
11 June 2019